A Love Story

By: Christopher Bonner

Dedication:
My family, friends, and loved ones.
LL Dane, LL King Mazi, LL Marion

Dreams without action are just that-dreams.

Part 1: Love & Happiness…or something like that

Introduction

Summer Jam was about to go down and I couldn't be more hyped. The first weekend of summer and I was finally gonna be able to spend quality time with my girl, Vanessa. The past two years working hard to get a solid foundation in our careers was definitely a reality shock for everyone. Our ride-or-dies, Alonzo and Jasmine, would also be tagging along too and we already knew what that meant-*we were about to cut the fuck up*, making up for all of the time lost dedicated to work since graduation.

Alonzo had just finished his internship while working as a part time coach and assistant athletic trainer for basketball conditioning and spring training at our alma mater, Highland University. Attaining his degree would guarantee both a promotion and bonus. Jasmine spent her time teaching dance classes at the local YMCA when not working as a dental hygienist with a prominent local cosmetic restorative dentist that personally chose her for her technical acumen and caring spirit. Vanessa also helped her out with classes, while honing her culinary skills and using the kids as guinea pigs for her latest culinary experimentations. Me, the official geek of the group, spent most of my time balancing managing my parent's real estate portfolio while being an actuary studying risk management from my financial engineering training. We were all grateful for this much needed reunion.

My little cousin Myles, who was more like a little brother, would be coming from Chicago to spend the summer and I couldn't wait to have him around to kick it with. I laid out my outfit so it would be ready to slide into after freshening up. Alonzo had lined me up the other day and I was feeling myself just a little bit. Other than Myles, I couldn't have a closer, more dedicated best friend. We had been through a lot together. When we went on to play ball together at Highland, we naturally opted to be roommates to keep each other focused. Some of the other athletes on the team roomed together, oftentimes with disastrous results.

There really hadn't been much time for partying too much, between school and learning more details about the family business, and looking out for Myles. One trait I definitely inherited from my old man James was using work as a distraction from things I wasn't ready to deal with or to take my mind off other things that were bothering me. It wasn't the healthiest thing to do, but it worked for the time being and brought much success and opportunities towards the later college years

I.

I had already washed, waxed, and detailed my other baby-my prized Shelby mustang custom painted metallic gray-a graduation gift from my parents. I was ready to show it off. I couldn't wait to see bae and couldn't even lie, even though I still carried my V-card, I was hoping to get lucky tonight. Ya boy was hurting something bad though I had other ways of taking care of myself. Alonzo and Myles both clowned me about it at times, but respected me holding out as long as I had. They both had been traded in their cards years back, with Alonzo going as far as creating a "mini-me" version of himself with his old girlfriend Yvonne, just before high school graduation. I could only hope to curtail Myles from following in his footsteps of early fatherhood, though given his current track record, I don't know if I was already too late. *112's Cupid* melody filled the room and I almost broke my neck to get to the phone.

"Talk to me," I answered, trying to play off the fact that I had hit my foot on the edge of the bed.

"What's good?" Vanessa asked. "Why do you sound distressed?"

"What are you talking about?" I replied, trying *not* to reveal how upset I was with myself.

"Stop playing Avant," she said to me, a little more concerned. "Bet you were just being clumsy again, and ran into something like you always do."

"Well thank you for being concerned," I responded, looking to see what damage had been inflicted this time by that damn bed rail. Thankfully just a couple bruised toes and my pride more than anything. "What are you up to?"

"Just finishing my hair and nails while waiting for Jas to show up." She said before asking. "What are you wearing to the Summer Jam?"

"I pulled out one of my Akoo fits out that I haven't taken the tags off yet and my all black Forces."

"Put on some of that cologne that I like," she said seductively.

"Don't start nothing, won't be nothing." I responded, feeling my soldier gaining weight. "But I gotcha. Make sure you put something nice on for me so I can see those curves-but no one else. I want you all to myself."

"You already know I stay fly," she said smartly. "Don't even play me like that."

"Aight then, I'll see you soon. Love ya."

"Love you too."

Just as I disconnected the call, Alonzo's number popped up in a text. "Open the door 'Vant, I'm pullin' up."

Right on time! The door was already open and I wasted no time coming in with my outfit bag in hand, wearing what the ladies would call "the official male *thot-wear* starter kit"-*durag, basketball shorts, tank top, and slides with footie socks*. A true athlete if there ever was one, no matter how old I got. Avant was my boy though, and had moved into one of his family's income properties after our college graduation, one of the more modest ones to be honest, to keep expenses low and save as much as possible while he worked to break ground in his new career. This had been a true blessing, especially with trying to find a house straight out of college. Plus it also allowed him to provide a somewhat peaceful sanctuary for me when I needed to escape from my 'reality show' life, or *get out of my own head*.

Both our parents were frugal and ruthless when it came to financial and business matters, and stressed the importance of being financially literate and responsible. His mother, now a retired rehabilitation therapist, opened her own integrative medical practice along with a team of other providers to provide holistic care for the body, mind, and soul. His father was a well respected one of a kind real estate guru within our community and was close friends with my family. He had been a male role model not just for Avant, but anyone who associated with him. He was also the only male father figure for his cousin Myles, and took all of us, including me, under his protective wings, though my parents were still married. I oftentimes would listen to Mr. James before my own father, though I knew my father loved me despite our differences of opinion and just about everything else when it came to life choices. My father was just very old school and didn't necessarily spare the rod when it came to discipline or holding me to a high standard.

Looking had me reminiscing.-Gone were the days of sleeping in Avant's room on one of the old Army cots his dad kept stored in the garage….Sneaking in with my eyes burning, being red and him knowing it wasn't just from a lack of sleep. I always kept that loud on deck. We would stuff towels all around the door frame to hide the scent while we burned our brain cells and smoked our trivial teenage problems away. I remember how when I went home to break the news of becoming a father, how my parents, not being surprised, still showed me support in between giving me the third degree even more about growing up and sacrifices.

Avant unfortunately was also on the receiving end of that lecture from both our parents, though they pretty much knew he knew better. I had waited a good while before telling them, not knowing mainly how my father would react. Luckily Yvonne fell into their good graces and really helped smooth over any rifts that were present between us, with her charm and personality, not to mention that we were expecting a boy. It was later on when Jas first came into the picture after we separated, that you would've thought my parents were dealing with a drug addict son currently heading on another downward spiral.

I took no time laying my attire out on the ironing board in the living room before heading to my "room" to get ready while listening to Yvonne ranting nonstop on the phone. I peeped Avant heading in the direction I had just come from, picking up the iron to go over them with the iron while trying to ignore the tension filled conversation that was taking place down the hallway. He could tell I was on the phone with Yvonne when I knocked on the door before opening to put my clothes on the hook behind it. My facial expression coupled with the yelling coming from the speaker phone let him know I was *getting the business* from her more likely about *Summer Jam* since she had forgotten I was going to pick up KyJuan tomorrow instead of today. I could tell he felt bad for me, but knew it was just another case of miscommunication. I motioned my head towards my left where three rolled blunts on the dresser, ready for later. I held up a super long one and he already knew it was the "pregame".

I wasted no time firing it up and we both took turns hitting it. I still had the phone on speaker and just let Yvonne vent uninterrupted. This was actually progress considering how badly things had been when we first separated. Despite our differences, we argued less and less though when it did happen, they were epic. Even our parents admitted we were more mature now than when lil man was first born. *All of the grandparents had a mutual dislike for Jasmine, but tolerated her since she didn't interfere negatively with me caring for my son.*

After successfully achieving a decent level of *namaste*, we hit the showers to start getting ready. About thirty minutes later we were ready to hit the scene. I had finished both a heineken and corona beer before we headed out the door. Quickly navigating through traffic to the park and finding a parking spot close to the exit, Avant carefully backed in-one thing pops taught me is never park where you can be blocked in; and always have an exit plan. *"Neighborhood*

Superstar" by the Hot Boyz played through the speakers as we waited for the girls to arrive.

II.

I couldn't wait to hang out with my day one's. It had been a long time since we'd all been out together, but hey we aren't in high school anymore and life does require sacrifices when you become adults. Officially college graduates and now out in the real world, the demands of balancing life and careers meant putting social events on the back burner while we all worked to establish our footings in our respective careers. I had been perfecting my culinary skills while working with different companies catering to events of all occasions and social statuses. It was very demanding learning the different etiquettes and procedures that came with each event and client's taste, but very rewarding as well. I even found time to help Jasmine with her dance classes at the YMCA in between, while also using it as an opportunity to provide nutritious and experimental meal ideas, with them as my guinea pigs.

Jasmine worked as a dental hygienist at a cosmetic restoration office, and was a true expert at her craft. Her acumen and charisma got her the prestigious position when it was virtually unknown for a young black female dental student to be chosen. I'm very proud of my girl for all of her accomplishments. I waited in the living room while she put the finishing touches on her hair and makeup before we headed out to meet the fellas at Diamond Lakes Park for the Summer Jam.

It didn't take long to get there and spot them leaning against Avant's prized GT Mustang. I parked not too far away and we both got out. We were both dressed to impress with both hair and nails accenting our outfits, and I could already tell something else had gotten excited as Avant shifted awkwardly after they spotted us and we walked their way.

"*Damn they're fine*!" Jas said as she looked towards me. "Over there trying to look cool. I'm so glad we all finally managed to be off at the same time for once!"

"Girl, who are you telling! This adult life is something serious." I agreed as Avant smiled, while looking my way.

I could feel my heart racing as well as my temple getting moist. I was also a V-card member and made it clear it would be on my terms when the time came to do anything. Me and Avant had been high school sweethearts and managed to stay together even through college. Every relationship has their tests, and we definitely have had ours towards the end of our degree journey. The hardest part was when I left to go away for a prestigious culinary internship that would take me all over East Asia for almost two years. Avant had his own internship working alongside some of the brightest and sharpest minds near Atlanta, Georgia, learning and fine tuning what he had learned within the world of financial engineering, while also gaining more experience with real estate, and risk management. With so much black business coming in, it was very obvious why it became known as the new "Black Mecca"of the south.

Now Jasmine and Alonzo were a whole different story. They had been childhood friends basically since elementary school, but hadn't really been cool until late high school, early college. He and Avant grew up together because of their family ties, and he had always been one to keep a crowd of girls around-he called it his so-called *charm effect*. And charm he did too many with not only his signature smile, good looks and smooth words. I couldn't be mad at him though I'm glad he didn't rub off on Avant. I actually took mental notes on the sly just in case Avant started to show any potential red flags, but he always reminded me that his parents constantly lectured to not get caught on the same wave. Sometimes Alonzo's actions unintentionally would lead to minor scraps or at other times, epic brawls between girls vying for his attention. Most of the time he managed to come out scotch free.

It was known that our mothers collectively didn't care too much for how Jasmine carried herself when it came to her dating life and extracurricular activities. Avant and Alonzo's mothers described her as *hot in the pants and a little too fast* for their liking. But after his official separation with Yvonne, he didn't take long to rebound. While I might have appeared as being absent minded when it first came to them dating, I'm sure Avant knew they had been smashing on the regular before that time. Unfortunately, they would become quite the toxic couple if I ever knew one during our time away interning. I must admit that she did play a pivotal role in him changing for the better when it came to managing his time so that he was able to really be active in KyJuan's life, helping Yvonne after his little arrival. Yvonne pretty much wanted to ensure KyJuan had a better life than she did, and knowing how good Alonzo had it with his family and support system, held him to the same standards that his parents did. She was his best girlfriend hands down, but it was the constant reminder of his parents coming from her that he wasn't wanting to deal with 24/7. Jas allowed him to do him while ensuring he didn't slack off, make excuses, or neglect being a parent.

III.

I stood leaning against the car as Vanessa walked my way. I was hard as a rock but maintained my swag. She was beautiful as ever and I counted my blessings every day. I planned to marry her in the near future but knew I had to be able to hold us down financially and everything else. Her dad was really strict like my mine, and especially with being a widowed father raising a biracial daughter that caught everyone's attention with her looks and aura. She slid next to me and we kissed.

"Bae you smell so good," she said slowly, taking in the cologne from my neck. I had put on my special Dior just for her. "You do too, *as always*."

"What's up Avant?" Jas said, giving me a hug too. "Y'all look like you're up to no good, posted up like that."

"Never that," I responded. "We always sit back and scope the scene out."

"Hell yeah," Alonzo chimed in. "I'm waiting for the Hot Boyz and Juvenile to come on. I ain't heard them in a minute."

"*Girl you look good won't you back that ass up*," we both rapped, with the girls slick twerking back against us.

"Alright now," Alonzo said as Jas went to work. "You gonna make me forget all about Summer Jam and take you back to the crib to handle that!"

“Boy quit,” she said as he helped her sit on the hood of the car. “You already know what’s up.”

“Aight then, we're gonna see later,” he said, *already knowing he planned to knock it out the park tonight.*

“Man you better be careful,” I said, elbowing him. “You already got caught slipping one time..”

“I was younger then,” he said, swatting my arm away while laughing. “Y’all better be safe-*Peter and Petunia Petty. Moving his two fingers back and forth between his eyes and us.*

“Whatever Alonzo!” Vanessa said as she slapped his shoulder playfully. “Don’t play me like that. And anyway, that was just a little more than a couple years ago, *so you're still young.*”

The emcee announced the lineup of performances and other activities slated for the event. It would be a mix of the old and new school, with a talent show, and some special guests we had to wait to see who popped up. The whole thing was lit and everyone was enjoying themselves. Alonzo pulled the blunt he had on his ear and fired it up. The girls didn’t smoke so it was more for us. I didn’t do it too often but wasn’t an amateur either. Just being around my close friends, more like extended family, always put me in a good place. I had a very tight-knit group of friends, with these being the closest of them all. We took in all that Summer Jam had to offer while enjoying all of the performances from Pastor Troy, TI, UGK, Lil Flip, 112, Next, P-Diddy, Usher, Hot Boyz w/ Lil Wayne, and Juvenile. The highlight was when DMX with Sisqo made a surprise appearance, performing "What these bitches want", causing a frenzy. We headed to the parking area early to try to beat the crowd. Just as we pulled out gunshots and sounds of fighting could be heard. *Can't ever have a good thing.* Alonzo rode with Jasmine and Vanessa and I followed as we went to Charlie's Diner, a local longstanding black-owned spot that always had good food and entertainment. We found a booth quickly and ordered something light. Alonzo had the munchies and ordered like he hadn't eaten in days. We all watched and tried not to laugh.

"Slow down baby," Jasmine teased while swiping a piece of bacon. "That food ain't going nowhere. But, thank you for the bacon."

"Try it again and we'll be up in here throwing hands," he said, blocking his food.

"Skinniest fat person I know," I teased. "You sure you aint hiding something?"

"What I told you about that?!" he said, dropping his food on the plate.

"Aye! Can I get a to-go box? I've lost my appetite."

"Calm down fat kid," we all chimed in. "You're all serious and shit."

"Aye man, Myles will be here this weekend for the summer," I said, switching topics to brighten the mood. "He said he has some skills to show you on the court, and in the ring if you are willing to spar with him again."

Myles had been learning some basketball tips from Alonzo and Coach Webster when he came to visit each summer in addition to the boxing training from my dad; he already had different scouts and schools offering him scholarships if he kept focused on his books and not on the girls and the corner with the street katz. He had both street smarts and book smarts and could go head-to-head with the best of them. James taught him boxing and he kept it up through the years and incorporated it into his daily workouts. The only person he really only had trouble with was his step-dad, Ollie, whom his mom treated like 'God's gift to women' though she didn't get anywhere near the same treatment in return.

Why she stayed with such a bum was beyond him but he promised he was gonna get them out of that situation '*by any means necessary*'-as the late Malcolm X spoke during the days of the Civil Rights Movement. They had suffered so much abuse from Ollie that Myles looked forward to getting away each summer, though he always feared what could happen to his mom in his absence. I was so caught up in my own head and thoughts that I hadn't noticed that everyone was staring at me when I came back around. I signaled for the check, paid, and then we left.

Alonzo stopped by to pick up his overnight bag and stuff and left with Jas, leaving me and bae to chill and get in that quality time. Grabbing myself a corona and her peach wine cooler (she really didn't drink like that either), after changing into some gray shorts and a tank top, we watched *Jason's Lyric* and started *Love & Basketball* when Vanessa started kissing on my neck. Still feeling the buzz from the last blunt I smoked with Alonzo working with the beer I was nursing, I turned towards her and kissed her gently, kinda surprised and excited at the same time. I pulled her on my lap and started kissing and caressing her entire body. Then slowly pulled my shirt off and she did the same. I could feel myself at full attention and became even more aroused as she slowly grinded on top of me. Though nervous, I tried not to show it and was about to let my pants down when she suddenly hopped up and grabbed my hand. I took one more long swig from the beer, before letting Vanessa lead the way to the bedroom and I picked her up and laid her on the bed. She grabbed the remote to my stereo set and turned on some slow jams that were already loaded in the CD player.

Luther Vandross "*Here and Now*" started playing softly through the surround sound. She then got under the covers and undressed, throwing her lace panties playfully at my face. I held it there for a second as I undressed and slid next to her. We kissed and I sucked on her velvety soft breasts. They were just big enough for me to cusp with my hands; I used one hand while gently sliding my other one further south. It was so smooth, warm, and moist. She sighed as my fingers slowly slid in-one then another in and out, a little deeper each time. She held my manhood and gently stroked it up and down. It took all I had to keep from nutting prematurely all in her hand. Feeling under the pillow, I found a condom that Alonzo had told me to always keep available in case I needed it. *My boy was always looking out!*

Please don't fail me now!-I prayed as I rolled over to unwrap and slide it on before going under the covers. I wanted to taste all of her. Starting with her thighs I kissed her gently while still exploring her temple with my fingers. I licked them and tasted her juices. Her breathing got heavy and she started squirming as I approached it with my tongue. I teased her for a bit with it then went in for the kill. She squeezed her thighs against my head and I eased them back apart as I made my way up to her belly button, breasts, chin, neck, and finally her lips.

As we kissed, she slowly pulled me towards her and guided my manhood towards her temple. It was a combination of wet, warm, and tightness. I stopped when I felt some initial resistance and she let out a soft cry. As I inched deeper and deeper inside of her, I could feel her body tensing up and then relaxing into a smooth rhythm. This was the most amazing feeling ever! I looked down at her and she let me know with her eyes that it was okay. I put my face into the pillow next to hers and slowly rocked back and forth. She moved along with me like we were a boat riding an ocean wave. I slowly lifted her as we rolled over, not skipping a beat. She slowly worked her hips while tightening her grip around me, riding me and pushing me back against the pillows, *OHHHHHHHH, this was good!* I moaned as we continued to rock back and forth; I didn't even care that I was making noises and curling my toes. Vanessa leaning down, kissing my neck only excited me even more. I flipped her back over and went all the way in with us making love for what seemed like an eternity, taking breaks to catch our breath and me ensuring I had my raincoats. At some point we fell asleep holding each other, completely exhausted.

IV.

We wasted no time getting down to business when we got back to my crib. I wanted her to own up to all that shit she had been talking about earlier. We got inside, had the door locked and stripped out of our outfits in record time. Before Jas could get to the bed, I lifted her up from behind by her hips, slid her thong aside, and commenced to go to town on her with my tongue. She grabbed the bedsheets attempting to get away from me, but I pulled her away and lifted her petite ass up, then turned and sat on the bed. She took no time returning the favor by taking me all the way into her wet mouth, signaling me to lay back as we pleasured each other. We kept this up for a while as I was too horny from drinking and smoking. I finally moved her body aside so I could catch my breath while she continued to suck me up.

Feeling myself about to bust, I gently held her head down as I released all my juice down her throat. I leaned back as she drained me dry while still working to keep me rock solid. Then instinctively, I retrieved a condom from my nightstand drawer, opened and slid it on before pushing her forward towards my ankles and sliding inside. The arch in her back only gave me more reason to thrust harder and deeper while gripping her thighs. Any noise she made was muffled by the bed as I hit it from the back while holding her down with my body weight. Smacking her ass I talked shit to her.

"What was all that shit you were talking about earlier?" I asked. "Naw, don't run now. Bring it to daddy. Take all this."

"Oooh, you're so deep daddy, don't stop!" she said as she purred like a cat before arching back towards me and turning to face me, swinging her legs around, all without breaking her stride. "Lay back and enjoy the ride."

She rode me like she was on one of those mechanical bulls. Anyone walking in would've heard the bed frame knocking against the walls. Thankfully my place had very thick walls between them and the neighboring unit. She tightened herself around me and she rocked me, her hands grasping the headboard. Not about to let her outdo me, I sat up and flipped over while holding her and gave her long, slow deep strokes as I held one of her legs high in the sky, that sent her catching orgasms back to back.

Soon I felt myself about to catch the big one, and lowered her leg so she was flat on her stomach feeling all of me as I went in deep one more time. I pulled out and groaned loudly as I felt the condom fill up and pop, spilling baby batter all over her ass and thigh. *Damn, that was close!* I thought as I saw the mess made. I slowly got up to get a warm wet towel to clean us up and also dispose of the condom remnants. After making sure she was good, I turned on the shower and began to wash up. Jas, sore beyond words, eventually got up and put on her shower cap to join me. We took turns lathering and teasing each other, which led to another round of sexing.

She had one arm around my neck and the other stretched to the shower door while I held her up against the wall, stroking for dear life. All of the stress from work, life, was being worked out as I gave her all I had with each stroke. It felt so good with the warm shower water running down over them. She sucked on my neck and gently bit my ear, which drove me crazy. Feeling myself about to bust and catch a cramp in my hamstring simultaneously, I held her up against the wall directly under the shower head, legs and hips wrapped around my waist as I went in real deep, releasing everything I had inside her.

I held her up against the wall as I struggled to catch my breath. I gently released my grip with her sliding off my exhausted manhood. I grabbed the portable shower head and spread her legs, gently scrubbing and rinsing, as I gently washed all of her intimate areas. I kissed the back of her neck and continued to lather and wash her body. She then reciprocated, while being very gentle with my now very sensitive third leg while ensuring we were good to go. We wrapped ourselves in towels and Jas wrapped her hair while I sprayed the shower down. While I went to get started on the bed and linen, she wasted no time taking a Plan-B with a bottle of water from the mini-fridge kept in their bathroom. Couldn't afford any unwanted surprises. It wasn't long before we both were passed out on the bed with *Sons of Funk's "Pushing inside of you"* fading out. And that was all she wrote.

Morning came quickly and I was up early like clockwork. I had to meet Yvonne at my parents house to get KyJuan today since I had my fun yesterday. I also wanted to touch up their yard since it had rained recently, allowing the grass to grow back fast. My parents, David and Viola, had made plans to go golfing with Mr. James, followed by a luncheon with some friends at the Carlyle Estates Country Club. I quietly got dressed and leaned over to kiss

Jas, trying not to wake her up as I made my exit. Pops was waiting in the driveway as I locked up. Accustomed to my routine, she stayed in bed a little longer before getting up and dressed so she could be ready for lil man when we returned. Even though she could be wild and reckless at times, Jas was no fool. She kept protection on her as a secondary precaution since her new depo shot. We hadn't used protection the second time, and she knew my baby juice was very potent. Plus she had big career plans and having a baby was not part of that right now. Neither she nor I needed that added stress. KyJuan was handful enough for the us and her mom told her she was *a damn good one* taking on that unnecessary responsibility given what all she was trying to accomplish.

V.

Yvonne loved Alonzo's parents despite not always seeing eye to eye with him. They co-parented pretty well though. She didn't care for Jasmine but that's because she thought he cheated on her with her but it was honestly her own *ex* best friend that ended up being the reason behind them breaking up. Victoria, aka Vic"horia", tried to hit on him at a party and when he turned down her proposition, she spread rumors that he was lame and wasn't acting crazy when she made time for him when Yvonne was busy working or too tired to put out.

Yvonne knew Alonzo had messed with her before they got together but Victoria timed her stunt right when it would hurt her the most-at the wake, a few days before her grandmother's funeral. Though it all turned out to be a lie, Yvonne and Alonzo had already been in a bad place and she felt betrayed by both of them, so the damage was done. Victoria still didn't end up with Alonzo, and after being ostracized by most of her close friends, ended up disappearing after graduation never to be heard from again. Also she felt Alonzo might have done it as payback for when Victoria lied to him about her supposedly having slept with her ex one time during their separation period.

The truth was she was sexually assaulted after getting separated from her friends during a girl's night birthday celebration, where she was found passed out in the VIP section of a club. It was only after going to have an examination and report taken that she actually found out she had been not only drugged, but even worse, was pregnant. She had started taking birth control when they got serious and only let Alonzo stop using condoms after they'd been going steady for almost two years. Fearing the worst and feeling ashamed for letting her guard down at the party, she kept everything to herself. None of her girlfriends knew about it; only her late grandmother who took it to her grave.

Any doubt that may have existed quickly disappeared when Alonzo showed up at the hospital with his parents when she was in labor. Little KyJuan "Dave" Carlson looked like a spit image of Alonzo when he was born. Unbeknownst to him she had a DNA test performed to clear her conscience. The detective working the case was able to get samples from her rape kit to use, and it brought her much relief knowing her baby was not conceived through rape. When they did get time alone from endless visitors coming to see the new parents, they had the painful conversation and agreed to let bygones be bygones.

Mama called my name as she watched Yvonne pull up in the driveway. They had settled in the living room by the time I came up the hallway having just finished talking with pops after showering up from the yard maintenance. KyJuan quickly took notice of my presence and walked right over to me. I leaned down to hug my growing little mini me. Senior wasn't too far behind and patted my shoulders while making silly faces to his grandson. Viola and Yvonne loved watching these rare kodak moments.

Three generations of the same face, personality, and character, all in the same room. She relished knowing that despite her own upbringing in the foster system, she was able to make the best of her situation with me for KyJuan's sake. She was grateful for her close relationship with Mrs. Viola. Pops walked over and gave her a warm hug and kiss on the cheek before sitting down next to ma. I sat down near KyJuan as he played with his Woody and Buzz toys. Yvonne's eyes met mine for a split second and for an instant it appeared that there might still be hope for us just yet.

I sometimes wondered if we had a future down the road but never brought it up out of respect for Jasmine. One day I'd cross that bridge, but for now just let it simmer on the backburner of my deepest thoughts. We couldn't hide our smiles. That spark was still there. The elders definitely caught wind of it but just put their hands on each other and squeezed as they finished their tea. *In due time things will be just fine.*

Just as I was making my exit from dropping off KyJuan, Jasmine arrived to pick the father-son duo up. We exchanged pleasantries. Alonzo had made it clear that Jasmine had nothing against me and was actually proud of how I balanced life as a mother with work and school. No matter how tired Alonzo was, she always pushed him to take KyJuan whenever possible because he had the support system I didn't and she felt for me. Secretly I knew Jasmine had a strong influence over Alonzo spending time with his son and was glad that she helped him honor his obligations.

We were all young working adults, navigating our ways through life. I unlocked the door to my Lexus suv and placed my bags in the back before getting in and starting it up. I told them when I'd be off so they could bring him home and left after kissing KyJuan.

Alonzo followed me to the car so KyJuan could see us together. He was very observant for a three yr old. He chewed on his apple slices while trying to wave at me. *"Oooh Child"* played softly in my mind as I watched her leave. *All in due time*.

VI.

When we got back home, Alonzo went into the kitchen to wash up and start fixing plates from the breakfast I had prepared for them. I could tell he had something on his mind but let it go. Today was family time and KyJuan was the focus. I took him while Alonzo gathered his thoughts and set their plates.

"What's your plans with KyJuan today?" I asked as we watched him feed himself cheese grits and pieces of bacon. He loved bacon just like his daddy.

"Nothing honestly," he said as he poured juice and they sat down. "Just wanted to hang out with my lil man. Might call and see if Avant and Vanessa are up to stopping through."

"It won't hurt to ask," I said to him. KyJuan let out a burp as he drank his orange juice. "Guess somebody's full."

"Let's put your plate in the sink and wash your hands," he said, grabbing their plates and heading to the sink. "You know I appreciate everything you do for me and for sticking by me with KyJuan."

"That's what couples do," I said as I stirred my cheese grits and added pepper to them. "My family always helped raise each other's children."

"You're gonna be a good mama whenever that time comes," he said.

"I appreciate it," I said, leaning over to give him a kiss. KyJuan tried to pull him away. "*Oh, no you didn't!*"

He cheesed hard as he pulled him into the kitchen. Alonzo sat the plates on the counter as he watched his son slowly climb up the step ladder. He passed him one item at a time to set down in the dishwater being careful not to drop or break anything. They were side by side as dad washed the dishes and son slowly held them under the running water to rinse. Jas then dried them with a towel and put them up. Just as she turned around ready to place the folded towel on the stove handle, father and son sprayed her with water. KyJuan squealed as they were soaking her up. She held up the towel to try to shield herself from their merciless assault. They finally stopped long enough for her to run down the hallway to change. Little did she know that lil man was hot on her heels with a small water gun-Alonzo peeped him slipping in right before the door closed, and held his side as he heard them going at it!

VII.

Bae and I woke up still cuddled together. I got up and went to use the bathroom. I heard her let out a loud shriek and almost pissed on the floor. My gut told me to look down. I saw red around me. My heart skipped a beat or two. I knew I had put on a condom and knew I had bought a three pack earlier just in case they were needed. *Had we used that many?* I checked the box and saw it was empty. *Aw hell*! I cleaned myself up before coming out. I heard her start running a bath and went to help her in. While she soaked, I stripped the bed and set them in the laundry area to be cleaned. I came back and sprayed the bed with Lysol before putting a new mattress pad, sheets, and comforter on it.

Vanessa called me as I finished tucking in the last corner of the fitted sheets. I walked in and saw her covered in bubbles. Sitting next to her on the edge, I could feel the heat from the hell waters below. I knelt down close to give her a kiss, trying to balance myself. She smiled and tugged at my sweats. I already knew what time it was and hastily loosened them, releasing my sidekick. I removed my tank top and stepped out of my boxer briefs, testing the water with my toes-*damn water hotter than hell!*

I quickly removed it and shook my head in adamant resistance. If it felt like that to my foot, I could only imagine how my twins would feel trying to sit down in it. Already feeling horny again, I took my chance. *The shit you do for love*. She came towards me and lay up against me, rubbing her body against mine. I slowly pulled her on top of my face, and explored her with my tongue. She moaned as I kissed and nipped at her inner thighs. I held her in place as I tasted all over her. I could feel her juices saturating my face and I enjoyed every bit of it. She slowly slid back down and I leaned my head back as I felt her insert my manhood inside of her.

She kissed me softly as she started rocking, the bath water in rhythm with her. I held on to her hips and ass pulling her closer to me. *Oh shit this felt good.* Feeling her hot breath on my neck, and listening to her moan turned me on even more. We turned to where I was now looking down at her and arching my back to give her slow deep strokes. She pulled me closer and closer, going deeper and deeper with each stroke. Pulling her back on top, I held her close as she wrapped her legs around my body. She nibbled on my earlobe and made her way down the side of my neck. I couldn't hold back any longer and moaned loudly as I felt myself about to nut hard. It felt like her walls were tightening even more around my sidekick so I couldn't pull out if I wanted to. As I released my seeds deep inside her I could feel her heartbeat slow down and match that of my own as we held each other close.

No turning back now. My nose was wide open and you couldn't tell me otherwise! No shame in my game, as we went at it til we were both wrinkled as albino raisins and the water had started getting cold. We eventually released our embrace and finished getting ready…but I went to the shower this time, with a slight limp, to prevent another potential session, while she drained and ran more water in the tub. *Today was going to be a great day,* I told myself as I showered, ensuring to congratulate my manhood for not failing me.

VIII.

I had Makaveli "Hail Mary" blasting loud as I finished packing my bags. I was too hyped about my trip. I looked forward to getting away from the hell hole I shared with my mom and abusive step-father Ollie. Only wearing basketball shorts, the most recent scars and wounds were starting to blend back in with my other skin tone as I looked back at the mirror on my dresser. Mama didn't know about these and I had succeeded thus far to hide them from her. I always did have a higher than normal pain tolerance since I was a child but the abuse was now starting to affect me mentally.

I had managed to avoid more severe physical abuse since working consistently to improve my boxing skills. But everything changed when my step-father pulled a gun on me; I knew the dynamics had changed and so I had to change my strategy to adapt accordingly. I had my own Glock-40 always close by in case I needed to protect myself or mama from Ollie or anyone else who dared to cross me wrong. Uncle James, Avant's dad, had gifted it to me not long ago and taught both of us how to use guns safely and effectively. He knew I was more street savvy than Avant but wanted both to be able to look after one another regardless of where we were and what situation we ended up in. Being a military veteran, he emphasized safety and only using it as an absolute last resort life or death option. I turned around upon hearing the door open to see mama come in.

"Are you almost ready, handsome?" she said just as I finished adjusting my Kobe Bryant Jersey. She walked over to knock some lint off my shoulders. She knew I was very meticulous about my appearance.

"I'm good ma," I said, giving her a kiss on the cheek. "Been looking forward to this all year long."

"I know you have," she said, giving me a hug. "Don't you worry about me. Jesus will protect me as he does you. You go have fun with your cousin and try not to drive your Aunt and Uncle crazy.... *And please steer clear of them fast ass lil girls.*"

"I stay with the protection mama, for all situations." I said as I slipped into some black no-show socks and my new Kobe Bryant customized Air Force Ones.

"Mama don't keep letting Ollie disrespect you like he does," I said looking her in the eye. "I don't want to have to hurt him over you."

"I know baby," she said, helping me with my bags.

We headed to the train station where she watched as I disappeared inside the train terminal and headed to check my bags and get my boarding ticket. I waved at her as I headed to the railway to wait for my train to arrive so I could board. Once I was gone from her sight she went back to the car and just sat there fighting back tears. She knew she deserved better and wanted better for me. She had contemplated letting my Aunt and Uncle adopt me when I started high school to give me a better life after I became more involved in the streets, but she didn't want them to be burdened with another teenager since they were both recently retired. Even with Avant there to help, they would still have their hands full with me. She watched the train leave from the parking lot, gathered herself together, and went on to her doctor's appointment.

She left the house dressed for work as she always did wearing her scrubs but didn't go to work. She had been diagnosed with glioblastoma multiforme, and had been going in for chemotherapy and treatments for over the past year or so. Always having short hair and a small figure, she was able to hide her pain and discomfort. When chemotherapy started thinning her hair, her good friend Clarissa had designed some custom wigs that matched her natural hairstyles. Me nor Ollie could tell the difference so she was good to go. She knew it would only be so much time before she'd have to tell. She prayed her Serenity Prayer and recited Psalms 90 and 91 perfectly in her soft tone as she drove to Agape Cancer Institute downtown.

I finally relaxed once I got settled on the train. Mama had managed to hit every new bruise when she hugged me, and it took all I had to muster up the strength to save face for her. I had been battered so much between boxing and street fights, gun shot grazings, and Ollie's abuse, that I stopped being able to differentiate which wounds came from the street war and which ones from the war at home. I popped a pain pill and drank some water before drifting off to sleep. I set an alarm that would wake me before we arrived at my destination. I closed my eyes and listened as UGK "*One Day*" played in my ear phones.

Alexis would pick me up from the airport and we'd chill before getting dropped by Avant's house. I couldn't wait to get back inside her guts. Lauryn also crossed my mind. I definitely wanted to link up with her too since we had kept on a regular basis. She was Vanessa's fine ass lil cousin I had met the last time I came down when she came to visit her. It would be cool to chill with her to help pass time when the others became busy, but not on a serious tip. Wasn't trying to cross any boundaries, or lead her on. My life already had too much going on to add anything else into the mix.

Alexis was waiting just as I expected when I disembarked and waited for my luggage to be retrieved by the staff. Those ass and hips could be spotted a mile away. She was a certified freak and I knew she was eagerly awaiting her much needed tune up from her favorite mechanic. She had a lil boy and was completing an advanced nursing specialization degree, but still found time to help out when she could. I hugged her and squeezed her ass while I could before putting my luggage in her car. Malachi, her son, walked beside her as we got in. I noted how he looked just like her as he held tightly to his stuffed ninja turtles. He would get dropped off at daycare along the way and then we'd be free to *chill.* I helped get him situated in his car seat while she started the car. Malachi looked up at me and smiled and offered one of his toys. Alexis watched silently from the rearview mirror and smiled. He had never done that before and usually was only friendly towards her family. She couldn't help to notice the similarities between them and how he'd make such a great father; but the uncertainty kept her from saying anything that might trigger a conversation she wasn't ready to have just yet. We cruised along while blasting Plies *"Bust It Baby, Pt. 2" feat. Ne-Yo.*

After we dropped lil man off we went to pick up food before heading back to her place. I left all but one of my bags in the car and followed her inside where I removed my shoes before walking over to make myself comfortable on her sofa. I removed my glock and ensured the safety was engaged before sitting it down on the coffee table. While she disappeared to do whatever she was doing, I pulled out one of my plastic bags containing some pre-rolled blunts. By the time she returned I had fired up one and was taking slow drags from it.

She was wearing a sequin lingerie set as her hips swayed back and forth towards me. I held it out and she took a long drag from it and pulled me close as she blew the smoke into my face. *I took it like a G!* She passed it back to me and cuddled up next to me. She wasted no time getting to what she missed. Soon as I went for a pull, she inhaled all of my manhood. I damn near choked on the smoke as she caught me by surprise. I reclined the seat back and continued to smoke while she topped me off. After making sure I was rock solid, she pulled a condom out and placed it on me before she straddled me and worked her magic-slow and easy. She lifted up my jersey over my head, while admiring my musculature and tattoos, barely being contained inside of my tank top.

She started with my ear and kissed and licked me all over. With all of the craziness going on in my life, just being here with her, I felt a weight lifted from my shoulders, even if only temporarily. I pulled her close and leaned back on the sofa sideways, holding onto her while sliding out of my clothes for a better position. We held each other closely as she rode me nice and slow. I flipped her over and wrapped my arms to keep us interlocked, enjoying every minute of our time together as she wrapped her legs around my waist. This reunion had been long overdue and I wasn't about to come up short. She moaned and squeezed her walls tightly around me as I stroked her deep and hard. I pulled out long enough to flip her into her favorite position—*face down ass up*-and continued my mission—*beat the pussy up*.

We continued for what felt like hours on end before we exhausted each other. When she thought I was close she pulled away to get her bearings back and get my soldier into her mouth; no longer able to resist her, I laid back on the sofa, closing my eyes, as she worked her hands, tongue, and throat with fury. She milked me dry as I felt my soul leaving my body filling the condom. I slid my fingers into her fiery wetness and worked them as a pianist worked the keys. She moaned louder and louder which only excited me more and gave me a second wind.

Seizing the opportunity, I quickly pulled her back towards me as we both ended up on the floor where I had her legs stretched back far behind her head. I went all in deep with my tongue and tasted all her sweet juices while sucking on her clit. She clawed helplessly as I took her to an unknown universe of pleasure. With her legs still stretched behind her head, I entered her raw on my tippy toes and stroked her something serious. Her moans only made it worse because she could do nothing but lay there helplessly as I inspected every deep crevice of her pussy walls with my soldier. Just as I felt her walls tighten and her legs try to hold me hostage, I jumped up-pulling out in just enough time to release my baby juice all over her stomach and breasts. I trembled uncontrollably as I felt all of my energy leave my body, before finally collapsing beside her.

Alexis finally managed to get herself to get up and tried her best to walk steadily to the bathroom using the wall for support. She turned on the shower, then relieved herself. After washing her hands, quickly opened her medicine cabinet to retrieve a Plan B-ensuring she downed plenty of water with it. After she finished showering, she then ran some bath water and went and helped me up, taking note of the scars on my back-my unspoken war wounds. She also couldn't help but take notice of the one thing that she loved about me most-*that damn bowlegged swag I couldn't help I walked with*. She watched as I eased myself into the hell fire water and proceeded to wash my back, careful not to irritate any of the wounds.

We looked at each other with an unspoken understanding of gratitude and appreciation. I gently pulled her into the tub to join me. As she lay back against me, I washed her body with the loofa slowly, enjoying their intimacy. She had been my ride or die for a long time, but knew that we could never truly be together. It was physical, but we shared that common chaotic upbringing, having to learn to survive on our own from an early age. We finished our bath and cleaned up, ordered and ate some Olive Garden, and chilled across her bed watching "*Menace to Society*" to pass time while my laundry was going.

She always made sure to get her health check ups, especially after becoming pregnant unexpectedly with Malachi. The timing was so off that she really didn't know who her son's daddy was between

Myles and Calhoun. In her heart though, she truly believed he was Myles'. *"Dilemma" by Nelly and Kelly Rowland in her head.*

Vanessa was on break at work, when she looked down to see her phone light up.

"Hey Lauryn, what's up?"

"Hey girl, do you know if Avant has heard from his cousin?" she asked shyly. "I remember him saying he was coming but don't remember when."

"He was supposed to be coming this weekend," she responded. "What's up,what y'all two lil fast asses got planned?"

"Nothing, I just wanted to finally see him again," she began as she described how they had connected last summer and stayed in touch after he went back home.

"*Not my Lauryn having a crush on Myles' lil thug ass.*" she laughed before getting serious. "Well looks wise, he's a tanned version of Avant, with more street savviness."

"I don't know what it is," she told her. "I just feel a connection."

"Just play it safe and take things slow," Vanessa answered. "He's a smart kid like Avant, but he's definitely a little rough around the edges."

"Kinda like different sides of the same coin," she cosigned. "Guess that's not too bad."

"You'll see for yourself when you meet him," she said laughing. "But I'm about to go back to work, gotta get this menu together for this client that's having some kind of *Soiree* at the end of this month."

"All right then," Lauryn responded. "I'll see you later on when we link up. I have to pick out something nice to wear."

"Whatever you wear will be just fine," Vanessa said confidently knowing that her cousin always carried herself well. "Love you and see you later."

A few hours later I received the call I had been anticipating. I immediately called Alonzo afterwards and told him. I was gonna swing by to get him and KyJuan on the way to get Myles from Alexis's crib. The father and s*on duo were on the porch waiting when I pulled up. I drove the suv since we had lil man riding-always safety first*. Plus I didn't know how much luggage Myles brought and rather be safe than sorry, space wise. Alexis lived on the far side of town, in Lakewood, near the county general hospital back in our old stomping grounds. The area still looked the same despite having more and more businesses closing down due to owner's retiring and others relocating for better opportunities.

I always looked for potential business opportunities to help give back and made mental note of a few properties to relay back to my dad. We pulled up to a quaint old fashioned brick house in a small, but well kept yard. I eyed the old school white *DeVille d'Elegance with whitewall tires* under the carport and smiled. My dad had one similar and drove it every so often when he and mom just wanted to go cruising on the weekends. Myles was already outside toting her son in one hand and his ninja turtle bag over his shoulder heading towards the house. Alexis was right behind him with the keys. She still looked good as she waved to us. Despite her being around our age, Myles didn't let that stop him from *getting to know her.*

They had been cool for as long as I can remember and spent a lot of time hanging out when I was busy at school or working. If only James and Vivian really knew what he was up to besides helping keep her family's yard *maintained* during his summer visits back in the day. Knowing them, they already knew but left well enough alone. Once he made sure they were situated he gave her a goodbye embrace, fist pounded Malachi, and came back out to transfer his bags.

Soon we were all tripping out. Myles played with KyJuan as we drove back to Alonzo's place. I watched how he had interacted with them and felt like he had an instant bond with her son in my gut. *I kept it to myself but made a mental note to bring it up once we were alone.* When we pulled up to the house, Vanessa and Jas were sitting on the front porch. As soon as we got out of the car, they came to greet us. Alonzo kissed Jas as they walked inside. Myles hugged Vanessa and spoke to Jas. As he walked into the house he was completely caught off guard when he bumped into Lauryn-he was instantly mesmerized. She looked exotic and he was definitely feeling her. He played it cool though. Lauryn could tell he was much more street than Avant though they could easily pass for twins.

After getting his stuff settled in his room and changed into something more comfortable he came back to see her. They went on the back patio for some privacy. Everyone watched as they disappeared. Vanessa was super overprotective over her younger cousin and narrowed her eyes unbeknownst. She wasted no time giving me the third degree about Myles and how he better treat Lauryn right. Jasmine grilled Alonzo the same way and told him he better help me keep him out of trouble. She then turned to me and repeated her threat-to keep the other two outta trouble or else I'd be dealing with her lol.

We all joined them not long afterwards. Myles went around the corner to get a basketball from the garage and cast a long three from far away. Alonzo turned at the sound of the swish and put his hands up to catch the rebound. He caught the ball and released quickly, hitting nothing but net as an answer to the challenge. He then caught the rebound and threw it out to me. I went inside for a quick lay up. Soon we were playing twenty-one. Myles ended up winning with Alonzo and me trailing close behind. He always knew how to lighten up the mood. The girls were all impressed and acted like cheerleaders. Myles came over and hugged Lauryn as she turned his way, totally catching her off guard. She pushed him off playfully as he tried to hug her, unsuccessfully fighting him off sweat and all. Vanessa and Jas both avoided the same potential embarrassment by running inside the house with KyJuan in tow. Lauryn finally got away and went inside herself. Making sure the girls were out of earshot, I dropped the bombshell.

"You serious bro?" Alonzo said, turning in his direction. "And it was yall first time?"

"Yeah man, I'm nervous and excited," Avant responded. "Guess it was bound to happen. She tightened up around me and I was trapped!"

"Don't sweat it man, it happens to the best of us." I chimed in. "The big question is, have you mentioned it to Vanessa?"

"Naw," Avant confessed. "She knew what she was doing!"

"She tightened her walls and it was over from there," Alonzo teased his boy. "Plus it's not like we are teenagers. Shit you held out longer than I ever could and I commend you for that."

"Hell yeah cuzzo," I said, giving us dap. "You and sis gonna be fine. You already basically set up with your own place and good jobs; just take it one day at a time *Cool Breeze*."

We all went in through the garage upstairs to hit the showers. Afterwards everyone met back up in the great room where the new love birds sat across from KyJuan. He made his little way over to them, leaving his dad behind to question his loyalty. I laughed and shrugged my shoulders as I picked him up and sat him between the two. Yvonne called to let him know she was on her way to pick up F since she got off early. Not wanting to cut his visit short, he offered to bring him by later since they were all hanging out.

She agreed to stop by later after she had gotten settled in from work. She had to come our way anyway, but appreciated his gratitude. Avant went into the kitchen to see what groceries were there to try to whip up a quick meal. Vanessa and Jasmine came in behind and wasted no time helping. Alonzo continued his daddy duties while also starting a game of spades. Lauryn and KyJuan watched as we talked shit to each other while becoming very animated. The others heard us and just laughed knowing I was more likely putting another beating on Alonzo and he was not taking it very well. We had more of a sibling rivalry than either of us had with my cousin. It took about an hour but a decent meal of baked salmon with broccoli and loaded baked potatoes and freshly made lemonade and Southern Sweet Tea made it all worth the wait. Even KyJuan got down on good eating. *Lil man was growing up fast.*

Me and Lauryn had kitchen detail once we finished dinner and didn't complain since it allowed us to have more time together. Vanessa kept a watchful eye on us two, with her eyes meeting mine disapprovingly at times. I stuck my tongue out at her when Lauryn wasn't looking, only further stoking the inferno already brewing. '*Keep playing, you gonna fuck around and fine out!*' she thought to herself as she made sure I saw her flash her brass knuckles on the side of the sofa, out of everyone's sight. I quickly straightened up, prompting Lauryn to look up and out towards the family room. Vanessa waved innocently while putting on her best '*Mrs. America*' smile. She smiled back, completely oblivious of the death threats passed between us.

Once we finished, we joined everyone where KyJuan was finally napping spread out across Alonzo like he had worked back to back graveyard shifts. He gently repositioned his son on the sofa and quietly excused himself just as his phone started vibrating. He went to one of the guest rooms to gather up KyJuan's stuff that Yvonne brought and set it nearby to be ready to take out when she pulled up. He hated that things were this way, but was grateful to be able to see his son. KyJuan must have sensed that it was time to go because he woke up fussy and was acting like he didn't want to leave. It broke Alonzo's heart to see KyJuan cry but he saved face and took him outside to her Tahoe and got him securely buckled in his car seat. He gave Yvonne a hug and watched as they backed out and drove off. Jas came out to check on him; she rubbed his back and held on to him as he stood silently, *his mind half a million miles away. Love Jones* was about to start so everyone got cozy in their own little space. It felt great to have everyone together again just like the old days when we didn't have much worries or responsibilities at all.

Waiting on the pregnancy test to change felt forever. Vanessa had been sick for about three weeks now and hadn't started her cycle. They'd been more careful for the most part after our first couple of times. Trying not to panic, she prayed that it was just late but knew in her gut it wasn't. Lauryn watched as she paced back and forth stopping momentarily to look at the test-then two lines appeared. Her eyes got big and she smiled as she showed her. Lauryn texted Myles and told him to have Avant come to the house asap. Avant was in the middle of a business meeting discussing risk analysis associated with a port client that was trying to expand and add new ventures with some overseas companies when he noticed one of the executive secretaries peek inside.

Thankfully the meeting was almost over, with him handing out an executive summary of findings and recommendations when she gave him a signal for an emergency call. After ensuring he was no longer needed he disconnected my laptop, gathered his briefcase and legal pad of notes, and took all back to his office. Myles told him something was up with Vanessa and that he needed to get home. Knowing exactly what it was about, he took slow deep breaths, asked his secretary to clear his schedule for the rest of the day, and headed to pick him from his parent's house where he had been spending time with them. Ten minutes later they were home.

"She's in the bedroom," Lauryn pointed down the hallway as the two walked in. "Aight, thanks," he told her, giving her a hug. "Y'all give us some privacy?"

"No doubt cuzzo." I said as we headed towards the front. I looked back and Avant tossed me the keys to the Shelby GT. "*GOOD LOOK*!!"

I was too typed about getting to drive the mustang every opportunity afforded. After he locked the door he prayed he wouldn't regret doing that, took a couple of deep breaths and headed back to her room where he found her curled up on the bed. He walked over to the bed and moved her hair away from her face and kissed her softly as he leaned over her. Within his line of sight sat three positive pregnancy tests on her nightstand. She was sleeping. He took off his clothes and lay next to her to just hold her. He was nervous and excited. They were going to have a baby; he was really about to be a father. They'd always heard about it happening after only having sex one time. Then again, he did recall their sessions the next morning in the jet tub; he was sure that sealed their fate.

Luckily they were both pretty stable financially, had their own spot, and he knew that he could hold them down on his main income for at least a year if she wanted to do the whole stay at home mom thing. He also had been ring shopping because he knew she was who he wanted to be with, and he wanted to do things the right way. He wrapped his arm around her under the covers and rubbed her belly thinking about the growing seed inside.

Me and Lauryn went to pick up some lunch and headed to the park to enjoy the scenery. We ate in silence and just walked afterwards taking in everything. The park had a lake with a private fishing dock that I took her to. I laid down an old blanket found in the trunk close to the edge and we sat there with our shoes and socks off and let our bare feet hang off the edge, swaying above the water enjoying each other's company and nature playing out all around. Lauryn looked up into my eyes and I could sense she was searching.

"What's on your mind, Myles?" she asked cautiously. "You seem to be deep in thought, like you're holding in a lot of pain."

"Nothing too much," I answered as I watched the ripples in the lake appear and disappear from the breeze flowing across it.

"Just glad to be here, with you, and visiting with my cousin and family."

"Y'all seem very close," she said. "Vanessa and I are the same way. I'm happy for them. I know Vant will do whatever he has to do. He's always been good to her.``

"Yeah they're gonna be aight," I reassured her. "Trust and believe Avant always has a plan. He may not act like it, but he's a planner. He's got more street smarts than he gives himself credit for. He definitely got that trait from Uncle James."

"I can tell," she said smiling and leaning her head on my shoulder as she watched the swans swim past with little biddies behind them." He really loves her. He's so kind and patient. He respected her wanting to wait before..."

"Oh that's for sure," I said, stroking her hair. "He's never been one to rush. He likes to do things the right way for the most part. His old man always preached that to all of us."

We stayed a little longer before heading back to the house to bring the others some food. Alonzo and Jasmine were there when we pulled up. Everyone gave us the side eye when we walked in. I brushed them off as I walked past to put the food in the kitchen, slick smiling and shaking my head while rounding the corner. sat down with the others. She knew they were about to give her the business. I came back and joined her in the oversized recliner putting my arm around her, eyes barely open but knowing that we were both in the hot seat.

"You took your *medicine* I see," Alonzo said, looking our way.

"You know me. Gotta have my therapy," I answered. "Still got half a blunt and some more loud and dro if you want some."

"Hell yeah I'm down," he said about getting up while looking back at Jasmine's disappointing glare. "*What*?"

"Y'all hold up for a minute. I have some news," Avant addressed everyone, looking nervous as he stood up and made his way towards Vanessa.

"What's up?" I said, sitting straight up, alternating between looking from his cousin and Vanessa. She was looking just as lost as everyone else.

"Vanessa, baby girl, you've been my ride or die since forever. You've held it down with me through so many hard times."

He said with a big smile as he held her hands. He then walked over to the mantlepiece and retrieved a small black box before kneeling down on one knee and opening it.

"Will you do me the honor of spending the rest of your life with me? Will you be my wife, to love and to cherish, and build a family? To grow old together?"

Vanessa tried to blink away the tears forming in her eyes as she looked at the rose gold engagement ring he held in the open box. This was truly happening.

"*YES, of course I will marry you baby!*" She said as she accepted him placing the ring on her finger. She pulled him up and hugged him tightly.

"*And we're going to have a baby!*" Avant beamed at the announcement and got down again to kiss her belly while placing his hands on either side of her.

"*Word?!*" Alonzo said, getting up to give them some love. He knew this was a big moment for them.

Avant embraced him with a brotherly hug. I did the same but locked up instantly when he clasped his arms together around my back. The pain hit me so suddenly but I tried to hide it. Everyone noticed but Lauryn, yet no one said anything. She didn't know my story. Right now wasn't the time, but she'd soon learn. Once everything had settled down, Alonzo and I went out on the back patio.

"Man what was that about earlier?" he asked as they sat back looking over the backyard. "I mean with your back."

"Just some injuries that haven't healed all the way," I told him. "You know how it can be out in the streets."

"Yeah but judging how you froze up I think there's more to it," Alonzo said, turning in my direction. "Be straight up man. It was Ollie again, huh?"

I looked down, lit the ends of the blunt, took a long pull from it, before looking back up at him tearfully.

"Damn man," was all he could say. 'Aunt Angie knows he is still doing this?"

"Naw she dont know, I don't want her stressing." I responded while shaking myhead. "She already has a lot on her plate so she doesn't need anything else stressing her out. Plus I can handle him myself." I lifted up his shirt to show my regulator.

"Man don't let it have to come to that," Alonzo warned me. "You know you got a place down here anytime you are ready to make the move."

"I know man, but I can't leave mama Dukes like that," I said, taking another puff before passing it. "Plus they're gonna need the extra space for the little one."

"Yeah, but you gotta look out for you." He reasoned with me. "Your mom is a fighter. Best believe she's gonna be alright; and if push came to shove, I bet you could convince her to come here too and keep your aunt and uncle both company. With the baby coming all hands need to be on deck. And y'all mightall be able to move into one of the many rental properties both of our families."

Avant watched as they headed towards the back when they came back inside. Avant waited before coming back to the room. Through the slightly ajar door, he watched in the doorway as his cousin took off his undershirt revealing many scars and bruises in various stages of healing to Alonzo. Not able to hold himself back, he walked in, closing the door and just grabbed him and held him close. Myles knew instantly what was going on and didn't fight it.

Alonzo joined in, and Myles let the tears fall as they stood there. Avant was not going to let Myles go back there to stay. Even if that meant moving Auntie Angie too. He went to look for the first aid trauma kit Vanessa always had kept ready and got some ointment and dressings out for him to use. After Myles came out of the shower, he tended his wounds and got them cleaned and covered. Both Avant and Alonzon's blood was boiling. They both wanted to fuck Ollie up, but knew they had to play it smart because he was cutthroat and didn't play fair; he would come with Pandora's box of arsenal. Myles could sense it and turned to look at the mirror where all eyes met. The look he gave back reassured us that all would be handled and we need not worry. Everyone took it in for the night.

Jasmine dropped Alonzo off so he could get ready for work. He had been called in and honestly was glad for the distraction. Plus it was extra money he could put away for KyJuan. Yvonne didn't have him on child support but he still made sure to pay for as much as he could to help take the load off her and also to show his parents he was focused on his priorities. She went on to the house, took a warm bath, and pulled out her books to knock out some work that was due soon. She called to check on Vanessa but she didn't answer. She probably wanted some time alone so she could prepare to tell their parents the "news". Her phone buzzed and she lifted it up to see a message and smiled before turning it back face down so she could study.

Lauryn laid in her bed thinking about all that had transpired over the past couple of days. She enjoyed her time with Myles and liked his swag. He was mysterious. She liked his street smarts and how he carried himself. She turned on her playlist and the remix to *Tamia's "So Into You" feat. Fabolous* played softly in the background. He stayed on her mind and she was glad he'd be here to spend the summer. She wanted to be in his arms. She felt safe around him. His eyes hid so much pain and sadness and she just wanted to be there for him, by his side. She looked at the picture of them from last summer in her mirror and reminisced about how she enjoyed talking with him on the phone. She was heartbroken when he had to go back home, but as promised, he came back to see her. *"Promise" by Jagged Edge continued to play softly as she drifted off to sleep.*

IX.

Sunday came around before we knew it and everyone was nervous. I was excited to see Aunt Vivian and get some of her good ole home cooking. Despite my Uncle and cousin calling me the *"devil in sheep's clothing",* I could really do no wrong in her eyes. I was in the living room sprawled across the sofa when I heard the door from the garage open. I quickly jumped up and played a joke on her by holding on to the door to force her to have to knock. I slipped in through their storage area in the mudroom into the garage and put my hands over her eyes. Uncle James just shook his head and went inside from the other doorway with some of her luggage, wanting no parts of my shenanigans. He had been in the garage organizing his tools when she pulled in.

"Avant quit playing and help me get this luggage inside," she said trying to move my hands off her eyes. "Boy move your hands."

"What are you gonna do mama? I got you," I said, sounding just like Avant. She lifted her leg up and stomped down as hard as she could, landing right on top of my toes. "Ahh shit!! You win, you win, you got it Auntie!" I hollered and quickly moved to open the door for her.

"Auntie?" she said, stopping and turning around to see me with my foot on her bumper inspecting my newest wounds. "Myles, I'm sorry baby!! Come here and give me a hug."

I cautiously limped towards her and gave her a big hug. I had gotten up early and worked out with Unc and took some pain medicine so I wouldn't be in too much pain. She "accidentally" dropped one of her bags on my other foot, almost crushing my damn pinkie toe in the process. I jumped back and whimpered, trying not to cuss. "Don't cuss in my house again! *You ain't too old to be beat!*" she said walking away. Avant came out rubbing his eyes and scratching his head to see what the commotion was about. The bags told him that Mama Dukes was back and he quickly picked them up and brought them to her room while she headed to the bathroom. He saw me limping back to the sofa and laughed. Still up to the same old charades and got outsmarted by the master herself, Aunt Vivian. Uncle James had gone and sat in the recliner, chuckling behind the newspaper he had been reading. He knew I stayed pestering her, but I was her only nephew.

"Hey mama," Avant said walking back down the hallway before stopping at her now closed door and knocking.

"Hey baby, come on in," she responded as she began unpacking her clothes and putting away her bags. He gave her a long hug. He was nervous about telling her the news later at dinner. "I see Myles finally made it. Now you two can keep each other company."

"I see he wasn't successful with his usual charades this time," he said laughing while reliving the moment of him limping to the sofa. "You know he's a fool over anyone dropping anything on his feet."

"He better be lucky that's all I did considering he was acting like you," she said, giving me the side eye. "Yeah, well he deserved it then. Better than my feet anyday. I need mine to make money." he said watching to make sure she wasn't trying to get him next.

"Tell Myles to bring me his tablet so I can see his grades," she said looking at me. "He better have improved from last semester."

She didn't play when it came to grades. No matter what other activities or events we had going on while in school, we were still students first and expected nothing but their best efforts when in class and exhausted all resources. Myles was no exception. They worked too hard paying for tutoring, for any of us to play around about our education. He went and dragged poor me in behind him. She looked at my grades and smiled. Now if only she could find a better life for me. They wanted it to happen earlier though circumstances prevented it from happening, but it was not too late to offer it.

"Myles, what would you say if I wanted you to stay, to be closer to Avant?" she posed the question. "You have so much potential and it would be a shame to waste all of your talents in the streets."

"I can't leave mama Dukes behind," I said, lowering my head. "She needs me, she ain't been right. Something's up."

“Let me speak with her and Uncle James and see what we can come up with?” she responded. “Because I know you and Ollie have history and it's not the good kind.”

“Bet,” I said as she gave me a hug before ushering us out of the room. “Yall stay out of trouble now. This spring chicken is tired and needs to rest up before helping your dad with dinner. Make sure everyone is here on time.”

I turned around to head out when I noticed Avant looking sick, hurrying out the room. Auntie was putting her good wig on the mannequin head so she didn’t notice. I closed the door and went to check on him. I went to retrieve some ginger ale from the refrigerator as I heard him appear to be hacking up his guts and all. I knocked on the door to get his attention. After a few minutes he emerged back out looking much better. I pointed to the drink on his nightstand as he sat down on his bed next to it.

“You aight brodie?” I asked as I walked around him to the opposite end to lay across the bed, still limping from Auntie’s assault on my poor feet.

“Man, I don’t know honestly,” he told me as I adjusted my head on a pillow. “It just hit me all of sudden.”

“Rest up champ. That’s *morning sickness.*” I informed him, while popping him upside the head. “You better get used to it.Yall both might be having more of these days but it should subside as the pregnancy gets further along.”

“Man what you know about that?” he asked me, turning my head his way. “You not holding out from me are you?”

“Not this playa! At least not that I know of,” I said confidently. “But I got a few home boys that done been where you are. Plus we can’t forget Alonzo and the epic cereal fiasco!”

“OOOHHH MANNNN!!!” He said trying not to laugh for fear of getting sick again. “He won’t ever, *EVERRRRRR,* live that down!”

“Nope! Not as long as I got breath in my body,” I reassured him. “But that’s my homie right there.”

“Aye I gotta ask you real talk,” he said to me. “You don’t think Alexis lil seed might be yours?”

“Man, to be honest it’s a possibility, not gonna lie,” I responded, looking him dead in his eyes. “But I’m going to let her bring it up when she is ready.”

“Understand that,” he told him. “Cross that bridge when you get to it. How do you feel about Lauryn?”

“She’s a whole vibe by herself, big dawg,” I said, cheesing hard. “I’m really feeling shawty. If circumstances were different, I’d try to pursue her. I’d only hurt her now.”

“She’s a good one just like Vanessa,” he reassured me. “I can respect that. I definitely don’t want to die at the hands of bae.”

"I ain't tryna cause any static," I said, giving him a fist pound. "Not perfect by a long shot, but I am upright. And if lil man does turn out to be mine, I'm gonna do right by him. He ain't asked to be here, so I gotta handle my business."

"Well til we know for certain, we'll just pray about it," we both agreed. "No need to stress yourself prematurely. I got enough going on for the both of us."

Avant watched as I gave that far away look as I turned towards the window like I saw on Alonzo the other day when Yvonne picked up KyJuan. He knew it had something to do with Aunt Angie and me being away with her unprotected, in the same household with Ollie bitch ass. I dropped my head down and sighed deeply. I felt him move off the bed and sit beside me, with his arm around my shoulder. I was just like my Uncle James than my late dad, not one to really express my emotions when it came to things bothering me. But even the strongest of us get overwhelmed at times, and this was one of them. I let him pull me close as I began to break down and let it all out. So much built up pain and anger finally being released. I continued to let him hold on to me til I exhausted myself and then he just pulled my pillow and comforter down to cover me while I slept leaning against him. '*I would always be my brother's keeper.*' Avant thought to himself as he watched over me.

I was awakened by Uncle James who was already dressed. Somehow I ended up in the bed. I stretched and went past him to freshen up. It didn't take me long to get dressed. After giving myself a quick look over in the mirror, I slipped on my shoes, and went to meet Uncle James. Auntie Geneva looked my way from the kitchen and shook her head in approval at us before we donned our fedora hats and headed to complete our mission. Avant was in his room sleeping. The Cadillac was already running, silently humming as we opened the doors. Refreshing cool air hit us as we clipped our seatbelts into place and I put the car in reverse. This was a tradition that dated back to as far as I could remember. Just me and Uncle James, spending time together. The weather was fair and not much of a crowd on the roads as we traveled through town. I handled the car with care as I drove. Uncle James wasn't worried about me behind the wheel. If anything, he was more like my co-pilot, or wingman.

The drive took just under half an hour before we reached our destination. We turned onto a gravel road that would lead us past the family church, to the cemetery at the very end of the road. We parked under a nearby tree and made our way across to a private area. I followed as Uncle James stopped to read the names, saying a few words, tipping his hat at some, kneeling at others. I kept walking until I arrived. I took off my hat but kept my shades on as I squatted down at the grave of my father, *Booker Moses "Peanut" Banks*. There was an imprint that had 4 hand prints between his memorial and the blank one for whenever my mom's time came. I traced my finger along them. I pulled out the flowers from the holder and replaced them with a fresh set, carefully discarding the others into a sack, and brushing away any dirt from the marble. Half of my family rested here-my Pops and unborn sibling, too young to know the gender. I lifted up the glass covering and pulled a small bear from another bag, placed it inside alongside other items over the years, including my favorite ninja turtle given to me by him, and closed it back. My baby sibling, forever a baby in my heart, would have something special to keep them company, in my absence.

Every visit I added something new. It became like a treasure box, safe from the elements, but right between the graves. I kissed my fingers and pressed it against his picture and once again to the imprints, before standing up. Uncle James was in the distance standing guard. I went towards him, placing my hand on his shoulder, indicating that I was ready as we returned to the car.

Vanessa felt a sharp pain in her pelvic area. She headed to the bathroom thinking maybe she was just cramping, and grabbed some midol. As she sat down, she felt something wet and noticed she was bleeding down her leg. She panicked and called Lauryn, who rushed into her room. As she tried to control the bleeding, Lauryn called me at my parent's home.

"Hello?" I mumbled half asleep. "Who's this?"

"Avant, it's Lauryn!" she said quickly. "Meet us at the ER. Something's up with Vanessa!"

X.

Two months had passed since Vanessa had emergency surgery because of an ectopic pregnancy. The doctors explained they ended up having to terminate the pregnancy to save her life. I was there with her everyday. Our parents, family, and other support system were very supportive and most thankful Vanessa was all right. We had all come together in the weeks following the incident and talked about everything recovery wise. We would definitely have to take it easy and not rush back into any intimate contact as she continued to heal. I wanted to make sure she not only healed physically, but emotionally and mentally as well.

I'm thankful for my mom being able to help us to understand the severity of the medical situation from her experience being in the medical field. As I wiped the tears off my face, I thanked God for sparing her life, knowing that I could've easily lost both simultaneously. I took an extended leave of absence from my job to take time for Vanessa and make sure she was okay. Lauryn temporarily moved in to keep her company, which was a plus-*more so for Myles than us.*

"Well, I want to ask you all something since we're all here," I said, getting nervous. I had their full attention.

"What is it son?" they asked simultaneously.

"I want to marry Vanessa," I said confidently as I held her hand. "There's no one I would rather spend the rest of my life with than her. But also I wanted to do it the right way-with y'all's blessings."

"You know this is a big step right young man?" Curtis asked. "Marriage is serious business and forever when with the right person. Y'all are still young,though grown."

"Are y'all sure about this?" my mom asked, looking at Vanessa. My dad looked at me.

"Yes, we are," We both answered. "We've been together since high school. We both have stable careers and our own space. We're still young, but we've been together this long."

"Well, Lord knows that's the truth." Her father said laughing. "Nothing I tried has deterred you away. But you've always been respectful and protective over her."

With that out of the way, I stood up, reaching in my pocket, then got down on one knee. I opened the box to reveal an upgrade to the engagement ring I had given her a while back. We agreed to keep it a surprise until I could formally ask Vanessa for her hand in marriage, with our parent's approval. Momma wiped tears of joy as bae accepted the proposal and I got up to hug her. Mr. Curtis gave me a big hug and welcomed me to the family. My dad put his hands on my shoulders, giving his approval as well. We took pictures by the fireplace where a picture of her late mother, Maria, sat on the mantelpiece. We all sat around and enjoyed each other's company before finally heading out to break the "official news" with the gang at the local karaoke bar that we liked to gather at. Myles was already there with Lauryn all boo'd up and Jasmine and Alonzo were running behind because of him picking up extra hours at work.

The Karaoke section of the Club Krucial was lit. Somehow word spread like wildfire and the place was filled with their old high school and college basketball teammates to congratulate us. Between the DJ spinning some 90s and 2000's hits and everyone dancing and trying karaoke, it was a fun time for all. Myles got up saying he was going to the restroom and just took in everything going on. Next thing she knew he was walking up on the stage. The instrumental sounds of *Jagged Edge "Promise"* filled the surround sound in and Myles serenaded Lauryn but not revealing anything so she wouldn't be too embarrassed just yet. When he finished he gave a shout out to me and Vanessa and signaled the DJ to put on the instrumentals to Montell Jordan's *"Fallin".* He took a swig from his corona and started singing. Everyone was grooving and chillin'. When that one was over he asked Lauryn to come up to the stage. She waved her hands like NO! But he instead came to her and started rapping T.I. "*Let Me Tell You Something*" to her. The crowd went wild and Vanessa and Jasmine were egging him on. He ended it with a kiss and bouquet of roses that me and Alonzo had hid from her. After that, the DJ set it off with some 112 *Peaches and Cream,* followed by Hot Boyz "*Hot Girl*" and Lil Wayne's "*Lollipop*" and "*Fireman*".He was gone off the weed and beers he had earlier, and rapped along to Lloyd's "*You*" in her ear as they slowly danced. Lauryn soaked in every minute of it and didn't want it to end.

Lauryn opened the door once they pulled around back and was about to see if I needed any help getting out of the car as I had passed out during the drive home. She figured I'd eventually get out of the car, and left me with the keys, to go inside and change. I did eventually wake up realizing where I was and got out and locked the door. I was still a little buzzed and started singing *Temptations "My Girl"*, as I walked inside, two stepping to the sound of my own voice.

I sobered up real quick as I rounded the corner and saw that she was standing in the kitchen with nothing but her t-shirt and panties on, watching innocently. I smiled and took off my shoes before slowly following her back to her room, making sure to lock the front door. I grabbed a Coors Light along the way. I changed into some basketball shorts and a tank top before cuddling up next to her in the bed. She laid her head on my chest as we watched *Jason's Lyric.* I played with her hair and occasionally looked down at her. Something about my swag and confidence ensured her that she was safe in my arms as she drifted off to sleep. I finished my beer as the movie played on, before eventually falling asleep too. I woke up early to get dressed and prepare breakfast for us, cuzzo and sis. After breakfast, we went to check on Alonzo at the mall while the girls hung out.

"You already know what it is playboi!" Myles said, sneaking behind him, forcing his hands up.

"What the fuck?" Alonzo said turning around to see him holding a gatorade and subway sandwich for him. "I was about to say."

"What up fool!" he said, giving them dap. "Thanks for the food. My stomach was pinching my back."

He let his boss know he was going on break and walked with us down to the food court. He was working a double today so he was grateful for the break from standing. He had no shame when he slid out of his shoes while sitting at the table. We ordered ourselves spicy chicken sandwiches and all ate and tripped out. Yvonne happened to walk by with KyJuan and stopped to say hello. He pepped up when he saw his lil man but didn't disturb him while he was sleeping in the stroller. He introduced her to the crew, and she was cordial. Alonzo told her he'd pick him up on his way home from work and keep him since he had a couple days off after working this double. We agreed to stop by and help. She was cool with the arrangements and then said goodbye so she could finish her errands while he slept.

"Man, you two have come a long way," I told him. "It's great to see y'all being cordial and co-parenting together."

"Yea, we try man." he said, massaging his temples. "Sometimes I wonder if we still have a future. I mean I got love for Jasmine and all, but I want KyJuan to grow up with both of his parents like I have."

"That's an easy one right there man," Myles told him as we all got up and gathered the trash. "Just see where shawty mindset is at and go from there."

"What about Jasmine?" I asked as we headed back towards his job. "She gone be bitter as fuck."

"Man, truth be told, I think she is seeing someone else anyway." he told us."I saw some suspect texts on her phone and she seems to always be busy through the weekends. She says it's school related, but looking at her schedule, ain't that much school work in the world."

"Don't sweat it man. It will all reveal itself in due time," Myles said to him. "I gotta eventually talk with Alexis about Malachi. If lil man is mine, I need to know so I can step up and do what's right for him."

"Man, I feel you on that." Alonzo agreed with him. "Better to know now, then to leave things in limbo. Especially if you tryna push up on Lauryn."

"Yall ain't gotta worry about that," I shook my head at him before he walked to the back to clock in. "I already told cuzzo I'm not even tryna go that route. I'm no good for her with how I'm moving in the streets."

Myles and I picked up some J's, under armour, and new balance shoes and looked for some outfits to match them. I asked him about what happened after the club, and he just started turning away smiling. He told me how they vibed but just went home to watch a movie. After some further pressing, he confessed that though he did want to hit, he couldn't do it knowing 1) she was a virgin, and 2) he wasn't trying to be her man. He didn't want to complicate things and just wanted to be cool with her, someone she could trust.

She was truly a good girl and he would protect her in that sense. If life had dealt him a different set of cards he'd be more willing to pursue her, but it's not worth the potential fallout that would inevitably come. His main focus was on finding out whether Malachi was his son. He thought about how they had naturally clicked when they were around each other, and how he seemed to feel safe even at such a young age. Just like he had told Alonzo about his feelings for Yvonne, he'd take his own advice…*All in due time. But he felt in his spirit that Malachi was his seed.*

XI.

The rest of the summer went smoothly and me and Lauryn became really close, though I did let her know upfront that I couldn't be more than friends with her because I had a lot going on in my life. I knew it would hurt her heart, but I wasn't right for her, and definitely wasn't in any position to be tied down with any *one* female. I didn't tell her about Alexis or Malachi. Lil man was my main concern. She expressed her feelings for me and I took it to heart. I think that conversation made things somewhat easier to deal with because we both knew where the other stood, so there were no misunderstandings.

We still spent a lot of time together before I had to eventually get back to Chicago. I balanced basketball, helping Alonzo with KyJuan when he went to start back lifeguarding and helping out with the different sports training camps. He was one busy man. Jasmine was more distant and it seemed like they were growing apart since they never really had time to be together. The week before I left, the girls went on a girl's trip, but she didn't tag along this time. Me and Lauryn said our goodbyes before she and Vanessa left. She was sad she wouldn't be there to see me off but knew it was probably for the best. They needed some girl time alone before she had to start back classes too.

Avant and I dropped Alonzo at the mall. *Speaking of Alexis*, she walked in the mall with lil man in tow just as we were exiting Alonzo's job. I was ready to get it over with. Alonzo just watched to see how this was going to play out. Even he could see how similar Malachi looked and had mannerisms just like me. Avant went on to the car. He knew what I had to do. We agreed to meet up here so I could go with her and handle our business. I could tell she was nervous because she knew the time would eventually come regarding paternity. Alonzo pulled me aside before I left and told me to be careful and meet him back here by five so we could go get KyJuan. I dapped him up and left with Alexis.

I played with lil man while we talked about the situation and why she waited before bringing it up. I'm thankful for her honesty and could do nothing but respect her for it. But I still just needed to know and now we were on the way to find out if I had a son or not. He had fallen asleep by the time we arrived, so I carried him on my shoulder as we walked into the facility. We signed in and filled out paperwork while waiting for our names to be called. It didn't take long, and we followed a nurse back to a room where she explained the procedure, verified necessary info, and swabbed both me and lil man buccal areas.

We had requested expedited processing, and were assured the results would be back within 24-48 hours. I'd delayed my return trip home for another week just in case. We thanked her for everything and headed back to the car. I fastened him into his booster seat all while watching how peacefully he looked sleeping. I admitted to myself that I had already gotten attached to him, but knew I had to be chill about the situation in the event that he wasn't my seed.

We dropped him off at her daycare before heading back to the family house. I needed time to process everything. My mind was on that test and Alexis knew it. She understood and dropped me off before heading back to her crib. I gave her a hug before exiting. I thought about how much time I'd potentially missed out on, how much my life would change if I was a father, how I'd have to break the news to ma Dukes and them. Shit was making me dizzy and I needed both some good liquor, and blunts to get me right. I went around back to the garage where the boxing bag was set up. I changed into some training gear from one of my tote bags, and got in some training. I was so focused on my technique and trying to keep my mind off that I didn't notice Uncle James slip in until I took a much needed water break and he tossed me a bottle.

"You've been practicing a lot I see," he said as he came over and put his hands on my shoulders. "Your moves are much more smooth and fluid."

"Can't afford to be reckless and sloppy Unc." I said as I sipped on the water and looked him in his eyes. "That gives your opponents opportunities to score unnecessary hits."

"Exactly," he said, agreeing with me. "Life is the same way, nephew."

"Man *whattttt??!!*" I said as I shook my head. "But God is still gonna look out."

"That is also true," he said as he removed the wraps from my hands. "Sometimes things are allowed to happen to help open our eyes. To help us refocus."

"Maybe it's what I need to help me leave the streets alone." I said as I thought about how ruthless the streets had been to some of my close friends, and how grim the work me and Jordan did as part of his *Clean Up Crew Company*.

> "*You were that for Peanut*," he said calmly as he placed the folded wraps on the table and hung the gloves and headpiece back along the wall. "You and Angie were his saving grace."
>
> "I miss my ole man," I said as I felt tears forming in my eyes. He stretched out his hand to help me up, pulling me in close knowing what I needed. "He's always with you. Never forget that."

I wiped my eyes with my shirt and just looked him face to face. Our shared pain made our bond very special. I had nothing but love and respect for him-he was the closest person to a father that I had, other than when I would hang out at Alonzo's house and be around his ole man. He patted me on my shoulder reassuring me that everything would be just fine. I nodded my head and headed inside to freshen up. As I passed my tote bag in the sitting area, I pulled out my last blunt and sat it on the coffee table while I went to see what Unc had to drink in his bar. I found some Hennessy and coke, and poured me a glass. I sipped on it before heading to shower and then returning back to the living room. I just sat back, sipped and smoked to ease my mind. I soon felt myself drifting off to sleep.

It was a little after noon that I heard the phone buzzing as I was about to swing by to check on cuzzo at work. I pulled into the parking lot to take the call. It was from the DNA testing place.

"Hello, Is Mr. Myles Banks in?" the caller said as the call connected.

"Yes, this is him," I said, feeling my heart rate increase.

"Yes, Mr. Banks. Your test results are ready," she said calmly. "Come in at your earliest convenience and be sure to bring your ID and reference #."

"I'll be on my way." I said as I took a deep breath. I shifted the car into gear, left the parking lot and sped towards the center to my results. The drive was quick and I parked in front of the building, making sure to pull up the e-brake and lock the door. Once inside, I stopped at the receptionist desk and signed in. It didn't take long for her to retrieve the envelope that contained the results. I thanked her for them, signed saying I had received them, and then exited.

I waited till I got to Avant's job before I mentioned anything. He was walking out as I parked so he didn't take long to get in. We then headed over to meet Alonzo at the college where he was doing his interning. Today was drill day, and he had the gym set up in different stations for skills training. They were finishing up and helping to move the equipment from the stations back into the storage room when we arrived. Once that was finished and the court was dust mopped by a few players, he released them. He locked the gym and met us back in his office. I pulled out the sealed envelope and held it up just long enough for them to read the info on the outside before laying it on my lap. They looked at each other and then at me. I took a deep breath and opened it up to remove the test results.

"The probability of paternity with regards to one Malachi P. Jacobs and Myles P. Banks is 99.999999998%." I read aloud, standing with the letter held high.

"*MY BOIIIIIIIII!!!*" Alonzo jumped up, pulling me in. "You got a lil Jr!!!!

"*OOOOOOH MANNNN!!*" Avant just stood and shook his head.

"Man please take me to go see my son," I said proudly. "I gotta make up for lost time!"

"HOLD UP!" Avant said realizing we gotta break the news to my parents AND Auntie Angie. Not to mention, Alexis's parents.

"Don't worry cuzzo," I said reassuringly. "I got it all under control. I just want to spend time with my seed first."

With that we all walked out of the office and waited as Alonzo locked everything up, activated the alarms, and then the gym exterior doors. He said he'd link up with us after checking on Kyjuan. I called Alexis to see where she was, and had with her, before letting her know I was enroute with cuzzo. When we arrived, I saw her parent's Cadillac shining from a recent detail, looking as immaculate as ever. Her father, Mr. Nelson Jacobs, was sitting under the carport admiring his handiwork. We walked over to him to introduce ourselves. He stood as we approached, hand extended for us to shake.

"Afternoon fellas," he said as he shook our hands. "Been a long time since I've seen yall around these parts."

"Yessir, it has been," we responded. "Much of it still looks the same, despite less traffic flow from businesses closing or moving,"

"Times are definitely changing," he said looking down the block to where a prominent grocery store used to sit but had long shut down after the owners died and their family abandoned the building. I'd seen it time and time again where people in my generation didn't want to carry on their family business when their elders became unable to keep them going. Mr. Jacobs maintained a decent sized vegetable and fruit garden on their property, and would give portions of their harvest to the store to sell to the customers as a way to give back to the community. He always had the best selections and prices when he was in full swing. Even though he has gotten older, he still keeps it going, though it has been divided to give space to his wife's flower garden. We saw her approaching from there and waved as she came to see who we were.

"Good afternoon Mrs. Jacobs," we spoke as she sat down her baskets, one with flowers for her vase, and the other one of fresh fruits that she would use to make a salad and other awesome dishes with.

"Avant and Myles?" she said, hoping she hadn't called the wrong names.

"Yes ma'am," we answered as she extended her arms for us to give her a hug.

"Y'all have grown up so much," she said, standing back to admire *how fine we've grown up to be.*

Alexis pulled up as we were sitting under the carport conversing. She waved as she got out and headed to unload his bags. As soon as she got him out of his booster seat with his backpack, he looked to see who was with his Papa and GiGi. He walked cautiously, making sure not to mess up his shoes or lose his balance. He smiled when he saw his two most favorite people in the whole world waving at him. But just as he was heading in their direction, Myles pulled out his ninja, causing him to stop dead in his tracks.

Malachi looked at it being held out. He bent his head to see who was holding it up, trying to figure out how he got it. Not sure what to do, he stood there with one hand scratching his head. Myles knew what he was doing and just waited patiently for him to recognize him. He sat his snacks down and reached in his bag to realize he was missing. He looked back up towards Myles and pointed at it. He held out his arms to reach for it, and Myles motioned for him to come to him. He looked at Papa and saw it was okay to go to him. He still headed towards them where he gave them both hugs. His Gigi showered him with kisses while his Papa gave him a big bear hug, which he both loved and hated. Myles and Avant watched the wholesome interaction. Once he was able to free himself, he left his bag but picked up his snacks to take with him as he went on his mission to rescue his ninja turtle. Myles welcomed him with open arms and watched as he confidently approached-holding out a cookie as a peace offering in exchange for his bear.

"*Daddy?*" he whispered softly as he looked him in his eyes. It caught Myles off guard and he had to blink away the tears trying to form.

"Yes, son," Myles said as he embraced him tightly. "I'm your daddy."

"*I love you daddy*," he said softly as he was lifted onto his dad's lap. Everyone watched the interaction between them. The light in their eyes couldn't be denied by anyone. Papa and Gigi wiped tears of joy as they watched father and son bond.

Alexis carried his bags inside while he was temporarily distracted. She knew this day would come but wasn't nearly as nervous since they had talked things out. The conversation with her parents had been rougher but they just wanted her to be truthful about who his potential father could be. They already had a strong idea who it was but wanted the test to confirm what they already knew in their hearts. By the time she came back up front, they had all made their way inside and were situated in the den. Avant had left so it was just them. Myles had his lil buddy in his lap, playing with his now rescued ninja turtle. She took a seat by them. All eyes were on them. Myles stood up to hand the envelope to her mom. She took it and moved close to her husband who shifted slightly in his seat. They carefully opened the envelope and pulled out the contents.

"Well, well," her father said, reading the results before looking up at them above his glasses. "It seems that our suspicions have been confirmed."

"Yes sir," I said, shaking my head and rubbing his lil head. "I am lil *peanut's* father."

"He looks just like you son," her mom said looking at them, now that he was sitting on his lap. "And he definitely has your charisma and charm."

Malachi looked up at me and I smiled proudly, giving him a kiss on his forehead. He immediately started cheesing wide at his grandparents. I couldn't help but do the same. His Gigi somehow managed to find a camera and took pictures of us-*kodak moments* she called them. I pulled out a couple pictures I had in my wallet of me and my late father, so they could see and compare. As they flipped through them, they would occasionally glance back our way, and shake their head at just how the same face, mannerisms, and charm had passed through the generations from Peanut Sr., to me, and now lil peanut.

I told them that I had planned to start the legitimation process so I could get parental rights and visitation set up moving forward. I had a lot of makeup to do and didn't want to waste any time. When they asked what my relationship status was with Alexis, I honestly told them we are just friends and co-parents. We both didn't want a relationship but would work together for the sake of making sure our son didn't go without. I reassured them that I had a stable job, was in school knocking out some general education classes at my local college, and had a stable place for him when he came to visit....I just had to break the news to *Mama Dukes*!

Unbeknownst to us, Uncle James and Auntie pulled up to the Jacobs' house, tapping gently on the carport door. We all turned in their direction as the Jacobs welcomed them in. They waved but just asked Mrs. Jacobs to come to the door to receive a basket from the church that she'd won during a recent raffle campaign. They were on their way to dinner and just wanted to stop by while on the way. She thanked her and promised to catch up with her later in the week.

Mr. Jacobs handed the wallet photo album back to me to return to its rightful place. Once she was free with that situation, she returned back to inquire as to how long I would be staying before going back home. I informed them that I had to get back in a few days but had extended my stay to be able to get the results, and now spend time with Malachi if permitted. They looked at Alexis who said she didn't see anything wrong with it, especially since the duo had already been bonding every chance they got. Malachi watched his Gigi and Papa move to get up from their seats and scurried to see where they were going without him. I didn't hold him back as he became their shadow as one went into the kitchen and the other down the hallway. He looked towards the kitchen before scrambling to find his Papa. Alexis laughed.

“Mama is probably checking on dinner while Dad is going to use the bathroom.” she told me. “You should stay and eat with us. *We’re practically family now.*”

“I don’t want to intrude,” I said, trying to be respectful.

“Y’all gone and wash up in the guest mudroom just down the hall,” Mama Jacobs called from the kitchen, “Food will be plated and ready when you finish.”

That settled that argument and we both headed to wash up. As we were exiting the mudroom, *lil Peanut Jr.*, was coming up the hallway pulling on his Papa with one hand while holding a death grip on his prized stuffed animal with the other. He stopped momentarily when he saw me and cheesed before continuing on his mission. Mama Jacobs motioned for us to have a seat while she and Alexis fixed plates and cups of iced tea and lemonade.

Once the table was set and everyone sat down, we all joined hands for grace. Lil man was flanked by his Papa on one side and me on the other. Gigi was across from him and Alexis beside her. The first “multigenerational” family dinner for Peanut. In due time he’d get to meet his dad’s side of the family, to be even more spoiled. But Myles knew he owed it to Alexis’ parents to meet them first.

I spent most of my remaining time bonding with Malachi, and working through things with Alexis’ parents. Alonzo brought Kyjuan over to meet him, and the two quickly became fast friends. They were very close in age and it didn't take long to tell that they would grow up to have the same type of close bond that their fathers had. On my next trip down, I'd make sure to introduce Malachi to my dad's side of the family. On the day of my departure, we went out to eat near the mall. Alexis put on a new set of scrubs so she could head to work. Her parents would be meeting us at the mall. Lil man lay in my lap asleep against my chest while we headed that way. I was a natural when it came to babies and got a lot of hands-on experience from having helped Alonzo when KyJuan was born.

When we arrived, I helped transfer Malachi's bags and toys into her parent's vehicle after getting him situated in his other booster seat. Just as I was fastening the last clip on the restraint and checking the seatbelt, he woke up and looked around confused as to what was going on. I bent down to give him a big hug as he stretched his little arms out for me becoming fussy. I calmed him down and gave him fist pound before finally closing the door so I could get ready to head to meet Alonzo. *Peanut* watched me the whole time. I hugged Alexis and told her I truly appreciated everything. Just before I walked in I turned back to see him holding up one of his ninja turtles. I smiled and pointed back at him. They all smiled back my way as they let up the window and headed out the parking lot.

Alexis waited til he disappeared within the station crowd before she pulled off. She stopped long enough to fix her makeup. It was too much for her but she needed to save face. She had a job to do. After dropping Myles off she had to handle her business. She was the "birthday girl" surprise for a bachelor party. She was supposed to dress like a nurse. A girl had to do what she had to do. Him being in the streets knew she was a hustler just like he was. She was a good mom and he respected that in her. He made sure to schedule another check up for when he got back home even though he was clean from the one he had gotten when he got there. Could never be too safe.

Lauryn texted him to have a safe trip back and that she already missed him. He smiled when he saw it and replied back with a selfie of him wearing his headphones and a peace symbol. He switched to *The Cool*, a new album by Lupe Fiasco he picked up earlier that day. "The Coolest" started playing in his headphones as he watched passing scenery. He thought long and hard about the offer Aunt Vivian had proposed. He wanted to be closer to his cousin and lil man but didn't want to leave his mama with Ollie.

He called to let her know he was on his way home so she wouldn't worry. He had his boy Jordan picking him up from the station. They had some business to handle before he went home. Jordan started a company called the *Clean Up Crew* and had an Uncle Harris who he helped with the funeral home business. Sometimes Myles helped him in the process. Jordan was no dummy by a long shot and he and Myles grew up together thick as thieves. They had some "processing" to do and he needed his help transporting their recent work order to the facility. Myles prepared himself to get back into work mode. *Time to get this money-grimey job but somebody had to do it!*

Part 2: Ain’t No Sunshine

I.

Jordan met me at the train station and we headed to the garage to drop off my bags and get changed for the job awaiting us. We jumped in the transport truck and headed to the pick up spot to get the loads. Because of the pick up location we were both wearing bullet proof vests and had AR-15s and a handgun handy in case things went south. There was war going on in the streets of Chicago, aka Chiraq, and bullets didn't have any names on them. We knew this first hand from our own dealings in the past. Thankfully we both found a legitimate way to help change our lives around, but still allowing us to be able to move through the streets without worry or concern. An hour later we were on their way to the Greenwood Funeral Home and Eternal Gardens.

Established over 60 years ago, the Greenwood Funeral Home, Crematory, and Eternal Gardens was the largest African-American owned and operated business of its kind, especially at a time when it was hard for blacks to own any businesses. Mr. Julius Harris and his wife Geneva had worked hard to maintain the business after inheriting it from the Watson family of Tulsa, Oklahoma, following the turmoil that ensued after the historical race riots of the Greenwood community, known as the Tulsa Race Massacre. Mr. and Mrs. Harris's desire to own their own business was a way to build a legacy for their family was instilled in them from an early age. Ole Man Watson, "Chap" as he liked to be called, was raised by his grandparents, J.C. and Louisa Watson, both former slaves, freed and rewarded a vast inheritance from the Watson Plantation back in the day, from their faithful services as an undertaker and midwife; this old money is what was used to educate their children and help them expand into real estate, medicine, law, and higher education. A long history of entrepreneurs made up Jordan's family, so much so it was predestined that he would continue when his time came.

It was only when he became older and spent more time with his Uncle Julius that Jordan truly began to see the complex intricacies that made up the "other" side of the business. It was truly Auntie Geneva who possessed all the power and control over what new "clients" or "customers" were taken in from the not so pretty side of the industry. It was her frugality and sometimes cut throat business tactics that grew the business from a small town mom and pop's undertaking service into the vast empire that it was today, with no limits anywhere in sight. Her sister Camille had married well with a man named Clarence, and established businesses in Atlanta and Miami. Since their businesses usually brought them in contact with many criminals of various types, it was only natural that Geneva would seek to offer her services to her sister whenever possible. Jordan was the perfect person to navigate both the corporate and underground world, with his street savvy skills and calm, business-like acumen and demeanor.

Jordan entered the access code signaling our arrival. We drove up the hill towards the old processing plant and backed the truck in the loading dock. I got out and opened the bay door and guided him back to the loading dock that led to the big assembly line. Jordan shut off the truck and lifted up the back door to the refrigerated truck. He then walked over to one of the control boxes and pulled one of the levers. Another door opened up to the incinerator and out came a big tray with a hook that grabbed the pallets that I had lined up. The hook dragged and lifted them one by one onto the tray until the truck was empty. The incinerator door was closed and within a few hours, there was nothing but ashes from the pallets remaining and smaller random artifacts fragments which were sent to the other side through another assembly line to be separated or dropped into the pulverizer to be crushed to a fine powder and distributed throughout one of many feeding pipes that pumped water and nutrients to the various gardens that made up the *Memorial Grounds….ashes to ashes, dust to dust…thou returnest to the grounds from which ye were formed*.

We shut down the machine, ensured all was done, locked everything down and headed to drop off the truck. Once we passed through the last gate and it closed, a unique confirmation code alerted Jordan that all was complete. Each job had its own confirmation that was automatically generated and a report was sent with the weight of the contents, which was what the company used to create their invoices for payment. Back at the office, we showered up and changed clothes before jumping back into the Cayenne. I fired up a blunt to smoke along the way. It felt glad to be back home, despite all of the chaos it brought.

"So, you enjoyed your trip?" Jordan asked as we entered I-85N.

"It was cool man," I answered thinking about everything.

"Finally got that DNA test done with Alexis concerning her son."

“That’s wassup man.” he told me. “It’s been busier than usual with Unc picking up new clients and doing more and more business with his old partner Mr. Chance and Mrs. Camille. He wants me to prepare to take over the funeral home business and I wanted to bring you in on it.”

“Word?!” I said, thinking it over. “I considered moving with my cousin and giving all this up. Get Mama Dukes away from Ollie before I have to make him disappear.” Jordan knew all about the history and tension between us.

“Man, you already know we can make that happen, just give the word.”

“Hell yeah,” I said, pulled out the blunt and looked for my *Bruce Lee* zippo lighter. “Just tryna make sure I make the correct move.”

“Oh yeah, he’s definitely my seed,” I said as I lit the end of the blunt. “You got a god son brodie.”

“*Really??”* Jordan as they slowed down at a red light before entering the off ramp from the interstate.

“Yeah man,” I said, shaking my head and passing the blunt his way as I pulled out my phone to show him pics of Malachi. “His name is Malachi, but I’ma call him *Peanut* after my ole man.”

“Dude!” he said vehemently, shaking his head left and right. “*Ain’t no way youcould deny his lil ass!*”

"He does look just like me, come to think of it." I admitted it to my best friend. "I gotta tell Ma Dukes."

We turned right on Shurlington Avenue and turned into the Turner Gardens subdivision. Jordan turned off his lights as he pulled up to the house. Ollie was the paranoid type anytime headlights shined through the front window and wouldn't hesitate to come out with a shotgun. Between the cocaine and other drugs he used, he was always on edge. Alcohol only intensified it.

Jordan was still speechless from the news as he sat while I grabbed my bags and headed towards the terrace level door quietly. We'd have to continue this conversation at a later time though. Jordan backed out and left just as quietly as he pulled up. Once inside the in-law suite, I dropped my bags and closed the door before flipping on a lamp on the desk. I jumped when I spotted ma asleep on my bed. This is something she never did. Not wanting to wake her, I covered her with a throw blanket and quietly changed clothes and put my bags in the closet before closing the door and heading to the living room. I hadn't sat down long before I heard Ollie come stumbling in from the front of the house.

"When you get back?" he asked loudly, cigarette dangling from his mouth while he nursed a Corona in one hand. "You deaf?"

"I ain't been in too long; why are you trying to wake up the neighborhood being so loud and extra?" I said, instantly becoming annoyed with his interrogation.

"Don't get smart with me nigga," he shot back, getting even louder. "Don't think you are too grown to get put in line."

"Man Ollie, I ain't even trying to be disrespectful," I said still looking at the television. "You're the one making all the noise. I'm just minding my own business, *in my own space*."

"THIS IS MY HOUSE! YOU DON'T LIKE IT, YOU CAN GET THE FUCK OUT PATNA!"

"*This is my MOMMA house-that my father left her*," I corrected him. "Fuck on with that dumb shit."

Ollie took no time launching his beer bottle at me. I caught it and hurled it back, shattering it on the wall adjacent to the hallway he turned to head back down. A piece of the glass nipped his ear. He felt the blood and turned around charging. I was already standing ready to lay him out either with my hands or with my glock, whatever it took. He grabbed his bat and swung at me, grazing my ribs. I leaned over, stunned temporarily, but managed to miss being hit with the full swing of the Louisville slugger. I stayed low as he came at me and threw him back before he could swing again. I seized an opportunity to catch him off guard and reached for the bat to knock it out of his hand. Ollie put his hands up to defend himself and I stood over him ready to beat him to a pulp.

"Take your drunk ass on somewhere now before I have to hurt ya," I said looking down at him. "I ain't no little boy. I'm a grown ass man."

Ollie looked at him half defeated, half embarrassed. He slowly gained his grounding and stood up. He cut his hand on the broken bottle fragments, setting off more anger. Grabbing pieces as he got up, he turned and flung him at my face. As I turned to shield from the glass fragments, Ollie grabbed the bat and pounced on me with it, hitting me wherever he could, with no mercy whatsoever-anywhere he could inflict the most damage. I fought him off as best I could using all of my training I had in my arsenal but knew Ollie had alcohol and drugs in his system working to his advantage. Remembering I had my glock, I managed to free it from its holster and clicked off the safety and fired, striking the wall just past his shoulder. He flinched and stopped momentarily.

"Next time will be in your **dome**," I said, locking eyes with him as I held my gun with both hands aimed straight at his head. Determined not to let him be bested, Ollie tried his luck. I quickly fired three shots-two to the chest, one to the head, square between his eyes. He fell back, landing in front of the fireplace.

Angela jumped up out of her sleep and fell on the ground. Not knowing what was going on, she stayed quiet until the gunfire ceased. Once she was convinced it was safe to move, she slowly crawled to the door and looked down the hallway towards the living room. Walking ever so quietly, she saw him lying on the floor bleeding from the head and chest. Upon walking closer, she saw I had my gun still pointed towards where he had stood, finger still on the trigger-*click, click, click*. I never lost sight of him as I saw her come into my view from my peripherals. Her presence allowed me to let my guard down temporarily for her to remove the gun from my hands. I then went to retrieve a broom and dustpan to clean up and dispose of the glass shards, before heading back to my room, where everything went black.

II.

I was awakened by mom sounding hysterical on the phone and my dad calmly trying to get information from her. I couldn't make sense of what she was saying so I got up and went to the bathroom. I could hear her crying and quickly got myself together to check on her. Walking down the hall, I could see her door was open, and saw her on the bed with her hands covering her face. Pops was already dressed and had a look in his eye that I hadn't seen in a very long time expressed. The same look I had when I saw the scars on Myles's back during the summer. I knocked on the door and I sat down beside her and hugged her.

"What's going on? What are you upset about?" I asked, rubbing her shoulders.

"It's Myles....there's been a shooting," she said through muffled cries.

"Is he going to be okay? What about Auntie Angie?" I asked, looking from her to my dad.

"He....he.....shot Ollie after they got into a fight. Now Ollie is dead and he's in ICU." he said with a calm that was incensed with anger.

"*FUCK MANNNN*!!!!" I yelled, jumping up from the bed. "How's Auntie Angie? Did Ollie hurt her?"

"*Son, you have to calm down and collect yourself,*" Pops said as he pulled me in very closely, putting his hands around my head and shoulders. "We all need to be level headed so we can be of help. I know you're upset but you have to get it together."

"She's a mess. She was in his room waiting for him to come back so they could talk, but fell asleep," she went on. "She was awakened by them fighting and then the gunshots and found Ollie on the floor and him near the sofa, both covered in blood and bruises. Myles passed out as they were trying to load him on the stretcher and now he's in ICU. There are police and other folks that want to talk to him about what happened."

I quickly left to gather my emergency overnight bag I kept in my closet. I checked it to make sure it had everything I needed for a couple of days' stay. I then went and helped get their bags into the SUV while they went back to make sure the house was secure. Dad was on the phone giving instructions for what to happen during his absence from his company. He also did the same for momma. We then got on the road to Chicago. I would call the crew once I knew more information but for right now, Aunt Angie and Myles needed us. The drive was mostly quiet except for the jazz music that played softly as we headed up the highway. We made the trip without incident and pulled up to the house where I saw auntie sitting in a rocking chair, smoking a cigarette, which was not like her.

"I knew this was going to happen eventually," she said as we walked onto the porch. "I planned to have him move. I wanted so much more for him. Now I don't know what's going to happen."

"Give it to God Angie," ma said, holding on to her hand. "It's all in God's hands right now."

"How's Myles doing?" I asked hesitantly. "Any updates?"

"He's in and out of consciousness," she told us. "He has a lot of unexplained injuries and they're also doing brain and other organ scans since he passed out and is pretty banged up."

"What hospital is he at?" I asked as I paced back and forth. "Can he have visitors?"

I noticed the white SUV pull up and went to see who it was. They had just gone inside. As soon as I got to the front, I knew exactly who it was. *Jordan Banks*. I walked over to the driver side window and dapped him up.

"What's good fam, long time no see," he said smiling wide. "I thought Myles just came back from seeing you?"

"Man, he's at Sinai Chicago," I told him. "I was about to head up there. You mind taking me, so we can go see him together?"

"Hop in, I got cha," he said unlocking the door.

I texted my mom to let her know I'd be back-I was going to check on Myles with one of his friends. She texted back to be safe and let her know when they made it. I filled Jordan in with what little information I knew as we drove to the hospital. I texted mom to let her know we had made it. We noticed a lot of police around the ICU and observed from a distance before heading to the desk to request access. Once in, we were escorted by a nurse to his room, 0532. I sat down in the seat closest to him while Jordan took one in the far corner to watch the door. I grabbed Myles's hand and just held it as I fought to stop the tears from flowing.. All of the wires, tubes, and dressings shook me. Jordan sat with his head in his hands. He was mad he left him to handle Ollie on his own.

A middle aged African American doctor came in and asked about our relationship to Myles, and once we confirmed I was on his emergency contact list, they started filling me in-Concussion, but no brain bleeds. Bruised kidneys and liver, several fractured ribs in various stages of healing, fractured wrists, compound fracture of his left tib-fib and ankle, dislocated shoulder and clavicle. The doctor was questioning how he got the injuries and I filled him in with just enough to confirm his suspicion of long-term physical abuse. He wanted to open a case to be investigated but I declined. I said it was already handled. The doctor's eyes confirmed an unspoken understanding and said no more. Myles was heavily sedated to allow his body to heal without him fighting it. The doctor said he'd fill us in if anything changed but for now we just had to wait and see how his body responded. We thanked him as he left.

I then breathed in deep as he pulled my phone out to text bae to call me asap. She called immediately and I filled her in on the situation but warned her to not tell Lauryn because I didn't want to ruin their trip. She agreed and told me to keep her posted on any updates. I then called Alonzo who almost flipped out. I managed to calm him down and told him he needed to stay focused; that I was there with Myles and so was Jordan so he would be fine. Alonzo was really close to Myles just like I, and was devastated. He prayed his boy would pull through. A man who looked like a detective came in and asked if we were family. I confirmed and asked who he was. He was Detective Monroe and was investigating the case. He wanted to get information about what happened. Right now no charges would be filed but the more information he could gather, the better it was for Myles. I gave him my Aunt Angela's number to get the details. Jordan told him that they had linked up from the train station and went to do some work at the funeral home before he dropped him off and that's all he could give him. Detective Monroe thanked us for our time and said he'd be in touch with any updates.

Vanessa took Lauryn to the beach to enjoy some time in the sun and to show off their new bathing suits. It was supposed to be three of them but Jasmine had something come up last minute and had to back out of the trip. She texted her but got no response. This had become a pattern and she was worried. They sat on the beach and enjoyed the scenery from under the one of many shaded umbrellas afforded to them. seemed at peace and Vanessa didn't want to disturb that. She had promised me that she wouldn't say anything and that was that. They put on their headphones, shades, and sunhats and enjoyed themselves.

III.

Jasmine texted Alexis for the address confirmation. They had linked up through a mutual friend that recognized her dance talent from the school and wanted to get her some money from side hustles. They were supposed to go to this private birthday party for a big client and make some money. She was nervous but Alexis would be there too so she wouldn't be alone. They met up in the covered parking deck of West Memorial hospital and waited for the private driver to pick them up and take them to the location.

Alexis was putting on her makeup and adjusting her outfit. She had changed from her scrubs into a tight skirt with a modified nursing scrub top, complete with a hat. Jasmine would be her assistant and they'd split whatever they made evenly. She thought about Alonzo and how she'd been lying to him but she was grown now and needed some breathing space from always helping him keep his life together. She respected Alexis's hustle and how she balanced being a mom and working and school. She asked about Malachi and Alexis told her he was good, growing fast and keeping her busy. She couldn't wait to be able to spend more time with him once she finished taking her boards. She showed her pics on her phone of him and Jas couldn't help but recognize some similarities between him and....*Myles*! She kept her thoughts to herself and the task at hand.

They pulled up this gated neighborhood full of multi-million dollar estates. Bentleys, Lambo's, Tesla's, Royce's, Benz Wagons, all filled the driveway of their location. They were escorted to a private entrance along the side that led to the "man cave" where the bachelor party private event was to be held. They recognized a few other girls as they settled in and got themselves together with their hair and makeup. They turned their phones on silent but kept their locations on in case they needed it. After securing their belongings, they got ready to make this money.

They all came in with their masquerade masks and trench coats and stilettos walking seductively. The guys went crazy as they walked in, to the sounds of Truth Hurt's "*So Addictive*" and started their tantric performance. You couldn't tell they were amateurs by their movements, nor nervous. Their moves seemed to hypnotize the crowd and they paid special attention to the guest of honor-Jimmy "Cool Breeze" Calhoun. He squeezed their asses and smacked them as they took turns grinded on him and giving him lap dances. They kissed each other seductively while feeding each other cherries and other delectable fruits available. This went on for as long as the guys allowed. They then went to the pole and did some pro-stripper twirls and acrobatics that had Calhoun ready to take them to the back for himself.

After the fun was over and the crowd dispersed, they followed him back to his private living quarters for some extra fun. Walking in one of his many bedrooms, he told them to make themselves comfortable on the bed as he got undressed. They did as directed and when he turned around they started teasing him by kissing each other and engaging in some foreplay. This turned him on. He hit a couple of lines and drank some hennessy. He offered it to them, with which they obliged with a shot glass each, but no drugs. They all then got on the bed and enjoyed exploring each other's bodies. One was massaging his feet and slowly making her way up his thighs with her tongue while the other one started at the top and made her way south, where they both met at his soldier standing eagerly at attention. They both worked him like a flute with their tongues and mouths. He took no time pulling Jasmine's thighs apart and going to work with his mouth. Alexis sucked on his jewels and stroked him with one hand while playing with herself with the other. Jasmine stopped sucking him and was turning around crawling towards him, ready to mount, when Alexis snuck up and started eating her from behind. She alternated licking her and sucking Calhoun. Jasmine felt like she was in ecstasy as Alexis ate her out.

He kissed Jasmine and sucked her breasts. Soon he pulled out a rubber before mounting her on top of him. His girth caused both pleasure and pain as she felt her walls stretch. She rode him like a stallion, nice and slow. He pulled Alexis to his face and started eating her pussy while the girls kissed and sucked on each other's breasts, and he fucked the shit out of Jasmine. She had never experienced anything like this before. Jasmine and Calhoun continued through the night and ended only in the wee hours of the morning. Jasmine's body ached but she felt so excited from that experience with Alexis more so than with Calhoun. He definitely gave her the business, but Alexis had opened her up to uncharted territory.

Alexis had stepped out and eventually linked up with her friend Trell in the main area after she freshened up. He was the main promoter and always looked out for her and whomever she brought. Trell was her other maintenance man she kept on standby. He was a good guy, like Myles, but really wanted both of them to get away from the chaos that came with this lifestyle. She loved how he respected her body and was gentle whenever they hooked up. She protected him and never let him risk his health. Like Myles, he encouraged her to continue to pursue her career goals and look at this as just a means to a higher calling for her and the wellbeing of Malachi. He was also finishing his degree in mass communications, and wanted them to truly be together.

After Jasmine had gotten up, they were escorted back to the dressing area to shower and change. Trell made sure they were good, before Calhoun's driver pulled up to transport them back to the pickup location. He had paid them generously for their time and made it known that they would definitely utilize them in the future. She checked her phone and noticed a few missed calls from Alonzo and Vanessa. She'd get with them later. She wanted to get home and rest. Alexis thanked Jasmine for joining her and said she was glad they worked together.

They hugged and got in their separate cars and left. She had the next week off and could focus on Malachi and her exams. Once she was licensed, she'd never have to work too hard and could be debt free from her student loans and the house she'd bought for them with money earned from hustling with Calhoun. She thought about Myles. She was thankful that the truth had finally come out regarding Malachi's father. Between his help and her upcoming promotion when she passes the last certification exam, she could cut ties with Calhoun for real. Myles had no love for him after the chaos he caused in her life, and unknowingly putting their then unborn son at risk.

IV.

I helped my parents as much as I could with Myles; even Jordan when he could, took shifts sitting and keeping Myles company during his recovery. Despite him being sedated, he did come around every so often. We all tried our best to act as if he was alive and well, and talked to him just the same. Our family was one full of faith, and never ceased to know that God had the final say so in whatever would happen moving forward. The investigation into Ollie's death didn't last too much longer, and even though the detective wasn't ever able to speak to Myles, there was enough evidence and probable cause to not warrant any charges against him in Ollie's demise. It was a clear case of self-defense and as the detective said quite frankly, *Ollie's ass had it coming and finally met his match*. Still it was of no true consolation to any of us.

Taking one's life was something no one should have to come to, and regardless of the circumstances, Auntie Angie still loved him as her husband, and wanted to ensure he had a decent final disposition. She held no ill will towards her son for his actions for he did what she knew he would do if it came to it. But the guilt was eating at her. The guilt of not having the willpower to remove herself and her son from the nightmare and abuse that terrorized their lives for so long. And now not knowing how Myles would be affected by this incident moving forward once he regained consciousness, in his long journey to recovery. Pops helped as best he could while giving her needed space and time.

Jordan made his business to help out with the final arrangements from a distance. Having personal knowledge and details surrounding the deceased, he removed himself from much of the process, instead opting for my dad, Uncle Harris and Aunt Geneva to formalize everything without any personal bias, while handling the administrative parts. Uncle Harris handled the remains and ensured that Aunt Angie's wishes were fulfilled for her late husband.

In a private service held in a very secluded part of facility grounds, the few of us minus Myles gathered to support her as she said her final goodbyes. This area was designed in the fashion of an Asian Zen Garden, full of peace with artificial waterfalls, streams, koi ponds, small temples and statues-all truly fitting for mental peace and meditation that was warranted. Mrs. Geneva knew that this was the appropriate place given the circumstances. In due time she also knew that Myles would be invited here as well for his own needs, but she'd let Jordan and I work through those details.

Vanessa and Lauryn finally returned from their mini-vacation, and started getting settled back home. She hadn't mentioned anything regarding Myles yet, but knew she needed to. Alonzo had reached out and they agreed to meet up and tell her together. They briefly voiced their concerns about Jasmine, but decided to not worry about her at the moment because there was no need for unnecessary drama right now.

About half an hour later, Alonzo arrived with KyJuan in tow. He looked stressed, while KyJuan appeared happy just to be with him. They both helped him get situated in the living room. KyJuan ran past Vanessa attempting to grab him prompting Lauryn to unexpectedly rescue him. Vanessa gave him the side eye. Alonzo couldn't help but laugh and add insult to injury "*Bombastic side eye!*"

"The audacity, *the betrayal*," she said, pointing at him teasingly. "You're going to need me before I need you."

"*Don't hate, Auntie Nessa*," said defending him. "You aren't the only *auntie*."

"I know that heifa!" she exclaimed. "But I am *the best one*!"

"Yall stop fussing," Alonzo said watching the two go at it. "Trust and believe, he always has a reason behind everything his little bad ass does."

Lauryn helped him up on the sofa where he smiled and closed his eyes while she laid down his blanket. She positioned him on his stomach, facing away from her. Both his dad and Vanessa watched. They knew from past experiences that he was known for doing something epic when he was sleepy, especially when being held by new people. She spread out his blanket over him. He turned his head ever so slightly and smiled, and Lauryn looked back at them, displaying her handy work. Just as she turned back towards him, her smile immediately turned to a grimace, draining all of the color from her face.

"What's wrong with you?" Alonzo said, trying to save face while watching her.

"Girl, why are you looking like that?" her cousin asked as well, knowing full well what was going on.

"Is that *KyJuan*??" Lauryn said looking crazy at them and back at KyJuan who by now was fully awake and had managed to roll over on his back, eyes wide open and smiling.

"What did he eat before y'all got here?" Vanessa asked.

"*Alonzo, come get ya chile!!!!*" she yelled while jumping up and heading back down the hallway.

"*Chili Cheese pups*," Alonzo laughed.

"Don't run now Lauryn!" Vanessa yelled while doubling over in laughter. "You wanted him!"

"Man man, you aint have to do her like that now," said his dad as he sprayed air freshener and checked to make sure it was only gas and actual feces. "But it was funny, wasn't it?"

KyJuan smiled with joy at his latest victim but it didn't take long to drift off to sleep knowing he was free of gas. His dad covered him with his blanket. He motioned for Vanessa to follow him so they could break the news about Myles. Vanessa knocked on the closed door to the room Lauryn had retreated to, to change her clothes. She turned the knob slowly and peeped in. Lauryn motioned for her to come in from the mirror. After ensuring she was fully dressed, they both came. Her eyes narrowed at the sight of Alonzo. They all sat down with Vanessa and Lauryn near each other, but both facing Alonzo. He had his head hung low with his hands together behind it.

"What's going on?" she asked, trying to break the ice of silence in the room.

"Cuz, we need to tell you some news," Vanessa began hesitantly reaching out for her hand. "*About Myles.*"

"But we need you to try to remain calm," Alonzo said, raising his head and moving his hands into a prayer position. "Avant and his folks are up there with them."

"What's up??" she said nervously looking back and forth between the two. "*Is Myles dead?*"

"No, he's alive, but hurt pretty bad," her cousin told her. "He got into a serious altercation with his stepfather."

She started shaking and crying uncontrollably. "How bad exactly, since his cousin, and parents are all up there?"

Alonzo restrained himself from breaking down and tried to save face while answering her question. "He's in a lot of pain and is heavily sedated. He's got several injuries to his body and the doctors figured that would be the best way to help him heal without him fighting it."

KyJuan woke up and started calling for his dad just as she broke down. Vanessa held her close while Alonzo found walking around the corner towards him. Pain and panic shot through her body to the point where she didn't know whether she was experiencing a panic attack, or potential heart attack, as her body started to shake uncontrollably. Fearing for the worst, Vanessa called 9-1-1 just to be sure Lauryn wouldn't crash out. Alonzo meanwhile brought him back up front with his belongings. Vanessa helped him pack up and get settled in the car so he could get him back to Yvonne. He told her to call him so he could meet them at the hospital as soon as he could but to keep an eye on Lauryn. They gave a friendly hug and parted ways, with him watching til she was back inside before leaving. KyJuan reached out his hand towards him as he looked back in the rearview mirror. Their eyes met and both smiled at each other. Alonzo looked away to briefly wipe away a tear before continuing the drive ahead. The ambulance arrived shortly afterwards, and after giving her a quick assessment, peeled out towards the hospital, with Vanessa trailing them and speed dialing Avant.

Myles was still in and out of consciousness, but was healing well according to his doctors. Mama, a retired trauma nurse and physical therapist, gently worked with his limbs and talked to him letting him know what she was doing. She made it her business to look after him in between the nurse and other staff's coming and going. Jordan and I helped Pops tend to Auntie Angie with whatever was needed around the house. Always a private person, we respected her space and didn't bother her much. There was always a list of things that needed completed while she was gone out or in some other part of the house. A month after the incident the scene of the crime was completely unrecognizable, and the house was ready back to normal use, for the future benefit of Myles and Malachi. Myles's belongings were also carefully relocated to the main house since he wouldn't have access to the lower level during his recovery. Auntie Angie didn't know he had purchased a house for them down that way, and no one would tell her until he was ready.

Jordan and I drove the moving truck back down to Georgia while dad and Auntie Angie trailed us not far behind. It was bittersweet leaving Myles but we knew he'd be in the best care in our absence. Mama had agreed to stay behind to make sure of that before we left. I called Vanessa and learned that she had finally broken the news to Lauryn and that she was taking it very hard. Alonzo was also taking it hard but was holding up as best he could. KyJuan was a welcomed distraction, along with work. Jas had been missing in action. *Maybe this was the best thing for them too, thinking back on the food court conversation not so long ago.*

"You alright *G*?" Jordan asked as we continued down the interstate.

"Yeah, I'm good man," I told him as my mind came back into focus. "Just thinking about Myles, and how this whole situation has messed up the entire summer.."

"The situation is messed up for real," he continued. "I'm glad Mrs. Angie is getting a new start somewhere away from Ollie."

"It's long overdue, and fucked up that it had come about this way," I responded trying not to be angry but not being able to help it knowing Myles's condition.

“True. Myles had mentioned y'all trying to get them to move a long time ago but she didn’t want to leave the ole man and he did not want to leave her unprotected.” Jordan mentioned. “I asked him about coming on full time with me working with my Uncle Harris at the family business. It would’ve gotten him away from Ollie but still allow him to be near his mom.”

“That’s wassup Jordan,” I told him. “He definitely needed the distraction, and also to keep him focused on something constructive.”

“He’s a hard worker and my family likes him,” he told me. “My aunt doesn't allow just anyone access to the affairs of the family business.”

“Yeah he’s always been a hustler,” I agreed with a chuckle. “He was never one to wait around for a handout.”

“He mentioned something else too,” Jordan said with hesitation.

“About Lauryn?” I asked curiously, raising one eyebrow.

“Naw. Yeah he did,” he said quickly. “But also about someone else.”

“*That Alexis chick?*” I responded.

“Yeah and how her son is his.” he said as we noticed a food sign on the upcoming exit. “He sounded like he kinda already knew but was conflicted until the test results confirmed it.”

Finally, the drive back to Georgia and home was complete. After backing the truck up close to the garage and ensuring it was secured, we both stretched and went to help Pops and Auntie Angie get the suv unloaded, and settled inside. Alonzo pulled up shortly after and dapped both me and Jordan up. He picked up some boxes and came inside.

“Hey Dad, Auntie Angie,” he said smiling as he sat a box down against a wall to give both hugs.

“Hey Alonzo,” he said, giving him a fatherly hug. “My other son. When did you get here?”

“Just now. Figured y’all could use the extra muscles to help download the truck,” he said, showing off his muscles. “How are you holding up Auntie Angie and my *bonus* dad?

“I’ve had better days but you know God is still good,” she said smiling, giving him a hug from the recliner.

“Amen to that,” he responded. “My parents said to tell y'all ‘hello’, and that they’re keeping everyone in their thoughts and prayers.”

He then made his way back outside to help us download and sort out everything from the truck. Auntie Angie would be moving into the rear upper balcony level of the house around the back that had direct access to momma's prized garden and infinity pool oasis while we would set up Malachi's new furniture in the lower terrace area. Thankfully wheeled tools were accessible to make everything easy to move and situate. Between the three of us, the truck was emptied and swept, furniture and other belongings moved and situated without damage. We were chilling, sitting on the back of the truck when Alonzo elbowed me and cut his eyes left, to the front of the driveway. I hopped up to find Vanessa and Lauryn had just pulled up. He and Jordan followed suit.

"What up lil mama?" I said she got out and closed the door behind her. "I would hug you but I've been working hard, and need a shower."

"I understand and appreciate the warning," she said, swatting me away. "We were just in the neighborhood and decided to stop by. Who is that?"

"Oh my bad, this is Jordan-Myles's good friend from back home," I said, introducing them to him. He extended his hand to her.

"Nice to meet you," he said to her before turning his attention to Lauryn . "And you must be the young lady that's stolen my boy's heart."

"Is that what he told you?" she said somewhat blushing. "I'm Lauryn. Nice to meet you. We're only friends. *That's what he wants*."

“Yeah, he was on cloud 9 whenever he spoke of you,” he continued. “You’re good for him.”

“Y’all go on inside and speak to Pops and Auntie Angie. We need to get this truck returned so we can come back and freshen up.”

With that the ladies headed inside and Alonzo headed to his car to trail us to the return location for the truck. After ensuring everything was good and the truck secured with keys in the dropbox, Jordan and I jumped in the car with Alonzo to head back. He told us he couldn’t stay long after we made it back to the house but that he’d link back up with us later in the week when he was off. I waited til Jordan had gone inside before asking him about Jasmine.

“You and Jaz officially over?” I asked cautiously.

“Might as well be real talk,” he said, sounding relieved. “She hasn’t made any time for me so I’m just gonna do me honestly.”

“I hear you man. You’ve definitely been on the grind hard,” acknowledging his non stop hustling. “Not mad at all. You're doing what you gotta do for yourself and KyJuan.”

“Yeah man, KyJuan ain’t ask to be here and it’s not for Yvonne to do everything,” he said through a yawn.

"Bet. Well, get home safely so you can rest up playa," I said dapping him up. "I'm about to go do the same. I'm tired as hell myself."

He lit up a blunt to hit, took a sip of some water, and changed the song on his stereo. "*Love & Happiness*" by Al Greene blasted from his speakers before he turned the volume down. "My bad brodie."

He laughed as he fastened his seat belt while backing down the driveway. I threw up the deuces as he pulled off and headed around the side steps, up to the upper level guest suite. I didn't hear any voices when I entered. I still moved quietly just in case Jordan was asleep and headed to turn on the shower in the bathroom on the far end of the hallway. Grabbing some clothes from the connecting closet, I wasted no time going to wash the sweat and soreness away.

I let the steam and water from the shower head flow and took slow, deep breaths. For the first time the thought actually crossed my mind about what would happen if Myles didn't pull through. Though his body was healing timely, he was still in and out of consciousness, and had a long road to recovery ahead. It all became too much-I couldn't tell my tears from the water as I held my head down under the shower head. It was only after the water temperature changed to lukewarm that I came back around and finished up. I checked on Jordan who was already asleep himself, and did too, once I finished cleaning up and getting settled myself.

V.

Jasmine heard her phone alert go off and grabbed it from her pillow. Everyone had been attempting to reach her but she was in no mood to deal with them. She needed time to herself. A couple days after the party, she got a call from Calhoun. Not really knowing how to react, she initially brushed his calls off. Not knowing if there was any history between him and Alexis, she was trying to play it smart. Plus she was busy trying to ready to take her dental hygienist boards so she could get a much needed pay increase and promotion. This would also entail her potentially relocating. Another alert from her phone-Calhoun again. She decided to call and see what he wanted.

"What's up shawty, you avoiding a playa?" Calhoun answered the phone with a big smile.

"Not even, I don't know you like that so what reason would I have to avoid you?" she responded.

"You don't know me like that?" he said pulling the phone away making sure he heard her right. "We seem to know each other quite well at the party. What you got going on?"

"'Hahaha, that was strictly business," she told him matter of factly. "I really didn't even know what kind of affair it was."

"But you enjoyed yourself right?" he asked as he reminisced back. "Other than the money?"

“Yeah, it was cool,” she said, reminiscing herself, getting quite moist in her soft spot. “So what’s up, since you hit me up.”

“Tryna see when I can see you again,” he laid his cards out. “I’m feeling you and want to get to know you better.”

“I don’t know about that,” she said, listening to him trying to spit game to her. “For all I know you might be some type of major drug pusher or high level gang affiliate.”

“Don’t worry about that, it won’t be a problem.” he reassured her. “Besides, my team ensures all my i’s are dotted and t’s are crossed.”

“So, back to my question,” he switched gears again to the task at hand. “When can I see you again?”

“What if I got a man?” she asked out of the blue.

“*Really*, shawty?” he asked as he brushed his hand over his fresh cut. “Go head now. Y’all can’t be really too serious considering…..”

“Everyone goes through rough patches,” she responded. “But since you’re on my line, it must be nice being able to set your own schedule’”.

“You know how it is,” he laughed it off. “But check this, enough with playing hardball, how about we link up for lunch, *my treat of course*. Just want to see you again. Afterwards, if you ain't feeling it, we can go our separate ways."

"Ill let you know," she said, still contemplating his offer. *What harm could just going out bring?*

"Bet, you got the math." he said and ended the call. He had other calls to make in the meantime. First one being to check on Azuri, his # 1 priority. Quickly dialing the number, he got up and started walking down the stairs of the covered pavilion overlooking his olympic sized pool with a fountain in the middle.He put his feet in the water of the step to the pool and sat back.

"HEY DADDY!!!!" she screamed into the phone, almost deafening him temporarily. "Where are you?"

"Hey baby girl, I'm taking a break from work," he said happily. "Glad to hear your voice. What are you up to?"

"Nothing, just playing with my dolls," she told him as she combed "Isabella" her favorite one. "When are you coming back?"

"Soon. Gotta few more things to finish up and then I'm all yours," he told her.

"*Forever?*" she asked. "You *always* have to go away for work."

"How else will I be able to buy you nice things and take you on trips?" He said knowing that she'd rather have him with her everyday than all of the materialistic and other things he provided her in an attempt to make up for his absence. His life had gotten much better since he made the transition from illicit entrepreneur to a legal one. It wasn't easy and things were more scrutinized but it was definitely worth the risk, given how he no longer had to look over his shoulder, and had patiently taken the proper steps to ensure his exit would be without any regrets. *Azuri* was his saving grace, literally.

"I know but I still miss you," she said sadly.

"I know sweetie," he said softly-she knew how to soften him up. "I'll see you soon. Love you Azuri, always and forever."

Jasmine hit Alexis on her line. While the phone rang, she checked the weather on her phone and stepped outside to also gauge the temperature. *Perfect for a sundress*! She went back inside and pulled out a pastel orange sundress that she'd never gotten around to wearing. After matching them with some naked toned sandals and a nice hair wrap, she went to turn on the shower-*set on hell, just like she liked it*. She got Alexis's voicemail and left her a quick message before disconnecting the call. She then turned on her stereo and tuned to 97.4, known for playing some of the best old school R&B tracks. *"Freak Like Me" by Adina Howard* was just going off, and *"Always on time" Ja Rule and Ashanti* played as she undressed, put on her shower cap, and jumped in the shower. She used some of her coffee scrub to exfoliate her skin and then made sure to apply some of her shea butter moisturizer all over, ensuring it was absorbed, before turning off the water and grabbing a towel to wrap around her body. Moving to the sounds of the music jamming from her speakers, she continued her pampering and preparation, and eventually freed her hair and styled it in a simple layered style that showed the highlights.

After brushing her teeth and flossing, she washed off her facial wash and dried, and applied a little natural toned makeup lightly with her brush. A natural beauty, she never required or relied on makeup to enhance her beauty. She put on her dress and gave herself a lookover in the full-length mirror. Satisfied, she grabbed her sandals, and sat on the bed while attempting to reach Alexis one more time, slipping into them.

"*Hey girl, sorry I missed your call earlier,*" Alexis answered, sounding exhausted. "*A bitch been tired as hell from working these doubles!*"

"It's all good. I'm preparing myself for the same thing once I hear back from these boards." she said thinking about how much longer she had to wait for her own results. "You wouldn't guess who hit me up trying to link up?"

"*Who?*" she said with excitement.

"*Calhoun!*" she responded. "I wonder how he got my number?"

"I kinda slipped and gave it to him," she confessed. "He wouldn't leave me alone about it, and I gave in."

"*You did WHAT?*" she said, almost falling off the bed. "*Well, I don't know whether to be happy or mad.*"

“What did he say?” she asked her. “You know he's a true baller right?”

“Yeah, I can tell by his smooth talking.” she told her. “He didn’t care about me having a man either.”

“Shit to be honest, it didn’t seem like you were thinking about *Alonzo or any other man* while we were at that party.” she told her flat out.

“*Anyway,*” she said, rolling her eyes. “I did what I had to do to help us make that money.”

“*I know that’s right!*” Alexis said in agreement. “But seriously, are you going to meet up with him?”

“What harm can it do?” she answered. “It’s not like I’ve been dealing with Alonzo. He’s old business in my eyes. He got his priorities and I’ve got mine.”

“Well I say go for it since you’re not technically tied up with him anymore,” Alexis told her.

“Yeah, taking a much needed break to enjoy myself. I’m still young and need to enjoy life.” she said mostly to herself.

“True that! But just be careful as always and trust your intuition.” Alexis warned her.

"I definitely will." she told her. "But I won't hold you up. Get some rest before Malachi has you running around like you're training for a marathon."

"Girlllllll, you said a mouthful then!" she said, throwing her comforter back and stretching. "I gotta get ready to go get his little bad ass now."

"All right, well I'll talk to you later." Jasmine said before disconnecting the call. Her mind thought back to when she saw her son and how much he looked like Myles. She knew it was none of her business but couldn't help but wonder-sometimes children can look like one person, but be from another. She knew that Alexis and Myles were real tight and spent a lot of time together, but couldn't shake the feeling about Malachi. She'd just keep that thought in the back of her mind for now, along with all of her thoughts about Alonzo, Vanessa, and the rest of her old crew. Though she missed them, it seemed like they were all in different places in their lives. She texted Calhoun and waited for his response so she'd know where to meet him. '*New day, new me'* she thought gave herself one final lookover in the full length mirror that she had stopped in front of as she walked out of her bedroom.

Calhoun was busy looking over some overseas vacation properties when his phone alerted him of an incoming message. He saw "lil bit" and already knew who it was. He smiled as he saw she had accepted his invitation for a meet up. He walked away from his computer and went to the closet to see what he was going to wear. He then sent her back a text and asked to send a picture, so he could complement her outfit, unknowingly. She obliged without incident. He chose a white linen outfit and straw hat, and sandals, that would complement it well with the nice weather outside. He then went and showered and was ready for a day/night out on the town within the hour.

Jasmine had looked at her makeup one more time while waiting for him to come meet her at the same parking lot she had parked during the party. She really didn't want him knowing where she stayed, especially in case he was on some stalker type mess. A man particular about his time, he made his way there early to scope the scene. She saw him pull up in his Jeep and quickly finished.

"Hey there *lil bit*," he said smiling as he watched her exit and lock up her car. He got out and gave her a hug before walking around to open the door for her, taking in all of her beauty. "You're wearing that dress!"

"Thanks, it's the perfect weather for it," she said while checking out his outfit, "You clean up well yourself. *Not often a man will wear open toed shoes without socks*."

"Well what can I say," he said, flashing his killer smile. "I grew up in Belize, and I believe in looking good from head to toe."

"Ain't nothing wrong with that *papi*!" she said, enjoying his suaveness."Where are we headed?"

"I figured we'd check out this nice spot near the water called *Albatross Acres* for some drinks and tapas," he told her. "That way we can sit on the patio and enjoy the breeze while we get to know each other."

He opened the door to his Jeep and made sure she was comfortable before closing the door and walking back to his side. He knew he had to be careful with her. He couldn't afford to have another Alexis situation again. It almost cost him everything to get her back right, but he did what he had to do because he allowed her to get too involved. Plus she had a lil man who depended on her. He questioned whether he was the daddy since they had never used protection when they hooked up. He knew she was seeing other people but she was one of his main girls so she let him have his way with her. She had also been messing around with this young kat named Myles and he knew it could be a possibility that *he could be the daddy as well.*

Either way, that was old business now that she was back on her feet, though they still linked up when business called. She could pull both men and women along with the best of them, and he enjoyed still having access to that pussy cat and mouth whenever business opportunities allowed. As they pulled up to the venue's valet parking area, he put the jeep in park and waited for the attendant to open his door. He stepped out, handed over the keys and proceeded to her side to open the door for her to step out like a runway model. She did so with an air of confidence she knew fitted her perfectly but did not appear conceited. Little did she know who the valet attendant was that observed the whole scene without incident…*Alonzo*.

"Welcome to Albatross Acres," said the hostess who greeted them as they stepped through the thick automatic glass doors. "Do you all have a reservation number?"

"Good day, and yes we do," Calhoun responded calmly. "457291-Calhoun, party of two."

"Awesome, let me just confirm it is ready for your visit," she said, entering thenumber into her system and gathering the VIP menus. "Looks like everything is set. Please follow me this way."

Jasmine took in the scenery and intimate details of everything as they walked through the establishment. Whoever was in charge of the interior designing paid superb attention to every detail when it came to choosing the furniture, art and wall decor, paint colors, to accent each individual view of the panoramic windows that showcased magnificent views of the Albatross Bay and skyline in the distance. They were seated in an upper secluded booth that opened up a rooftop sky bar. Just the right amount of wind, sunlight and shade to complement their visit. Calhoun ordered a Long Island Iced Tea while selecting a Peach Sangria for her. She smiled at the thought of him anticipating her beverage choice. She looked over the menu and selected the Chef's special sashimi deluxe paired with their seasonal fresh fruit.

"I see you know how to pair food and drinks well," Calhoun complemented her as they handed the menus back to the waitress.

“Well since you picked out the drinks so perfectly, I figured I needed to do my part,” she smiled. “Too nice a day to ruin it over wrong food selection.”

“You got that right,” he co-signed. “So tell me about yourself.”

“Okay, well I am a dental hygienist intern preparing for boards.” she told him confidently. “Looking forward to getting certified soon and hopefully relocating for better career opportunities within the field.”

“That’s wassup. It takes a special person to want to deal with folks' mouths all day.” he chuckled. “I applaud you for that.”

“Well thank you,” she said, placing one of her hands on the table. “I am very fortunate to be working with one of the best African American female cosmetic dentists, *Dr. Gwendolyn May Rollins*. She’s one of my role models.”

“That’s very impressive,” he said, placing his hand over hers. “Don't ever limit yourself. Let this just be a stepping stone on your career journey.”

“Amen to that. Maybe one day I can carry on the torch and do more for disadvantaged families within minority communities.” she said reminiscing about her future outside of her current location for the first time in a long time.

“Make it happen, you don’t have anything or anyone holding you back do you?” he asked her, taking genuine interest in her.

"No honestly I don't. Only maybe myself." she said taking off her shades and looking him in his eyes.

"Give yourself some time once you get certified and more experience in the field to get a better idea of exactly where you want to be and what speciality, so you can tailor your time around that to help when the time comes." he told her.

"I will," she said, feeling his genuineness. "Enough about me, what about you?"

"Well, I'm Jimmy Calhoun, serial hustler turned legit entrepreneur," he said as he readjusted his glasses. "I have a three year old daughter, Azuri, who basically saved my life and made me change for the better."

"I dabble a bit with the music industry, mainly providing a space to produce local talent and other artists that want to learn more about the production and engineering side." He told her. "Otherwise I own a couple of laundromats, dry cleaners/alterations shops, all while maintaining a commercial and a residential cleaning company."

He showed her his daughter's picture and she smiled looking like an exact mini replica of him, except with longer hair but the same stunningly beautiful natural blue-green eyes and smile. She could tell that he was really involved in her life as they flipped through the multiple pictures on his phone. Their food and drinks arrived shortly afterwards and they dug in. Everything was so fresh and carefully selected and prepared. They complemented the drinks and thankfully the light refreshments didn't give her a buzz. She wanted to still be in control of her mind and be able to make clear judgments. They sat back taking in the breathtaking views of the bay and perfect weather. *I could get used to this type of treatment!*

After so many years of taking care of family and then helping Alonzo with KyJuan, she was ready to step out on faith and pursue her own dreams...but she'd tread lightly with Calhoun. While she wasn't in any hurry to start another relationship, she didn't mind having his company. She felt a different type of energy that gave her a comfort she wasn't able to feel when around Alonzo. He played his role and while she enjoyed the ride, it was time to move on to bigger and better opportunities. KyJuan she'd miss painfully but just she'd get over it as she'd done with everyone and everything else that came and gone in her life.

VI.

Jordan, Alonzo, and I drove Auntie Angie back to Chicago. We had to delay the trip back for a couple days because had suffered a panic attack upon hearing the news about Myles and had been hospitalized temporarily under observation. After getting the greenlight from the doctor that she was good to go, Vanessa helped her register for a brief internship with her-assisting with the upcoming soiree like event. The rest of us packed up and hit the road to come check on Myles. Once he got better he'd be coming back with us to Georgia, and having his care and treatment transferred to one of the network hospitals so there wouldn't be any interruption to his care.

More than likely he would be flown there due to his fragile state whenever the time came. The ride was smooth for the most part. We made a stop at a local diner called *Sadie's* that was a hotspot for tourists and travelers near and far. They specialized in southern cuisine, desserts, and delicacies. Everyone took the necessary time to stretch and relieve themselves before sitting down for some good ole southern cooking. Alonzo, Jordan, and I ordered southern fried catfish filet meals with peach tea while auntie opted for baked fish or chicken with roasted veggies and rice. She played around with her food for the most part as she didn't have much of an appetite. Her mind was on her baby. She would end up packing her food to take with her on the rest of the trip. I called Pops to check on everything and let him know where we were. He said to make sure to bring him and mama something good too. They were long time friends with the owners and made it a thing to stop there whenever they came through.

Myles heard faint beeping noises and voices around him but couldn't figure out where they were coming from. Panicked, he started trying to move his arms but couldn't get them free. It was all he could do to cry out for someone to help him. He didn't know what was going on but felt trapped. Gunshots and blood, screams and sirens, all added to the confusion. He continued to cry out for help for what seemed like forever. He felt helpless. Then he felt a comforting hand on his heart and forehead. A comforting voice telling him it was okay. That he was safe and no one was going to hurt him. He knew the soothing voice but couldn't place it. Whoever it was was telling him not to fight. Just rest.

He had nothing to worry about. He saw Malachi holding his ninja turtle out for him to hold….he saw Lauryn pushing a baby stroller coming his way, smiling. He was walking towards them when all of a sudden everything turned very dark. He looked around to see what was happening and lost sight of them. He heard screams and searched frantically but couldn't see anyone. He yelled out for them but couldn't find them anywhere. He yelled louder and louder. Then he saw a large man attacking them near an intersection. He tried to run towards them but was being blocked by two younger men.

He fought hard to get free, but couldn't. The man had grabbed Malachi and was lifting him up as if he was getting ready to throw him. No one appeared to be bothered by the scene unfolding around them. The man turned his way and his face struck him with fear. OLLIE! He held Malachi up like a rag doll as Lauryn tried unsuccessfully to grab him while holding onto her baby stroller. He finally managed to free himself and ran at full speed towards them. Ollie had this pure evil look on his face and grinned knowing he had the upper hand. Just as Myles reached them, the motherfucker threw Malachi in front of an approaching metro streetcar with one hand, while trying to use his other hand to pull Lauryn and the baby stroller in the same direction. Right before impact, Myles opened his eyes and screamed at the top of his lungs,

Ma Dukes was so frightened all she could do was pull him close as if to bear hug him. She'd never witnessed anything like this in her life and knew whatever was going on was truly traumatic and devastating. The nurses and doctors did their best to help hold him down as another one came in with a powerful sedative to put into his IV line. Just as quickly as it happened, it was over. He went limp and fell back. He briefly made eye contact with his aunt and looked around to see that he was in a hospital before releasing a single solitary tear that she gently wiped away with a nearby wash towel.

He was safe. His breathing slowed. He saw her angelic smile and felt her comforting energy. He felt her hand on his heart. Her mouth was moving but he couldn't make out what she was saying, though it was enough to give him some peace as he began to relax. All he could do was cry. He didn't know what was going on. He saw his left leg and ankle slightly elevated. His arms were strapped to the bed. He had pain in his throat. He could still hear the beeping noise. They were starting to become faint and softer again. Everything became blurry, and then it all went black.

Pops was in the waiting room down the hall. He looked stressed as he took off his glasses and gave the crew all fatherly hugs. Auntie Angie was the first to go in his room when we arrived.

Mama gave her a quick update and stepped out to give them much needed privacy. She and Pops were gonna head over to the cafeteria to enjoy their food. Unbeknownst to them, Myles had become quite the super star with the young nurses and techs. Everytime she came back, he had something new in his room, and appeared happier when he was conscious. They kept up his appearances as best they could, even going so far as having a personal barber come in to keep his hair and goatee groomed as he would do himself. One tech even convinced him to let her clip his finger and toenails. He was not a fan of people touching his feet, only his mama.

Through the grace of God Myles hadn't had anymore episodes like the initial one though he still suffered from what the doctor's called PTSD, or post-traumatic stress disorder, and would be connected with both counseling and a psychiatrist free of charge because of his circumstances. At least he was now more conscious and able to breathe without the aid of a ventilator. He couldn't speak much but was able to tolerate some solid food. We were all at the house having breakfast and enjoying each other's company.

"Myles has been through something awful I tell you," Mama said as she sat down in the closest rocking chair in the quaint living room when we walked in. "He's come a very long way since he first arrived."

"Has he seen the psychiatrist?" I asked curiously. "I hate to think that he might have to take medicine because of all that he's been through."

"Yeah he has, but he will be on a combination of therapies-medication, one-on-one counseling, and others as the need arises." she explained. "But seeing y'all will be the most helpful. He's been asking about everyone. Especially Lauryn. He's also mentioned a *Malachi* person."

We fellas just looked nervously back and forth but tried not to let on to give anything away. We told her Lauryn was Vanessa's little cousin and he had become good friends over the summer. She blushed at the revelation and shook her head. We were filled in about his hospital groupies and fan club. All we could do was hold our sides laughing at knowing that no matter how fucked up a situation he was in, Myles could still charm anyone. Alonzo took credit for teaching his lil *brother* well. Jordan said he had to go check in with his family as they still had some jobs to finish that required his presence. He actually asked Alonzo if he wanted to help him and make a few bucks in the process. That was music to his ears, plus he was ensured that all he needed to do was drive one of their trucks back and forth along with Jordan. Once they left, I sat down to catch up with what was really going on with my Ma Dukes.

"He feels really guilty and remorseful for how things went down with Ollie," she told me after she made some hot tea for us. "It's like Ollie keeps haunting him in his dreams."

"That was one evil SOB if I ever knew one," I responded with as much restraintas I could muster up given who I was talking to.

"You sound just like your father James," she said in between sips. "But we have to forgive him. For ourselves."

"*How though?*" I asked her trying to understand why he deserved such treatment.

"He can't ask for forgiveness," she explained. "Whatever he did he will have to give into account for with the good Lord, unless he did so right before taking his final breath."

"But we are commanded by God to forgive," she went on. "When you pray the 'Lord's Prayer', that you learned in Sunday School as a child, the part that goes 'forgive our trespasses, as we forgive those who trespass against us', that's where it comes from. It is not for us to always understand, but just to trust that God knows best."

She stretched out her hands across for me to grasp onto. She knew I was struggling to understand and that she was doing what she always did when it happened. She prayed. I bowed my head and closed my eyes as I listened to her pray. In her angelic voice, she started with the 'Lord's Prayer" followed by thanking Him for all that he has done, known and unknown, seen and unseen, and then going into specifics about what was on her heart. One thing about Ma Dukes, she was a prayer warrior and didn't need to be boastful. She stayed calm and let her concerns be known. Though I felt she would break my hand bones as she tightened her grip, I knew she wanted me to know how serious she was.

By the time she ended, I felt a peace and calm that I know could only come from God. All hurt and pain had temporarily subsided and I was most thankful for it. She opened her eyes and patted my hands, letting me know it was okay. I looked at her with tears in my eyes and allowed myself to become that little boy once again that needed mama's comfort. No matter how old I got, I knew I would never be too old to get one of her wonderful, comforting hugs. Thank goodness the rocking chair was strongly built because I just knew I was going to fall and break my hip as she rocked while holding onto me.

VII.

Vanessa and Lauryn kept busy at the Youth center where she was the head chef. Due to her medical emergency a while back she missed out on the initial Soiree that was supposed to be her moment to shine. Thankfully it was rescheduled, and would be featuring her children at the center and she was more than ready to do it big. Lauryn volunteered to help her since she didn't have much to keep her mind off Myles. Jasmine came back around but with a different aura that Vanessa knew meant she didn't want to really be bothered. They kept things as copacetic as possible for the sake of the children and upcoming events. Even Lauryn picked up on the *stank* aura and tried to steer clear from any extended alone time with her. It didn't last long.

"Jasmine, do you have an issue with me?" she asked innocently as they were sitting down after having helped the girls group finish their final rehearsal of a difficult dance choreography she'd been drilling them on without ease.

"No, I'm just trying to make sure the girls do their best," she said, clearly deflecting the conversation. "Why would I have an issue with *you*?"

"I don't know but it seems like you want to say something but are holding back for whatever reason," she responded. "Whatever is going on, you can just say it."

"Really now," she said sarcastically. "But right now is not the right place *or* time."

Vanessa overheard the conversation but stayed in her lane Lauryn could hold her on and she was going to let her do just that unless things became too heated. Jasmine was her girl true enough but she knew that if given an opportunity, she'd spit venom from her tongue more vile than any other person she knew. Lauryn on the other hand was an angel, but held her own hidden 'mean girl' spirit as well. She just watched from a safe distance while monitoring the young men she had assisting her in the kitchen. They'd pulled off a hell of a spread without her having to micromanage them.

This Soiree was to honor victims of domestic violence, as well as women who were part of a transitional program being given a second chance to rebuild their lives and reunite with their children. Some of the children had no idea their mothers were some of the nominees. It would definitely be a tear jerker. She just had to make sure everything went smoothly. Unbeknownst to her, a potential monkey wrench was about to make a guest appearance.

Alexis arrived early to the Soiree event. Jasmine had invited her as a return favor. They had become best buddies and she wanted her to see the performance. Jasmine didn't know Lauryn would be there helping her cousin. This would be very interesting to say the least. Vanessa had to do a double take when she saw Alexis walk in looking naturally flawless in her simple, yet elegant evening gown attire. In between ensuring the young men had everything set up and the presentations were in their appropriate places, she kept a watchful eye as Alexis greeted Jasmine with a friendly hug. She was very cordial to Lauryn, who she didn't know from a dead-end alley. She had brought her son with her and he was dressed to the nine's with his little cute self. She decided it was only right she came over to say hello.

"Hello, and welcome," Vanessa said, extending her hand. "Please make yourself comfortable and feel free to enjoy the refreshments set out on the other side."

"Thanks girl, this setup is awesome," Alexis said looking at the food spread and how everything complemented each other. "Yall definitely did your thang with this!"

"Thanks, it was definitely a team effort-with the young folks definitely deserving most of the credit." she said humbly. "Are you staying for the performance too?"

"Oh yes, Jasmine said she helped the girls with a very tough choreography and she's nervous," Alexis said as Malachi tugged on her hand with his. "Yes, Malachi?"

He pointed to the fruit assortment and looked up at her. "Okay, we will go get some fruit."

"Where are my manners, Vanessa, meet Malachi, my knight in shining armor." She held him up so he could see her face to face.

"Hey Malachi, don't you look mighty dapper in your tuxedo!" she said as she couldn't help but notice how strikingly familiar his face looked. "Y'all go ahead and eat. We will have time to catch up later on."

"All right," she said, letting him down and letting him lead the way towards the fruit spread. He was so careful as to not mess up his shoes or spill the fruit bowl she allowed him to hold as he pointed and she filled to his little delight.

Vanessa kept it to herself as she continued back to the kitchen to see how the other food was coming along for the multi-course dinner that was soon to be served once the rest of the guests arrived and were seated. Lauryn was being a mini dictator having the gentleman executing orders with the precision of a drill sergeant overseeing drill and ceremony. That lil lady had some spunk about her. As she peeked out the window she could see the room almost filled with guests. She said a silent prayer and watched as her workers made their way around to each table with the first of many dishes for the guests to enjoy as the night's emcee laid out the order of events and introduced VIP guests. She looked for Alexis and Malachi and prayed they wouldn't cross paths with Lauryn too closely.

Lauryn monitored her group of gentlemen and also kept an eye on the young ladies who tried not to look nervous as they were about to put on the performance of a lifetime. With Jasmine giving the signal, they effortlessly made their way around the guests and towards the center stage. Just then a woman dressed in a stunning silver gown made her way to the microphone with her escort, who then made his way to the Bosendorfer Imperial Grand piano and took a seat.

Without missing a beat, he tickled the ivories as the group on stage began to execute the first part of the dance. As he played specific keys with a dynamism of a virtuoso, their fluid movements captivated the audience. The woman then began singing in the most angelic voice, signaling a shift in the performance. The group behind her assembled in a choir formation as she belted out a song called "Change". Lauryn instantly recognized her as *Heather Headley*! She had worked on her costumes one summer during the production of "Aida", and she was such a joy to learn from. As she sat captivated by the performance, she caught Malachi out the corner of her eye about to drop the bowl he was trying to dispose of. Her quick reflexes saved him from messing up his tuxedo and shoes. He looked up at her and she was left completely speechless. She didn't even notice Alexis heading her way, probably wondering why he hadn't come back to sit down.

"*Malachi*, what are you up to little man?" she said as he looked up at her smiling.

"He almost dropped his bowl on the way to the trash can," she told her. "He was trying so hard not to mess up his clothes and shoes."

"I don't know what I'm going to do with him," she exclaimed. "He is so much like his Daddy, it's a crime and a shame! "Nothing wrong with looking good," she said as she noticed his lower lip starting to stick out like he knew he was in trouble. "Don't worry Malachi, you're not in trouble, *right mommy?*"

"Yeah, you're not in trouble." she said, rubbing his back. "You're being quite the perfect gentleman and little helper."

Malachi perked up at that and had a full grin now that he knew he had escaped trouble once again, this time *thanks to his guardian angel Lauryn*. Alexis thanked her and headed back to her seat at a nearby table, leaving Lauryn speechless once again. Upon standing up, she was hit with a spell of nausea and bolted for the nearest restroom. Vanessa just happened to be making her exit, when she was blindsided. She moved just in time to see a blur disappear behind the door leading to the handicap stall and someone heaving up lungs and guts.

"Excuse me, are you okay in there?" she called out softly as she stood outside the stall door.

"I don't know, oh God it happened so quickly," said as she felt intense pain in her stomach.

"*Lauryn*, is that you?" Vanessa called out a little louder before realizing the doorwasn't secured.

She helped her cousin up and walked with her to the sink so she could clean her face. She wondered if maybe something she ate didn't agree with her, but couldn't remember seeing her touch any of the food. Lauryn rinsed her mouth out and looked in the mirror attempting to fix her now disarrayed look. Vanessa helped her fix her hair while she touched up her makeup. They then headed back just as the girls were finishing up another final performance and the gentlemen were rotating food plates in and out of the prep area to the guest tables without missing a beat. Lauryn chose to sit at a seat far away from any food to avoid a repeat. She didn't know why she was so nauseous all of a sudden. She hoped she wasn't getting sick from the new birth control. She pulled out her phone to try to call Myles.

Auntie Angie had just finished putting lotion on his feet after carefully clipping his nails when noticed his phone light up and saw it was Lauryn calling. He looked her way, smiled and shook his head for her to answer.

"Hello," she answered. "Who's this?"

"Hey, I'm sorry," she said, caught completely off guard. "Do I have the wrong number? Is Myles around?"

"No baby, hold on let me put you on speaker," Auntie Angie said as she fidgeted with his phone clumsily. "Here we go, he can hear you. I'm his mother Angela. What's your name?"

"I apologize, Ms. Angela. My name is Lauryn. I'm Vanessa's cousin," she said, trying not to break down. "I know you might not be able to talk back to me Myles but know that I'm praying for you to have a full recovery. I'm coming to see you as soon as I can. You keep fighting okay. Don't you give up Myles."

"He can hear you sweetheart. " Angela reassured her. "He's smiling and shaking his head in acknowledgement. He's getting the best care and doing his part as well."

"That's great to hear," she said, getting some relief. "Have Avant and Alonzo come to see him yet?"

"No, they accompanied Vivian back to the lodge so she can get some rest." she told her. "They should be up later on. They're probably tired from the long drive up."

"Okay, well I'm glad y'all made it up there safely. I'll call to check on him later. It was nice talking with you." she said reassuringly.

"You as well, I look forward to meeting the young lady that's captured my son's heart." she said before disconnecting the call.

Myles was grinning full on when she looked up at him. She smiled at him and shook her head. *That damn son of hers, always the charmer.* She looked at her watch to see what the time was getting to be. She heard a knock on the door. She turned to see me, Alonzo, and Jordan. We all gave her a hug as she stood. She went back to give Myles a hug and kiss. He saw her eyes tear up and he started to do the same. He clutched her hand tightly and uttered just barely above a whisper, "don't cry ma, I'ma be alright." She wiped her tears and then his before walking towards the door. Jordan came and gave him a hug and said he'd be back once he made sure she got home safely. He shook his head and watched them until the door shut. He then focused his attention on Alonzo. He motioned for him to come his way. Alonzo treaded carefully so as to not hit his leg as he maneuvered around to his left side. He took a seat and clasped his hands around Myles'. Myles mustered up what little strength he had and pulled him close.

"How have you and KyJuan been?" he asked him slowly.

"We're hanging in there," Alonzo reassured him. "KyJuan gave Lauryn the silent killer gas treatment."

Myles tried to laugh without inflicting more pain. "That's my hitter."

“You all right?” he asked him as he surveyed the scene. “I can’t imagine how you survived what you did, but God knows you are a real soldier.”

“Taking it day by day,” Myles whispered to him. “You gotta look after Avant for me. He's gonna need you just like you're gonna need him.”

“I got him, don't have to worry about that,” he reassured him. “We're gonna help Vanessa with Lauryn too.”

“Avant, come here man,” he said, motioning for me to come closer. “I’m alright.”

“I know you are. It’s just hard seeing you like this man.” I said hoarsely. “But God is so good.”

“Amen to that,” Myles said pointing up out the window towards the sky. “How’s *my boy* doing?”

“He’s all right. He and his mom showed up at that Soiree that Vanessa and Jasmine helped coordinate.” I told him. “Here’s a picture.”

He looked as I pulled up the picture Vanessa had sent me. Alonzo looked and smiled at Myles. Malachi looked just like him, mannerisms and all. There was no doubt that he came from Myles. No DNA test was necessary. I thought about the text that Vanessa had sent regarding Lauryn getting sick and how it had happened coincidentally just after her encounter with Malachi and Alexis. I told

Myles about it and he just looked from me to Alonzo then to Myles, who just shook his head defiantly.

"She is not potentially pregnant…" Alonzo asked as he moved his head to try to find his line of sight. It had Myles' mind wandering back to the nightmare he'd had and tried not to think about it too much.

"Nah, can't be that," he reassured us both. "*At least not by me*."

"That's a huge relief," was all I could say as I sat back to take it all in. My baby cousin did not need that level of stress; he was only twenty. Auntie Angie would flip her wig otherwise, and I would never hear the end of it. Myles continued to watch us. We had no clue how much pain he was carrying behind his eyes.

"You know you need to gone and cuff Lauryn," Alonzo said, tapping his arm. "She's wifey worthy."

"Not to change the subject," he said as he looked my way. "You wouldn't guess who I saw the other day like she didn't even know me…"

"*Jasmine*?" I asked as I was still processing the damage Ollie had inflicted on Myles.

"Hell yeah, with ole buddy Alexis used to deal with back in the day," he said snapping his fingers as he tried to recall his name.

"Calhoun. *Jimmy Calhoun*, the former big time weight pusher from the Southwest," I helped him out.

Myles eyes narrowed as he shook his head. He knew more about Calhoun than the both of us because of his dealings with Alexis. Calhoun was bad business back in the day. You didn't want to cross him wrong. He had deep, deep connections to go along with his even deeper pockets to make happen whatever he wanted. Supposedly he had gotten out of the game though, but that didn't mean he kept his nose completely clean.

"If that's who she chooses to be with then that's her," Alonzo said defeatedly. "I gotta do what's best for me and KyJuan."

"'Lonzo," Myles called out as he watched him move towards the window. "It's a blessing in disguise."

He turned to look his way. Myles was wiser than his twenty years. "Everything is going to work out for you, just as you want it to. Give it a little time."

"I trust and believe you," he told him. "This ain't the first time you spoken something into existence regarding me or any of us."

"Don't stress about Malachi." I reassured him, fully prepared to help out wherever I could. Alonzo patted his arm in unison. "We're gonna take care of him for you."

"Well we are all brothers and in this together," I told him as he tried to sit up. "I am my brother's keeper."

We all joined hands as we repeated that mantra. With that Myles was ready to eat so he hit the call button to alert his nurse. It didn't take long for her to respond. She sounded *fine*! We wanted to wait to see what dime piece walked through the door. We didn't have to wait long either. A quick tap on the door and in walked a couple of nurses and techs. They looked around and smiled as they saw all of us, looking like a pack of hungry wolves, and we were their snacks. Alonzo looked at me, I looked at Myles. He looked back at Alonzo and then at me. I moved my head towards the door and Alonzo took that as our cue to dip out before we all got in trouble. Myles innocently threw his hand up and smiled as we made our exit. *He was gonna be just fine.* Alonzo started to shoot his shot since he was back on the market temporarily and turned around to see one of them coming in his direction. Her name was Charice and she offered to walk us down to the cafeteria since she was headed to lunch herself.

"Lonzo," Myles tried to call out before we left. He turned back at the sound of his name to see what was up.

"About what you said earlier," he said as a smirk filled his face and he pointed his way. "You still *NOT* eating cereal?"

Completely caught off guard but fully knowing what he meant, he instantly shot two birds as we left. He heard me doubling over in the hallway and shot me two as we headed to the car. Charice had no clue what had just transpired.

Part 3: Can You Stand the Rain?

I.

“Thoughts aren’t racing as much as before. Therapy has been going well and I’ve finally adjusted to my medication. Uncle James and the crew have helped me with my boxing training and physical therapy.” Myles told Dr. Flewellyn as they sat in her office.

“That’s great to hear,” she responded, making a few notes on her notepad. “What else is on your mind?”

“Honestly, forgiveness, so I can continue to heal and be a better man for my son,” he told her. “I found out about my son the same summer that I got into it with Ollie, when I went to stay with my cousin Avant.”

“Oh wow, how did you react to the news?” she asked him, readjusting in herchair. “Did you have any idea prior to?”

“I did honestly, but the situation was complicated with his mom, so I just took it in strides,” he told her. “I met his mom’s family and we talked things through. Other than that I’ve just been working to get healthier-spiritually, physically, emotionally. Gotta get stronger so I can keep up with lil man.”

“Sounds like you’ve been a busy young man,” she said to him. “How’s the adjustment being to fatherhood and everything? Are you dating?”

"Fatherhood is fun and challenging," he told her while thinking back to how Lauryn found out about Malachi and Alexis through Jasmine being messy and petty. He recounted what he could remember.

They all were together for the Soiree that took place during the Winter Holiday Gala where both Vanessa and Jasmine had been a part of their youth groups. Apparently Jasmine had known about Malachi and had some suspicions early on. She had become tight with Alexis and had worked with her on some other side hustles involving Alexis's ex-James Calhoun, unbeknownst to him. She innocently invited her to the event as a sign of gratitude since it also was to congratulate and recognize women who'd graduated from a domestic violence/second chance program. Alexis showed up with Malachi in tow, and had crossed paths with Lauryn. Jasmine was sitting at the same table with them and told her who she was. Vanessa had been coming out of the restroom when Lauryn rushed in feeling sick to her stomach.

Eventually they all crossed paths and revelations came about, leading to a very painful situation for everyone….Jasmine and Vanessa weren't speaking to each other because of how she handled the situation. Alexis and Lauryn really didn't know what to think but tried to remain civil since it was he that they had to work things out with. Lauryn was trying to understand whether he had brushed off wanting to date her because he wanted to be with Alexis since they had a son. She felt slighted but knew she owed it to him to get his side of the story. Malachi was caught in the middle but in spite of all the drama ensuing, they all managed not to act an ass at least in front of him, nor cause a scene during the event. After talking it out with Vanessa, she made the painful call to Myles. He just listened as she spilled her heart out to him and how conflicted she was about having to find out about Alexis and Malachi. Eventually he was able to explain his side and fill in any gaps. He didn't try to mislead her or string her along.

She was still in her feelings about it but couldn't deny that he had been honest, though not completely forthcoming since there were details he couldn't confirm at that time. She could hear the pain in his voice that he was caught in the middle of a life changing event and had to respect him for trying to make the best decisions in light of it. So she told him to focus on his own healing journey and do what he needed to for Malachi, since he needed to make up for lost time. She would be in touch. Though they were only friends, she had made "*Keep it to myself*" by Monica, his ringtone on her phone. Yet, as she laid on her bed as the sounds of Whitney Houston singing, "*Why Does It Hurt So Bad,*" played softly through her stereo speakers. Suddenly she wanted to watch 'Waiting To Exhale'.

Alonzo managed to open the door while toting groceries and supplies he picked up for his parents. He saw KyJuan sitting in his grandfather's lap as he passed through and spoke to his father. He figured he was deep into the program on the tv, *In the Heat of the Night*, so he didn't bother to repeat his greeting. He continued on to sit everything down and began to put the items in their respective places. His mother would be coming back from Bible study soon and he wanted to have dinner warmed up for her since she had been helping out at the church all day preparing for their upcoming

Pastor's Anniversary and annual revival service, which their church would be hosting this year.

Their own wedding anniversary and his and Avant's mom's birthdays had recently passed, with the fellas and their dads surprising their wives with VIP tickets to see Anita Baker and Babyface in person. Little did they know Anita Baker would give them a personal shoutout on the two special milestones, as well as serenading Alonzo's parents to "*Just Because*" as one final gift request from Alonzo himself. Avant's parents and Auntie Angie had accompanied them, his mom and aunt unbeknownst that *he and his Dad* had sent a request for him to surprise her by appearing on stage for a special performance of "*Every Time I Close My Eyes*", just as the saxophone solo portion of the song began, dedicated to to them and as a tribute to his late baby brother Peanut who played the Sax. They were so thrilled that their sons and husbands had kept it a secret the whole time!

As he pulled the food from the refrigerator, he called out to his dad to see if he had eaten. He continued to set it all out and took down plates for everyone. KyJuan had a new found love for black eyed peas, cornbread and "pot liquor". While the food was warming up he went to check on the two. As he walked up from behind, he saw KyJuan moving his grandaddy's hands up and down as he watched the show. He put his hand on his dad's shoulder. His dad had his arms around him to hold KyJuan close to his chest. His Bible was next to him, as was a pad where he often took notes.

I've done many things over the years to provoke my son into anger, but as many times as I have, I've asked the Lord to forgive me many, many more. I know none of us are perfect, especially not me, but I know my son is trying his best and I am so proud of him. He's much more of a father to my grandson than I ever was to him. He taught me to be a better father, a better husband, a better man. I thank God for allowing me to see that despite my doubts at times, Alonzo has continuously proven to me how much he listens through his actions. He's helped me to grow in my older age, and also how to let go through watching him as he journeys through fatherhood. All the Glory to God the Father and my Lord and Savior, Jesus Christ. In His name I compose this prayer, Amen.

He tapped his father again to see if he was asleep, but didn't get a response. He shook more forcefully, still eliciting nothing. Lastly, he tried checking his carotid pulse-again nothing but a slight cool feeling. As reality set in, KyJuan looked up at him and he reached down to try to lift him up. He pulled away and turned to hug his granddaddy and lay his head against his chest. Tears fell down his eyes as he watched KyJuan-he knew that his grandaddy had transitioned to be with God.

His pillar, his rock, his best friend, was now gone. He took his glasses off, folded them and placed them on his notepad. He wiped away his tears as he went to turn off the food. He had no appetite to eat himself, but fixed a plate for KyJuan. When he came back into the room, KyJuan had gotten down from his granddaddy's lap and walked over to him, using the coffee table as his helper. He picked him up and held him closer than ever. As he looked him in his eyes, KyJuan wiped away his tears and hugged and kissed him. The three of them shared that lasting moment. It was his turn to carry on the torch. *He was his father's keeper.*

I was startled out of my sleep by my dad. I looked up to see him with a serious face, knowing something had happened-not like Myles's situation, but just as serious. He was too calm and that bothered me. My mom was already in the car but no one said anything. We were inside the Cadillac which was definitely not usual. Dad also had on his Vietnam Veteran cap that he only wore on certain occasions. Mom sat quietly holding her bible-I could see that she was reading Psalm 23. I sat quietly as we drove towards the country club subdivision. We were going to Alonzo's house. As we continued towards his family's house, I noticed a lot of cars parked along the side leading towards his driveway. There was still enough space for us to pull in and park. My parents went on inside. I went around back towards the basketball court where I found him shooting the ball. KyJuan was watching from his power wheel.

"What's up lil man?" I said as he drove his car towards me. He held his hands up for me to pick him up and I gladly obliged.

Alonzo turned around and I could see the redness and dried tear streaks on his face. "*He's gone man.*"

I stopped to take in what he had just said. "Gone where? *Who's gone?*"

"He's *gone, gone* man!!" he said, taking a shot but not bothering to retrieve the ball. He just squatted down and covered his head. I walked over to him and sat down with KyJuan. He walked over to his dad and wrapped his little arms around him. That made Alonzo cry even harder. I felt helpless. So I just sat near him with my arms around them both. I knew they didn't have the best relationship and that he would come talk to me and my dad when he had disagreements with his father. But I knew that they loved each other more than they ever allowed others to see. It was in the small things that you'd see it. Yvonne had quietly made her way to the court and tapped ever so lightly as to get my attention. I pulled KyJuan up with me and he saw her and became fussy. Alonzo looked up to see her and embraced the both of them. I wiped my face and pointed towards the house. I understood the assignment and went to go check on his mom.

Inside I could see that most of our fellow crew had arrived to pay their respects. Some of whom I hadn't seen since high school. Alonzo's dad, Mr. David, was very popular amongst our group. Just like my ole man James, he was highly respected and a pillar in our community. They were said to be thick as thieves back in the day, almost like twins, since they had also grown up together. I made sure to check on his mom, Mrs. Eva who was surrounded by my mom and a flock of other church members.

We all spoke to everyone and then paid our respects to her one at a time. She was overjoyed seeing all of her 'babies' all grown up now. They eventually made us leave because we were causing her to weep, even though they were clearly tears of joy. My mama squeezed my hand to get my attention. I focused to see where her eyes were and saw bae and walked in. I got up and went towards them. They waved towards her from behind the crowd. Lauryn kept a low profile and sat down and looked around. I wondered if she had spoken to Myles and how they were doing. I hugged bae and then hugged her. They went to speak and I walked outside to see Jasmine getting out of her car. I went to speak to her.

"Hey Jas, long time no see. How have you been?" I said, giving her a brotherly hug.

"I'm good, just taking a new look on life and everything," she said softly. "How have you been?"

"Taking things one day at a time, looking after Myles, and now Alonzo," I told her. I saw him and KyJuan heading our way. Yvonne went back inside. I took KyJuan from him so they'd have some privacy. He waved his little hand towards her and she responded warmly. When we walked inside I could see Yvonne had congregated with Vanessa and amongst the other females in the room. They all showered KyJuan with love and before I knew it, they snatched him away from me. When I tried to get him back, he emphatically shook his head in defiance, clearly enjoying the attention. I threw my hands up and let him have his moment in the spotlight. The fellas shook their heads and we all went outside. Soon as I stepped out, I heard a distinct whistle, and I looked up to see Jordan and Myles with Malachi in tow.

"*AYE YO*!" I responded by jogging in their direction and squatting down to get a good look at Malachi, wearing a matching outfit to his dad. "What's good fellas? *What up lil cuzzo?*."

"Can't call it," Jordan said while dabbing me up. "See oh girl over there with Lonzo. That's that Jasmine chick who's dealing with Calhoun?"

"Yeah, that's her. I guess she came to pay her respects to him. I doubt she'll go inside though." I said honestly knowing there wasn't a chance in hell she'd walk into that awaiting inferno after the scene she tried to cause at the Soiree Event.

I watched as she got back into her car and left peacefully. Alonzo was still numb to everything and appeared to be glad she was gone. Myles and Jordan walked up and dabbed him up. He was happy to see them, especially Myles-who had made great progress and was thankful for his help to get him back in shape. Jordan came through on the clutch with his extra bonus payment for helping him with that job when they were up visiting Myles.

He checked the mailbox and noticed a couple of letters for him, and a big heavy flat box. He opened the first one to see the notification of his achievement of his coaching & sports management degree, and that he was being offered a full time position with benefits to be retroactively paid from the day after his internship ended. This would allow him to not have to work multiple jobs as much and concentrate on building his skills and experience. Eventually he'd like to move into sports rehabilitation later on. He showed the letter and his framed degree to us and we all gave him his due credit. He made a prayer sign with his hands and pointed up while holding his cross pendant on his necklace towards the sky.

"This is for you ole man. God is good." he said as he wiped his face. "Wish you were here for me to hug you but I know you're proud of me. I'm going to make you proud too, I promise."

"We're all proud of you man," we all said collectively. Myles instinctively pulled out some Cuban cigars and looked around before lighting one up. He passed each of us one, along with a customized zippo lighter with a Bruce Lee design on it. We all took turns lighting ours up, and then he took one and placed it in a special holder case and gave it to Alonzo to put up.

My dad came out to join us and Myles gave him one. I wasn't surprised when he partook in the celebrations. But what did surprise me was when he ushered us all out back to the lounge area and pulled out a ginormous bottle of Hennessy to pour in small shot glasses for all of us to partake in. He spoke proudly of each of the young men that were out there. He lit a candle, a cigar, and poured a solo cup in remembrance of his ace, and sat holding vigil while we all chopped it up, having an official 'gentlemen' moment.

Once the cigars were all put out, KyJuan and Malachi managed to sneak out the sliding door and make a run for it to their dads. Me and dad watched how Malachi was interacting with Myles while KyJuan was doing the same with Alonzo. They had become inseparable. Not long afterwards, Yvonne and Alexis appeared to pick up the dynamic duo. Lauryn and Vanessa weren't too far behind them. Dad and I watched to see how it would go.

Yvonne and Alexis both watched as KyJuan played with Malachi. Lauryn watched cautiously as she and Vanessa came to where me, Myles, and Pops were sitting. Lauryn sat on the arm of the chair with Myles and bae did the same near me. I watched as Pops waved Alexis over and she came without incident. Myles watched in between taking sips from his cup. He was just taking everything in. She sat down next to them and Yvonne took a seat next to Alonzo. They all had bottles of water with them. I turned to bae and gave her a kiss. Dad just smiled as he watched everyone interact. Apparently someone had gotten through to the ladies and smoothed everything over. There was no tension, no animosity of any type, nor ill will from anyone. Yvonne and Alonzo had rekindled their relationship for the sake of KyJuan, and Alexis had agreed to share custody of Malachi with Myles and had wished him and Lauryn the best if they chose to become a couple. No one made mention of Jasmine. She had made her peace with Alonzo and he wished her the best with whatever she had going with her life and whoever she was with. He made no mention of seeing her with Calhoun as it was not his concern. There was nothing tying them together, so it was what it was.

"Well young folks, I guess it's time for this 'not so young man' to get his young lady and head home," my dad said as he started to get up.

"Stay a lil longer OG," we all said as we all had enjoyed his company just as much as we knew he enjoyed ours.

"Naw, she'll be looking for me if she hasn't already become restless," he said looking at his watch.

"*JAMES, you out there with them young folk???*" My mama called out from the sliding door.

"Speaking of the 'proverbial devil'," he chuckled as he raised the still full shot glass he held vigil for his departed friend.

"What did you say, *ole coon*?" she said knowing he had said something smart.

"Here I come darling," he said with a crack in his voice as he held the cup up as if making a toast. "To David, my best friend, more than a brother, now our guardian Angel. Take your well deserved rest my friend. I'll see you afterwhile. Don't worry, I'll take care of things down here till then."

"*Don't do that mannnnnnn,*" Alonzo said, getting up to give him a hug while taking the halfway empty bottle and twisting the top off while raising it up in the air. "This one's for you Pops. A great husband, best friend, father, and best grandfather to KyJuan."

With that Pops turned the cup back and took his final shot. Alonzo turned the bottle up and passed it around for all of us to do the same until it was empty. Mama came out to help him to the car. He and Alonzo gave each other a father-son hug, with Alonzo almost breaking down on his shoulder all over again. We all surrounded them as they had their moment. I'd never witnessed such a powerful moment and knew it needed to be cherished. Yvonne was finally able to get Alonzo to calm down. I helped my mom with getting dad to the car so they could get home.

Alexis was leaving with Malachi in tow. He wasn't ready to go but knew he had to listen to his mama. Myles hugged her and told him to listen to his mama and not give her any grief, that he'd come get him so they could hang out again. He shook his little head and gave his dad some dab. Myles hugged him and made sure he was securely fastened in his booster seat. Most of the crew had also started to leave and we made sure everyone was safe to drive. I wanted to make sure his mom was okay before I left so I went back inside to find her still surrounded by a much thinner crowd of church members. She welcomed my hug and told me she would be all right. I hugged each of my other 'mothers and aunties' church members before looking back for Myles and Alonzo.

Jordan had left with Myles and Lauryn to go check on Auntie Angie at the house. He was crashing there till after the funeral. Alonzo would be alright. Yvonne and KyJuan would stay with him. Vanessa drove the rest of us back to the house so I could check on my parents before we headed home ourselves. Once we made it back to the house, I turned on the shower and just stood under the water for a moment before finally showering and going to lay down next to bae. She had changed into a nightie and I just lay next to her in spoon position. She pulled my arm over her and clasped my hand with hers as we drifted off to sleep.

The others silently crept in through the terrace door where Myles showered, changed, and cuddled next to Lauryn. He admitted to himself that he missed her company, though still also knowing he wouldn't cross any boundaries to complicate things. He realized how truly blessed he was and wanted to do whatever he needed to ensure his family would be secure. They fell asleep with his arms protecting her. Back home, Alonzo and Yvonne fell asleep with KyJuan between them.

II.

Jasmine felt a sigh of relief now that she was no longer attached to Alonzo. She had gone by and showed her respect to him and spoke her piece at the wake earlier that week while she had come back to visit family. They kept things very amicably, and now she was back in LA, preparing for dinner with Calhoun. Even though he was older, she felt safe around him and that he was who she needed at this point in her life, even if it was initially a “friends with benefits” type of situationship. She had temporarily relocated to help work at the new LA office that was catering more to the nonprofit end of her boss’ business ventures.

Calhoun had gotten his realtor to help her find her ideal place. Right now she wanted her kitty scratched. She hadn’t been on any birth control since she stopped messing around with Alonzo, and hadn’t had any since the move. She texted him and told him to meet her at her place around eight. She stopped by to pick up some dinner and got home in enough time to shower and lay out the food. Her new place was closer to downtown and with her recent promotion and side hustles, had saved up enough money to get a loft with spectacular views, at a deeply discounted price.

She had just put perfume on around her ears and neck when she heard the doorbell ring. She opened the door to see him dressed in a blue linen outfit with some loafers on. He smelled of Dior and it made her wet in her soft spot. He hugged her and took in the Chanel perfume she had applied just moments earlier. He kissed her neck as she secured the door behind them. He removed his shoes as she led him to the dining area where she sat him down and put his hat on a nearby chair. She then retrieved some champagne flutes and poured them some merlot. She then brought out dinner plates and sat across from him. He smiled at the food spread on his plate. They said grace and enjoyed the food and wine.

Later she refilled their wine glasses and led the way to the adjacent living room area where she had the fireplace going steady. He peeped her sound system and went to check out her music selection. Not really finding anything to his satisfaction for the current mood, he opened one of the CD mixes he created, and inserted it into the changer, selecting *"Knocking da Boots*" before rejoining her. They got comfortable in front of it and just enjoyed each other's company on the floor against the sectional.

He held her close as she looked into his eyes. He smiled and leaned down to kiss her softly. Something about her made him want to protect and guard her. She was so delicate. He gently moved his free hand lower towards her panties and slipped one finger in to feel her temple. It was hot and moist, which turned him on. She moaned as he massaged her clit with his fingers and slid her panties away. He kissed her neck and cupped her breasts, sucking them softly and gently. He continued his journey until he stopped just shy of her temple, teasing her belly button with his tongue. She massaged and loosened his linen pants to free his soldier. He could feel his tip get wet as he slid out of his pants and boxers. He positioned himself near her thighs and spread her legs as he began tasting her temple. He held her up by his hands as he led his tongue further and further inside while sucking on her clitoris. She held his head down as he made her cum over and over again all over his mouth. He stopped long enough to lick and nibble at her thighs before going back in for another taste. She wanted to taste him too.

As he flipped her over so that she was sitting on his face, she turned so she was facing his soldier standing at full attention eager waiting for her. She gently wet it with her tongue while massaging it ever so slowly with her saliva. He moaned as she teased him, getting him fully wet before slowly devouring first the tip, then eventually his entire soldier. She could see his toes curling as she continued to work him slowly with intention. She massaged his jewels as she stroked and sucked him to a premature climax. She then got up and pulled him with her as she positioned her ass in the air, ready to receive him.

She purred as she backed up against him, guiding him into her fire hot temple. Her walls wrapped tightly around him as he entered her slowly and deeply. She winced as she relaxed to accommodate all of him inch by inch. He held on to her hips as he stroked her nice and slowly at first. Then as he got into a good rhythm, he got into position and went in for the kill. She was so wet that he thought he would bust too quickly. He could feel her cum as he stroked her deeply. It turned him on even more. He pulled out and started licking her from behind which sent her clawing the edge of the sofa.

He laid down so he could have her ride him while he took her to ecstasy. He then slid her down on top of him and she wrapped her legs around his waist to help as she rode him like a stallion. She gripped him tight with her walls as she thrust her hips, making him close his eyes as she moved back and forth. She leaned down to kiss him and lick his neck while he fondled her breasts. He sucked on them and kissed as he pulled her closer and closer to him. He sucked on her neck and left passion marks all over her. He felt himself about cum and flipped over.

Now in a missionary position, he pushed her legs behind her head as he went in for the final act. Getting his head comfortable on the arm of the sofa, he lifted her up as he stroked her with all he had in him. He felt his legs catching a cramp and curled his toes as he released all of his seed deep inside her. He moaned loudly as he tried to keep going, not wanting to end just yet. Jasmine held on for dear life as he kept rocking her with his deep strokes like he was digging for gold. She dug her nails into his back which caused him to cry out in pain. He held her close as he continued to make love to her, kissing and caressing her body. She bit his left nipple gently as they rocked, causing him to bust again-sending out another batch of baby batter deep within her and him collapsing on top of her, trembling as he struggled to catch his breath. They fell asleep intertwined with the warmth of the fireplace, him still inside her. Too weak to move. *"Fallin"* by Montell Jordan played softly in the background.

Auntie Angie woke up early to fix breakfast for everyone. Myles and Lauryn stirred around quietly, listening. She was no fool but trusted Myles to make mature decisions. He knew she had gone to bed early, so they used the back entrance to not disturb her. She knew who he was with and the occasion so she didn't mind him being out late.She heard him coming up the hall from the back stairwell but continued on with her cooking. She cut up fruit purchased the day before and made waffles and eggs and cheese grits, turkey bacon and french toast. She expected everyone to come over so made sure to have plenty to go around.

Surprisingly Alonzo and his family were the first to arrive. He and Yvonne helped while Jordan entertained KyJuan. They eventually went to terrorize the other two around back. Jordan opened the sliding door for KyJuan, who crept down the hall to the open door and peeped her laying on the bed. She welcomed him in, and he climbed up to cuddle up next to her, resting his head on her belly, under the blanket. Myles came out of the bathroom after freshening up and was about to climb back into bed when he saw her look at him and then back towards the bed confused.

He cocked his head at her as if to say, "what?" when he saw movement from under the blanket. He threw the cover back to see KyJuan knocked out and she just laughed while covering her mouth. He picked lil man up and while trying to act like he was gonna toss him out the room, slammed his shin against the edge of the bed frame, causing him to howl out in pain. Not wanting to drop the lil man, he limped towards the door, hitting his foot against the dresser as he yelled through the door.

"Aye bruh, come get your youngin!!!" he said as he didn't know which wound to tend to first. KyJuan squealed as he ran back up the hallway where Jordan was waiting to rescue him. Jordan stuck his head in and laughed before shutting the door back.

"Come here baby," Lauryn said as he limped towards the bed mad as hell. She rubbed his foot and leg as she continued to laugh.

"That's not funny," he said pouting but thankful she was looking after him. *The payback would be epic*!

He helped her make the bed and then after getting dressed, both went to help his mom set up. Vanessa and I swung by to pick up my mom and dad. Her dad would meet us over at Auntie Angie's house. We parked our car and jumped in the suv so we'd have more room. Mom packed more food to add to what would already be a large breakfast spread. Alonzo's mom had already arrived when we got there. We parked and dad and I helped bring everything inside. Surprisingly Myles and Lauryn were on kitchen duty cleaning up and setting out plates, silverware, and glasses, while Alonzo and Jordan helped keep KyJuan and Malachi away from the fruit and danishes.

Everyone helped fill in wherever there was a need while the elders sat back and enjoyed each other's company. Mr. Curtis finally arrived and we all gathered around the table. The two youngest sat in the middle, one on each side across from the other, while everyone else filled in seats around the large oval table. We all joined hands while Auntie Angie said a powerful prayer that had everyone moved. We then all passed food around after fixing Malachi and KyJuan plates. Alexis and Yvonne watched their sons feed themselves as they tried to eat too. Soon it was them getting fed by the youngins. Everyone laughed as they made messes on their mothers. After everyone was finished, we all helped take care of cleaning up while the elders went to help plan Mr. David's memorial at the funeral home. Auntie Angie went to her doctor's appointment. Jordan helped clean and take out the trash while the rest of us made ourselves busy tending to the rest of the house.

III.

The wake set up was real simple and everyone from our crew helped the church members ensure Alonzo and his mom wouldn't have to lift a finger doing anything. Leading up to the actual funeral we all gave them space to mentally and physically prepare for the homegoing. KyJuan clung to his grandmother more than ever and Malachi stayed close by to keep his new best friend company. Auntie Angie helped her as well with the dynamic duo. Malachi was finally warming up to his grandmother and she was delighted to have someone else to spoil. She was still getting used to the fact that her baby boy was a father. She wasn't exactly thrilled but knew it was too late to be upset. She tried to keep her mind off of it by staying busy. Her cancer was in remission and she was thankful to be off chemotherapy. No one broke the vow kept since she revealed the news to us about the initial diagnosis. Myles still didn't know and we left it at that.

The morning of the service Alonzo had a breakdown. It was really sinking in that he was about to say goodbye to his father for the last time. He smoked two blunts specially prepared by Myles and Jordan, and was higher than a kite by the time he made it to the church. We all sat behind him and listened as the church choir sang different selections picked out by him and his mom. "*I pray we'll all be ready*" was being belted out by one of the younger female members. My mom dabbed her eye with a tissue as the choir joined in. Alonzo's mom and my mom got up and sang a Shirley Caesar and Patty LaBelle rendition of "*What a friend*" that moved the entire church to tears. Alonzo sat still between me and Myles, while holding

KyJuan who managed to sleep throughout the entire service. Malachi was fighting sleep with his mom, but gave up after my dad got a hold of him. He too eventually fell asleep.

Pastor Johnson gave a moving sermon on 'What a friend we have in Jesus and the importance of seeking a personal relationship with him.' Afterwards we all took turns giving remarks to the family. Uncle James surprised everyone by singing a tribute of "*Don't Look Down*" by David Ryan Harris, dedicated to Alonzo. As the service came to a close, the crew lined up as pallbearers to escort the casket to the hearse that awaited outside. We would all join them at the Veterans cemetery for the committal and military salute.

KyJuan carried a tiny American flag as he walked to the front of the chapel and placed it in the holder that lay next to a full sized picture of his granddaddy in full dress uniform. He even gave him a final salute as his daddy held him up and hugged the picture, before climbing up in the seat next to his dad. Malachi followed suit and they sat there watching the flag being folded and presented to Mrs. Eva. "Taps" began to play as the rifles fired off their salute somewhere in the distance.

Myles jumped initially but stayed calm once he realized what was going on. His uncle James sat beside him and placed his hand on his knee to let him know it was okay. Malachi climbed up in his lap and hugged him to help as well. He placed his arm around Alonzo as he felt him start to tremble and cry silent tears. KyJuan lifted his glasses and wiped his dad's face with a tissue he pulled from his pocket. Alonzo let him have his way. He was only trying to help and he appreciated it more than he'd ever known.

After they'd returned to the house, Alonzo unloosened his tie and undressed. He changed into some gray sweats and a t-shirt, slipped on some slides and went to check on his mom. She had also changed and just laid on her bed with the folded flag close to her chest. He came in and sat on the bed with her back to him. She patted the bed letting him know she wanted him to lay next to her. Even with their backs facing each other they provided an unspoken comfort that would go on for a while. His stature being so close to his dads' brought her a peace that was beyond his understanding, but deep inside he knew she wasn't ready to sleep alone just yet. KyJuan wanted to see his daddy but Yvonne knew he needed his space and so she kept him busy around the house. He was growing up fast and she knew he would be starting to want to explore more and needed to be enrolled in daycare to socialize with other kids around his age. She was glad he bonded with Malachi since he was more introverted and KyJuan helped him break out of his shell.

One day after KyJuan had been dropped off at daycare, the two finally had a moment to themselves. They had waited till he had become distracted to make their exit. It would be the first of many days they'd have to repeat the same thing until he finally just didn't pay them any attention at all once he got there. But Yvonne wasted no time getting comfortable in her short shorts while cleaning the house from the tornado that KyJuan and Malachi left around with his toys. Alonzo snatched at her waist playfully and she didn't resist him. He pulled her close and they wrestled as he finally led her down the hallway to the bedroom. She knew what he wanted and she wanted it too. He turned her towards him and backed her against the wall, kissing her passionately all while lifting her shirt over her head. She moaned as he removed her clothes piece by piece, until she was completely naked. He lifted her up till she was resting on his shoulders, and his face was square between her legs, *ready to feast*! She held his head in place as she felt herself cum all over his face. *This nigga still had it going on!* He was gentle, yet focused on making sure she enjoyed every bit of his tongue lashing, as he spread her legs as wide as he could.

Once he had had his filling, he used one hand to loosen the strings on his grey gym pants and boxer briefs, freeing his aching soldier. He slowly lowered her down while moving closer so she could guide him in. She helped him remove his tank top, as he slowly went to work, grinding up against her. *Shit, it felt so good as he stroked her deep, trying not to nut early!* She held on as he took her for a ride, gently nipping on his ear and kissing on his neck. He tasted and sucked on her breasts as he moved her up and down rhythmically. Trying not to lose his footing, he held onto her as he untangled his feet, losing his socks in the process. He carried her into the room and the bed where he sat down, them still interlocked. They slid back together in one fluid motion towards the center of the bed.

She pushed him back as she gently straddled him, before sliding all the way down, stopping face to face with his soldier. He smiled as she teased him with her hands, and then her mouth, returning the favor. He laid back, gently guiding her head with his hands, as she topped him off. *Ooooh weeee*, she had him squirming with her mouth and tongue action, so much so that he nutted hard before he knew it! He moaned loudly as he held her head in place, as if she was sucking his soul out of his body. She kept going but more gently this time knowing he was now very sensitive until he was back rock solid. He pulled her back on top of him and held her close as she leaned down and kissed him, wrapping her legs around his waist. He licked between her breasts and cupped both of them as she held onto him. She threw her head back in ecstasy. She increased her stride to let him know he wasn't the only one who'd learned a few tricks along the way, and it turned him on so that his toes were curling.

This reunion was long overdue and the love and passion they brought was raw and genuine. He held her close as he rolled her onto her back, not missing a beat as he gave her slow, deep strokes, ensuring she felt all of him inside of her. Knowing he was about to cum, he didn't try to pull out, but instead let nature take its course-and released all of his seeds into her fertile womb. He kept going, rocking with her as he worked hard till he released again, deep inside. They held onto each other until their breathing eventually slowed, both covered in sweat.

"So where do we go from here?" she asked as they lay intertwined, and she played with the curly hairs on his chest.

"Let's just continue to take it one day at a time." Alonzo told her, enjoying their post-coital moment. "No need to rush anything, though I really do want us to be a family again."

"I agree, and I'd like that too," she told him, pulling his face towards hers to kiss. "We've both grown up and are in a better place."

"You really helped me become a better man and father," he told her rubbing her shoulders. "You and my parents forced me to grow up by showing me tough love. I couldn't have done it without yall. God knew exactly what I needed to happen. So I definitely can't NOT give him his due credit."

They continued to lay there enjoying each other's warmth before finally getting another session in the shower and getting ready to face the new normal that awaited them. Alonzo was fully aware of the vulnerable moments that transpired during their *morning workout*, but was ready for whatever came of it. He loved Yvonne with all of his heart and wanted to make things work not just for the sake of KyJuan, but for them to be a real family again. They all deserved it, and he wanted to make his ole man and mama proud. He knew that he'd have to help his mom sort out the estate in the coming days, regarding his father's assets, and then rely on the fellas to help them go through his father's belongings to best determine what to keep and part ways with.

So much had to be done, but he refused to stress himself or his mom about it. Knowing his dad, there was a list with everything laid out in the way he'd wanted it done in the event of his passing. Alonzo would look in the safe when he went to his father's study when he went to check on his mom later on. Right now, he just wanted to be comforted by Yvonne and her peaceful spirit. She helped to bring him the much needed peace he needed in his life at this moment. It would help him to bring the same peace to his mom as well. She would definitely need him more and more, and he couldn't afford to not be in the right headspace for whatever duties she had for him to handle. He kissed her forehead as they laid in bed again, this time just enjoying the peace of being together. They fell asleep, but managed to get up and clean the house before having to go pick up their son. *Everything was going to be just fine!*

Mama and Pops sat at the table just holding hands when I came up the hallway to greet them. They'd been spending a lot of time just enjoying each other's company, and not so much being focused on work or anything else. I guess Mr. David's passing really made them take a step back and look at how quickly life could change, and how time was limited and we best make the most of our fleeting moments together. It was great catching them in these moments, that I just stood silently in the doorway of the opening and cherished what wonderful love they shared and how dad still managed to make my mom's eyes sparkle and have a flame that never seemed to dim after so many years.

"Good morning handsome," my mom said as she looked up, feeling my sleepy eyes watching her.

"Morning mama, pops," I said, walking in and giving them both hugs. "What are yall two love birds up to early this morning?"

"Just enjoying the moment," my dad said, rubbing my mom's hand with his. "You'll understand as you get older."

"I pray bae and I have a long love story like y'alls." I said as I brought a mug of coffee in to sit with them at the table in the sunroom. These were rare moments that we shared and I wanted to enjoy them while I could. Dad had started back reading his newspaper and mom was fidgeting with her tablet trying to find some new audio or ebook to download to keep her company while she was hemming up a dress she'd recently purchased for Vanessa. My mind had been on talking with them both about how to go about planning a wedding, and what part I needed to focus on.

I knew Mom, Vanessa, and Mr. Curtis would handle certain aspects, and me and Pops would have other things to focus on. Mr. Curtis had to play dual-roles and I could only imagine what was going on in his head. It was hard to think about this knowing my best friend was still mourning and grieving the passing of his father but I knew that life had to go on and he would need some welcomed distractions in his life. I was truly glad that he and Yvonne were going slow and steady again, especially for KyJuan. They'd been through so much and grew on each other. They'd all have to be part of the ceremony. I'd let bae decide on if and how to approach Jasmine. At least extending an invitation to attend would be a kind gesture on both our parts. She was still her friend, though now somewhat estranged. Lauryn and Alexis would also get invites, though I don't know if Alexis would show up. Myles and Malachi would definitely have to make cameo's, though they'd better not try to steal the show. *Well Malachi and KyJuan might just steal the show. They were quite the showstoppers whenever together!*

Myles was folding up clothes and arranging them in his drawer while Lauryn entertained Malachi on the bed. He was sitting up playing with his ninja turtle stuffed animals as she lay on the bed leaning back against a stack of pillows. She would look into getting one with an adjustable base to better help accommodate her back, and also with him having his own issues stemming from his injuries. He looked into the mirror and watched his family. He smiled to himself as he thought about how blessed he was. His mind was still healing from the trauma but he took it one day at a time. Thankfully he didn't have too many side effects from the medication, and was purposefully being mindful and trying to apply the coping skills he learned in his therapy sessions.

He needed to see what was up with his mom. He noticed she appeared smaller than usual, like she was losing weight, and he also took notice of her always wearing her hair shorter and in the same styles. She used to always keep her hair nice, but it just seemed like she tried to keep things *too simple*. Something wasn't right but he knew it would reveal itself in its own time. He loved that they were in a better place and not around Ollie anymore. I managed to get his gun returned to him after his mom had surrendered it to the police during their investigation. He wanted to go back to the range but was advised to wait by his therapist. He was told to seek out closure from the incident with Ollie so that he could close that chapter and continue on his healing journey. As much as he hated that man, he knew he needed to go get his closure. He would go to Auntie Vivian's zen garden to handle what he needed done. Unless he was going back to help Jordan with work, he had no intentions of returning back to Chicago.

Once he finished, Myles came out of the closet to see Malachi laying against Lauryn's belly with one of his ninja turtles close in tow, and the other one on top of her belly. She tried to move it and he stubbornly placed it back down. Lauryn smiled his way as she rubbed lil man's head. They were his little world. He knew his mom was safe down here, and that gave him peace of mind. His secret plan to use the money saved from working with Jordan to purchase a small townhouse for his mom and them had worked out. Lauryn understood where his priorities lay and didn't pressure him any. He crept out of the room and headed towards the small study area where he needed to get back on his computer to work on his classwork.

He had been working on his classes through distance learning, but still had to go attend physical classes for some of the tests that required proctoring. He didn't care for the formal education system, but knew it was a necessary evil to help him be able to succeed in life later on. He planned to open his own gym, offering a variety of services and activities to help keep young children and adults from being on the streets potentially being led astray. Though he still had some connections to the streets with Jordan and his family, he tried to stay focused and not end up doing anything that could take him away from his family. He had already missed too much time from Malachi due to his mom and her recklessness but he wasn't mad at her, they were both young and dumb and still trying to figure out life. He had managed to land an internship working with Alonzo at his job and was grateful for it. They had planned a family outing touring historic Atlanta, and he wanted to check in with his mom before he left in case she needed anything before or while he was out.

Angela was getting herself ready and had the door to her room slightly ajar as she continued to dress and fix her hair. Though she was back in remission her hair had continued to thin and she had more and more alopecia resulting from it, making it so she had to switch up her wigs. She had recently started simultaneously having migraines, along with pains in her back and sub pelvic area and wanted to get checked to make sure nothing new had developed. She had been so careful not to let Myles see her in pain but she knew it would only be so long before she had to tell him. As she continued to adjust her wig and pull on her scrubs to cover up her mastectomy scars, she never noticed him watching her through the doorway.

Myles knew she had been through a lot but had no idea just how significant they were. Him watching her through the door wasn't intentional, he had intended on knocking on her door to let her know he was about to head out, and hadn't counted on the door being ajar. He felt like he was about to have a panic attack and quickly went back to the study where he closed the door and tried to collect himself before calling his cousin.

"Cuzzo, we gotta talk man," he said as he talked to me, almost in a ramble. "Something's up with ma Dukes."

"What's going on?" I asked sitting up from my bed so as not to wake up bae. "Is she okay?"

"She can't be after what I just saw homie," he said as he began recounting what had transpired. I knew this day would come but I couldn't confirm or deny what I knew. I listened and silently prayed he didn't have a panic attack or setback. Lord knows he'd been through enough already.

"Man, just ask her about it," I finally told him, not knowing what else to say. "You know you can talk to her about anything. You're her son, she'll be open about it."

Alonzo and Yvonne were taking KyJuan on a trip to the King Center in Downtown Atlanta. It was part of a city pass they had found a good deal on that included many different activities. He had asked Myles to bring Malachi and Lauryn, but she wasn't feeling up to going so instead told him to invite Alexis. She had no problem with them hanging out since she wasn't a threat to their relationship, plus Malachi would like that. They all met up in a nearby parking lot and headed to the King Center first to pay honor to one of their heroes and to teach their sons about why they were there and who Dr. Martin David King Jr. and Mrs. Coretta Scott King was.

They watched as their sons looked through the fence at the memorials that were in the center of the fence and the wreaths that were on display. Myles and Alonzo each picked up their sons so they could have a better look and then stood side by side as the ladies took pictures of them. They switched places and did the same, finally getting individual family pics and one group picture with the help of one of the younger volunteer tour guides who was a local college student interning at the center as part of her degree studies requirements in Africana studies and African American history through Spelman College. Once they finished there, they headed over to get a personal tour of the King Family house and Ebenezer Church.

Everyone was equally mesmerized by the intricacies that went into preserving both establishments. Alonzo was caught by surprise when Myles pointed to a picture that showed his late father Mr. David, walking behind Dr. King in a march along with a group of younger black men who were holding up signs saying "End Voting Discrimination". He also spotted a young Avant's Dad, looking just like him. They had no idea how involved the elders had been with the Civil Rights Movement right in their own hometown. He broke down for a minute there as he held onto KyJuan with one arm, and held out the other to touch the photo. He missed his father so much. He never knew this part of his life. His lil man lifted his little hands and wiped his dad's tears away with a tissue his mom had handed to him. Alonzo held him close and kissed his cheek. They left a donation with the center before heading to the Georgia Aquarium area for lunch before letting the boys explore the museum.

Myles and Alexis enjoyed the time spent with Alonzo and his family. Though they weren't together as a couple, they made the most of co-parenting Malachi. KyJuan was helping him become more outgoing and they seemed to help each other adapt and adjust to different things as they explored different animals and played with the different activities in every area they explored. They were really excited to watch the dolphin show. By the time everything was done, the two little explorers were fast asleep in their father's arms, exhausted from their adventure, and potentially recharging their batteries for later rounds. Alexis and Yvonne were chatting while the guys walked behind them.

"Guess we wore them out today with the tours," Yvonne and Alexis high-fived each other.

“Yeah, we did that girl, it was nice to spend time like this,” Alexis said, agreeing with her. “No drama, just pure fun and enjoyment.”

“True, and the fellas were just as excited as boys,” Yvonne added, looking back at them carrying their sons who were peacefully sleeping in their arms. “It really helped Alonzo get his mind off everything dealing with his dad.”

“Yea and Myles has been making progress as well,” Alexis said thinking about how far he’d come with Malachi and how had stepped up to help him. “I just wish him the best as he continues moving forward.”

“Myles will be fine, he’s definitely a fighter. He’s Alonzo’s biggest supporter, little does he realize.” Yvonne was so grateful for Myles and Alexis tagging along.

They made it to their respective cars and loaded the small people in before saying their goodbyes and heading in separate directions. Alonzo was ready to get home to take a nap. He had been feeling sleepy a lot lately and just wanted to get them home safely. Yvonne took his cue and switched seats so she could drive. He adjusted the seat back and was gone before they hit the interstate. Yvonne smiled as she watched her two men sleep in almost the exact positions, unknowingly.

She had been feeling a little sleepy and queasy lately herself and was wondering if it was a sign that her cycle was about to start. She sure hoped that was what her body was trying to tell her. She and Alonzo had been going strong for a while and his sexual stamina had seemed to increase ten-fold since their first time back together. They hadn't been using protection and though she knew she was on her depo-shot, she still prayed it wouldn't fail her anytime soon.

Myles and Alexis rode back to her spot with Malachi in tow. He was knocked out, with his arms fiercely guarding one of his ninja turtles. Myles was grateful for this babymama co-parenting situation, and how everyone in his circle was getting along well. Alexis put her hand on his leg innocently, but moved it once she realized she triggered another type of response. He chuckled as they continued to drive back to her house. He helped get Malachi inside the house and settled before giving her a friendly hug and heading back home. Lauryn had left earlier to pack up because she had to go back to school.

Jasmine woke up feeling refreshed, though a bit sore. Calhoun was cuddled next to her with one of his arms holding her close. They had somehow managed to make it to her bed at some point in the night. She felt so safe around him. Not wanting to leave his embrace but knowing she had to get up, she fought against her conscience and got up to make her way to the bathroom to relieve herself. She then turned on the shower and let the water heat up really hot before commencing to scrub her body clean and wash her hair. Using her Japanese maple scrub she exfoliated herself and conditioned her hair well before finally rinsing and drying herself off.

As she was washing her face and getting ready to exfoliate it she heard him start to stir around through the ajar door leading to the bedroom. It didn't take long for him to make his way past her to go handle his business. When he came back around he stopped to wash up and then attempted to give her a kiss and let his scruffy stubble rub gently against her face. She turned around and let him lift her onto the vanity as they embraced. She could feel his third leg gaining weight and knew what that meant.

Calhoun slid her legs open and moved the silk robe aside just far enough to let his soldier slide inside of her warm wet temple. She let out a slight moan as she felt him stretch her walls as he slid deeper inside her. She pulled him close as he stroked her while lifting her off the vanity to gain better positioning. He leaned down and nibbled on her neck and licked her all over as he continued to give her the business. She licked on his ear and bit softly on it as she held on for dear life while he rocked her up and down on his soldier.

He carried her from the vanity back to the bed where he let her down long enough to spread her legs far behind her head and dive in head first to taste all of her. She shrieked at the intensity of his tongue lashing. She felt herself cumming over and over again all over his face as she wrapped her legs around his face. When he was satisfied, he flipped her over and slid in from behind and positioned himself on top of her, with one of her legs slightly up, and stroked her slow and deep. She threw herself back against his rock hard abs as he held her legs spread like scissors.

He seemed to be stretching her in every direction with his strokes and rocking motion and speeding up the intensity against her small body. Knowing he was about to cum, she flipped on top of him and locked her legs around his waist and went to work until he had no choice but to bust all inside her, filling her all up. If she became pregnant, it wouldn't matter to her at this point. She'd adjust to the change and make it work. She was in love with Calhoun. She never truly felt this way before.

They had each other's noses wide open. The sex only made it only so much better. She lowered herself down to kiss him gently-first on his lips and then neck, while slowly making her way down south to his now half wake soldier. She took him into her mouth and slowly nursed him back to health with her hands and tongue. He moaned as he lay back and allowed her to do her thing. It was too good for him and before he knew it, he busted again hard, all down her throat, almost choking her. She took it like a pro and continued massaging him with her mouth til she had drained him of every drop. Suddenly remembering the shower was still going, she got up and went to check the temperature before jumping in to wash up. After finishing and brushing her teeth, she slid back next to him, wrapping one of her legs around him, and he guided himself back inside of her as she lay on his chest and wrapped his arms around her under the covers. They fell asleep late into the day. She didn't want the moment or feeling to end.

Bae was still in the bed when I came over to check on her. I leaned over to give her a kiss and felt her tug at my sweats. I knew what that meant and obliged willingly, freeing myself so I could help her out. She took no time sliding me inside and *oh how good and warm she felt.* It felt like a sauna and I could feel myself stretch her walls as I went in deeper and deeper til I got all of myself inside. I lifted her up so I could get better positioned for the task at hand. At some point during the passion, I had to pull out to keep myself from busting too early. She didn't like that and took no time guiding me back to where she wanted me to be. She pulled me down on top of her and wrapped her arms and legs around my body as I rocked her slowly in a rhythmic trance.

I pressed my face against her neck and I stroked her. She felt so good and I wanted her to enjoy every bit of it. I didn't want to hurt her but wanted her to feel all I had to offer. Her moans were turning me on and made me move faster and faster. She bit down on my ear and caused me to moan in both pleasure and pain. I freed myself long enough to reposition us to where I was able to palm her ass while sliding back inside, not missing a beat. She grinded back against me, turning me on even more and caused me to cum hard as I tried my best to give her *the business*. She moaned as I hit her g-spot and nibbled on her breasts. They were so soft like velvet. I stroked her hard and deep until I couldn't hold back anymore and released all of my baby juice deep inside her again, convulsing hard as I drained myself. I held her close as I felt myself breath hard and drift off into a deep sleep, still inside of her. She kissed my forehead and held me, our hearts beating in sync.

IV.

Jordan sat down with his Aunt Geneva and Uncle Julius as they prepared for their monthly meeting to review the business performance. Business had picked up a lot recently and they were still looking to add more people part-time or on a temporary basis to help fulfill the orders and jobs that were last minute, or emergencies. Jordan thought about Alonzo and Myles, along with a few others locally that would be willing to help out. There had been a recent street war going on and a lot of casualties resulted from it, which caused the need for extra manpower.

One of his uncles had recently been killed when his car exploded while he was in it. Both his aunt and uncle were furious and hell bent on getting revenge on whomever was behind the attack. This went way beyond a personal vendetta. He told them he would reach back out to the crew and see what their availability was like and what housing accommodations could be made to house them during their work period. Jordan always kept his eyes and ears to the streets for intel.

Surprisingly Calhoun's name seemed to be very hot lately though he was supposedly not heavily involved in the street life anymore. Apparently whatever business he was legitimately involved in still had some street ties and some people were looking for him to clear up information that didn't sit well with them. Knowing where he was but not at liberty to speak on it, Jordan stayed in his lane and played his part. He'd get word to wherever it needed to be but for the time being he had to continue to play it safe. Right now there were too many confounding variables to factor in, and any unnecessary collateral damage would have to be avoided, unless push came to shove. He'd have a contingency plan in case one was needed in order to fulfill the task at hand. This street war was about to seriously get ugly and Lord only knew who would all fall victim to its rage.

Myles and Alonzo simultaneously received a text from Jordan asking their availability for a job order that needed fulfilling on short notice. The money would be guaranteed, with half paid up front, and the remaining upon completion of the job. Housing and meals would be arranged for the duration of their work period as part of the packaged deal. Myles was already game for it and ready to get back to the grind, while Alonzo would have to check his current schedule to see how things would work out. He'd also have to check with Yvonne to see if she'd be okay with him being gone for a while since she hadn't been feeling well and had an upcoming doctor's appointment.

He didn't want to put too much stress on her nor his mom, though the latter wouldn't mind helping out with her grandson to keep her mind distracted from everything else going on in the world. He'd just started back working in his new position as assistant basketball coach for the school since taking leave due to his father's passing and he didn't want to mess that up. The salary and benefits package offered had allowed him to quit working his part time job at the shoe store for good and allow him to focus on what he was passionate about. Plus it allowed him more flexibility when it came to KyJuan and Yvonne. He needed to call her and see how she was feeling. He had been so caught up in his own head that he didn't want her to feel ignored. He dialed her number from the office phone.

"What's good lil mama?" he asked when she answered, sounding groggy. "Are you getting ready for your appointment?"

"Yeah I'm up," she said as she made her way to the bathroom while still on the phone. "Gotta get KyJuan ready too."

"Okay, just take it easy and let me know what you find out," he responded to her.

"I will, you take it easy too, and try to focus on work," she reassured him. "I'll be fine."

"Aight, love you bae," he said before disconnecting the call and turning to check his emails.

Yvonne stood up to flush the toilet and immediately felt nauseous and turned just in time to vomit into it. She felt a tight cramping in her stomach. Her gut told her she was pregnant and she slowly began contemplating whether to tell Alonzo. She had taken a pregnancy test before but it came back negative. She waited til she felt ok and then flushed the toilet and went to brush her teeth. She needed to get into the shower and then get their son up and ready to go too. She was excited and scared at the same time. Alonzo was already under enough stress and having just started getting the hang of his new position, he didn't need anything else added to his plate.

Thankfully they had been saving as much as they could from his other jobs in between ensuring KyJuan and the household was taken care of. His father had left him a sizable inheritance but he wanted to save it for the baby and also to ensure his mom was good on her end. She also received a nice gift for herself and KyJuan and had chosen to also keep it in its current location to continue to grow with compound interest. She finally got showered and went to get KyJuan ready. He was already up and moving around. Alonzo had gotten up early to pick out an outfit before he left for work. She got him freshened up and dressed before looking to see what was quick and easy for their breakfast. She settled for french toast sticks and juice for him, and a cream cheese and smoked salmon bagel for herself with some tea. She checked her time as they ate to make sure they were still on schedule. Luckily the daycare was along the way to the doctor's office so she wouldn't have to rush as much. After cleaning up and gathering their bags, she ushered him to the car, got him strapped in, bags loaded, and then herself. She checked her phone app to ensure all of the doors and windows were locked and the alarm set before fastening her seatbelt and making sure they were ready to go.

Jasmine woke up full of nausea and with her stomach doing flips. She went to her cabinet and took out a couple of pregnancy tests and got herself comfortable in the bathroom. Calhoun had left out early to go handle some business. He was on the phone and it seemed urgent because he didn't waste any time getting dressed and heading out the door without saying goodbye. She would check on him later. Right now she needed to determine whether or not she was potentially carrying his seed. She unwrapped the first test and read the instructions before following it and playing the waiting game. She tried to drink some pedialyte to hydrate herself while waiting for the results to show up. *Positive*. She took a deep breath and stared back at the test. She knew she had an appointment coming up soon and would also have a test done there for confirmation. Right now she needs to get ready for work. She was going to be training in restorative evaluations and assessments for a couple of cases for indigent patients who had been selected to receive complementary treatment. She loved this part of her job and was looking forward to being involved with improving someone's life through their smile. She would make sure to ask about permanently relocating so she could start a new life with a change of scenery. She tried to call Calhoun as she prepared to head out the door but got his voicemail.

"Hey Calhoun, I hope everything is ok. You seemed in a hurry this morning. Hit me back when time allows. Got some news for you baby. Love you, Jas." She disconnected the call, and made another one to her doctor to confirm her appointment.

Calhoun's head was spinning and he was trying to make sense of everything. One of his event centers, *Lights, Camera, Action,* had caught on fire and was a total loss. One of the female employees was a casualty and he had to deal with the police and her family. All he knew was that it looked like an arson case but nothing could be definitely notated until the investigation began and their report was submitted. He stood there looking at what remained of his business venture and wondered whether the family was near as he looked around at the crowd. His insurance agent and business partner both arrived shortly and were assessing the situation from a distance. He saw a police officer approach him and he identified himself as the owner of the establishment. They walked over to a squad car where more details were given and the identity of the victim. He would need to come down to the crime lab to do a formal identification but informally, he was aware of who it was. *Charlotte Reynolds*. One of his most trusted and loyal employees. She was ruthless when it came to business operations and spared no one the wrath of her tongue lashing when it came to running the business. That was what he loved about her. *But who would want to hurt her? Who were her enemies?* He knew she could be cutthroat but knew of no one with a personal vendetta against her. He saw Jas had tried to call him but let the phone call go to voicemail. He needed to focus on the situation at hand then he would take care of his *lil bit*. She brought him peace and right now he needed to get to the bottom of this so he could get back to his peace. He thought about how she'd make a great mom to Azuri.

He walked over to his business partner, Horatio, and insurance agent, Lucious, to talk about what the next move would be while the investigation was being conducted. They'd go do a positive identification for Charlotte and go about contacting a local funeral home connected to him to handle the arrangements. She would have a homegoing fit for the queen-mother that she was to him. Horatio had gotten some intel regarding who might have been behind this brazen attack as the streets were already talking. Lucious was working with the newly arrived arson investigator to get details crucial for him to file his claim. Calhoun wouldn't have anything to worry about as long as he kept his cool and didn't do anything rash. Lucious knew he was deeply hurt by Charlotte's untimely demise, but also knew that this was not the time to resort back to anything *eye for an eye* with so many spectators and witnesses present. They'd let things cool down before acting. Thankfully they were fully insured for all sorts of catastrophes and that other than the one casualty, no other structures nearby were affected. Just a part of doing business-losses will come and go. The payout would go towards demolition and the rest to Charlotte's family. Now that some of the affairs were now in order, he turned his attention to Jas. He needed to hear from his baby. He dialed her number.

"Hey baby, sorry for this morning, I had a situation come up." he said when she answered the phone.

"I figured it was something serious. I hope everything is okay," she responded.

"When is your lunch break?" he asked her hoping she'd be free to spend some qt. "Able to break away from the plantation for a bit?"

"Around one-thirty, and yes I am able to disappear for about an hour." she said smiling. "I got some news for you too."

"Oh yeah?" he said, mental antennas picking up on something in her voice. "Can't wait to see you baby. Imma let you get back to work. See you soon my lil bit."

"You too baby," she said before disconnecting the call.

He tried to collect his thoughts. He knew he had some unfinished business ties to straighten out but he hadn't been able to get in contact with his contacts, Law or Jason. He hoped to God that neither one had done any foul shit that caused him to be caught up in the middle of their recklessness. He dialed Horatio again just to double back and see if he had heard from either.

"Horatio, I didn't want to ask earlier, but have you got any word out on *Diablo* or *Renegade* (code words for Law and Jason)?" he asked as he drove back to his crib to get ready to freshen up for his lunch date with Jasmine.

"Word on the streets is that they *kamikaze*." he responded with a period of silence transpiring to allow the message to sink in fully. "They fucked with a powerful OG and got taken out in the process."

"What the *fuck man???!!!*" Calhoun said with a sick feeling in his gut that they were connected to this shit. "Call Sr. and see what he can find out."

"I had already been on it man," Horatio said as he began recounting what he had found out and confirmed after speaking with his father, Horatio Sr. One of his clients had cut business ties because of all of the heat that had gone down and the resulting blood bath, street war that ensued as a result. Calhoun's eyes got big and all sorts of internal alarms were going off in his head. Law and Jason had fucked with Ole man Chance and killed his wife Camille, who was related to Mr. Julius and Genieve, funeral home moguls. The dots were further connected when Jason had kidnapped one of the nephews' son and baby mama, and had been hiding out in Atlanta. His partner Lucius had tracked him to this posh condo up in Buckhead where he had his contact who was the property manager keep tabs on his movements using a tracker. She was there when he and some girl got snatched up by a gang of goons professional ninja style in the dead of the night. Law had got snatched up by another group and was taken out in the most heinous of ways.

Their final disposition was unknown, but their business operations had been falling to shit, and some kat named Blu was trying to pick up the pieces and do damage control. All of this was too much for Calhoun to digest at the moment, but he knew he needed to get the final piece of the puzzle to see why his place of business had been targeted. Horatio said he was still working on that part and would get back to him as soon as he could. With that they parted ways and he walked inside his house to jump in the shower. His heart hurt for Charlotte, she was the closest thing to a mother he had since he aged out of the group home when he was 17. She was related to his group home mother and had looked after him after they all had been sent to other homes when she passed away from congestive heart failure. Charlotte didn't have the financial means to keep the business going, and with all of the new policy changes making it difficult to keep things afloat afterwards, she made the difficult decision to shut it down and let the Department of Family and Children Services take over operations and cash her out. She later moved with Calhoun and helped him get set up in Atlanta after he made it clear he was done with the criminal and street life. He had a daughter to live for and had been somewhat riding the straight and narrow since she'd been born. Now it seems like someone or something from his past was trying to disrupt that. He shed some tears as he stood under the shower and thought about Charlotte and how he was going to have to call her family and also tell Azuri that her grandma was now in heaven. He finished showering and picked out an outfit and accessories that would allow him to somewhat brighten his mood while out with Jasmine.

V.

Jordan felt his phone buzz and unlocked the screen to see the message flash across the screen, "*Fini*!" He already knew what that meant and sent back an emoji to express his confirmation. He didn't care to know any details though he happened to catch a clip of it on the online local news page. Long as business was handled he couldn't honestly give a fuck who was sacrificed along the way, *as long as it wasn't a child*. He stood up and grabbed his sports coat to put on as he got ready to relay the news to Uncle Julius and Aunt Genevie.

Though you wouldn't know it by her sweet appearance, they both knew auntie was seething with rage over the death of her sister and pulled every string and connection she had to make sure whoever was responsible paid for it with blood. Anyone and everyone involved and connected directly and indirectly to those responsible would also pay, until she felt enough damage had been done to right this awful wrong. Her "zeroes" stretched *very, very* far and her reserves *even deeper* than her family knew about. Aunt Genevie was out in the greenhouse pruning her newest arrivals of bonsai trees to add to her ever growing collection.

Her collection ranged from the miniature ones all the way to the full size that were planted throughout her property. The small ones were her prized ones for they were cultivated for use in the children and pets section of the eternal gardens. She was always creating new ways to bring more peace and creativity to the business. She had a special set of gardenias she had been growing and harvesting to relocate in a private area she was dedicating to her late sister Camille. They were almost ready and she wanted to have them perfect for installation in a few weeks. The mausoleum was already completed and she and her husband rested inside.

Jordan knocked on the entrance and she turned to see him nodding his head. She acknowledged the signal and went on carefully arranging her trees on the cart to be transported out later that midday by her staff. She was preparing for a dedication in the children's area because she had recently formed a long awaited partnership with the city to help develop an area for the foster children and state wards that didn't have any family, or that couldn't afford burial costs. She had one special tree, a Japanese Maple, in the center of the section that was installed after she was inspired during one of her many trips in the Far East to visit for a much needed break from reality. One day she hoped to finalize her plans for vacation homes either in Spain, Italy, South Korea, or Japan. Those were her top four retirement and vacation destinations far away from home.

Jordan was taking on more and more of the business affairs and would soon inherit most of the business responsibilities as soon as he had his team in place to help him run things. She and Julius were overdue for retirement, but when you work for yourself, one's work is never truly ever done. She also needed to check on Kingston, Memphis, and Harlem to ensure they were all set up in their various new homes. They had all started having children and getting settled, so she wanted to ensure that whatever Chance had left them with was going to continue helping them live comfortably for generations to come.

Uncle Julius was wrapping up a phone call when Jordan knocked on the door before opening to peep his head inside. He was waved in and welcomed to one of the plush office chairs that faced the ginormous mahogany desk that was deadcenter. He looked around in awe, just as he had when he was younger and saw it for the first time. So much had changed over those years, but this room stayed true to its original character. He waited for his uncle to take off his head set and ensure the phone call was disconnected before he showed him the message he'd received earlier. Julius sat back as he contemplated the next move. He'd definitely have to call the others and let them know, but not until after he knew how Genieve wanted to handle the next chess pieces. Everything was working according to plan and thankfully no contingencies had to be activated at the moment. Jordan was finalizing his crew and other people to be in place for whenever the word was given for them to transition into the next phase of vengeance.

"I've reached out to the fellas for extra manpower and they should be arriving this weekend once they've worked out their individual schedules." he told his uncle.

"Great. I'll make sure the lodge is prepped and ready for their arrival and temporary stay," Julius responded as he stretched his arms in anticipation of the next phase of their plan.

Jordan felt his phone vibrate and saw that Myles had sent him a message about wanting him to consider coming to work with him and Alonzo with a basketball tournament being hosted at the University in mid-March. He was happy for his homeboy to finally be able to put his athletic skills to use and definitely wanted to join in to have some fun as well. He would reach out to Alonzo to get more info as soon as he got a chance. Jordan and Myles always looked out for each other like brothers, and both had made a pact to get out of the street life before it got to be too much. He was fortunate enough to have his family business to keep him busy while Myles looked up to Avant and his parents when he wasn't fighting with Ollie and the streets back home. Myles was the only person that Jordan had confided in when he had gotten locked up for mistaken identity and had been sexually assaulted when placed in a cell with an older male that was supposed to be a father figure to him. Though his Uncle and Aunt had sent him to the best therapists that money could afford, Jordan never completely healed from it and had always had lingering feelings about his sexual orientation. Myles and his family never passed judgment and made sure he knew he had their unconditional love regardless because he was family.

Alonzo checked his email and saw Jordan had inquired about wanting to help participate with Myles in the upcoming tournament, both as a helper/trainer, and also as a player if an opportunity presented itself. There was a possible opportunity for teams to be formed to compete in the tournament and he seriously considered having the old crew reunite, plus Myles and Jordan, to go up against his players and some of the other contenders to give them some serious competition. He'd reach out to each of them and see what the response is. As much as he enjoyed coaching, he missed the action himself, and wanted to show his players he still had it, and they still had a long way to go to reach his and his former teammates' levels of development and acumen. He crafted an email about the tournament, with an inquiry about the team formation, and sent it to all of his former teammates.

Now all he had to do was wait for their responses. He thought back to how he would watch as Myles worked with a few players on setting up screens and other defensive tactics to help develop their individual and team strengths. He was a natural athlete and leader, and Alonzo wished he would consider playing for the school seriously. He understood his boy's complicated life, but was willing to vouch for him to his bosses if he was truly serious about committing to it. He heard from Myles that Jordan was equally as talented but wanted to see him in action to see how he could use him.

He also entertained thoughts about potentially managing Myles if he decided to pursue boxing instead of basketball since he knew about sports management and always wanted to open up his own training gym. Avant had always pushed him to pursue his dreams in between fatherhood and working, and was always scouting out potential spots for consideration to visit for purchase or rental consideration to start off. A small portion of his inheritance left from his dad might be able to help make his dream a reality, though he'd talk it over with the family to decide how best to go about it. He looked over at the most recent picture he had of him and his dad and son, taken not long after him and Yvonne had gotten back together and she had come over for breakfast. Three generations of the same face, strong black men. Even the lil man had the same facial expression. There was a similar picture on his late father's desk only with Alonzo as a baby, and another one with him in high school when they won their championship. He honored his late grandfather by giving his son his nickname, which he took to immediately. He had passed shortly after his birth, but was able to see and hold him, and bless him the same way he had done Alonzo when he was a baby. So many memories had Alonzo on the verge of tears. He wiped his face and picked up his phone just as Yvonne's name popped up.

"Good morning baby girl," he said smiling, silently thanking God for his perfect timing.

"Nothing much, going to my appointment after I drop off Davie," she said as she fought off the nausea that is hitting her more often now. She knew she was pregnant and just wanted to get her medication and prenatals.

"Oh ok, well you make sure to take it easy and if need be take the day off." he told her knowing she hadn't been feeling well lately. He wondered if she was pregnant since she had been extra cranky and sleeping a lot lately. He thought back to when they were expecting their son and how he hadn't had any symptoms other than sleep and a strange craving for spicy pickles and ice cream. Crazy how things like that happen. He dreamed of having a little girl sometimes but knew he'd then have to deal with young men just like himself trying to date his daughter. He prayed for whenever that time came that he'd be a better role model for her to learn from then how he was when he was out sowing his wild oats. He then thought about his little indiscretion when they had visited Myles in the hospital. *Ole nursy girl had given him the business…head to toe treatment*, down in the hospital parking lot with no shame whatsoever. He technically wasn't dating during that time, but *was* trying to work things out with Yvonne, so he did feel somewhat guilty. Hopefully he wouldn't run into her when they went up to help Jordan with his latest big job assignment. He couldn't afford to potentially end up in a situation like Myles, though by the grace of God, and Avant and Vanessa's family, everything managed to smooth out.

"You got time for me to swing through for lunch after my appointment?" she asked him as she pulled into the medical office's parking lot.

"I think the Coach can make time for his favorite player," he chuckled. "But you gotta do something for me,"

"What's that *Coach Lonzo*?" she said, trying to sound sexy while the nausea subsided.

"Bring ya boy something good to eat today," he said thinking how he had forgotten his lunch *again*. "I walked out and forgot it."

"I gotcha covered babe," she confided in him. "Well let me go get this over with and I'll be on my way. Love you baby."

"I love you too Queen." he said as he disconnected the call and saw a quick meeting had been set up for him in about an hour regarding a list of student athletes that were in jeopardy of being placed on academic probation. He shook his head as he looked at the list and recognized quite a few students on the list. One caught him off guard and he knew he needed to look into asap. He made a quick note on a sticky pad and placed it on his screen as he logged off and grabbed his keys and notebook for his meeting across campus. Myles would be coming in shortly and could handle things while he was away.

VI.

Vanessa sat in the doctor's office waiting for her annual well woman's check up when she saw Jasmine walk in. She appeared to be glowing, and blossoming since the last time they saw each other. They caught each other's eyes and smiled in acknowledgement. Something was different but she couldn't put her finger on it. They hadn't been in touch for a long time and she had heard that she relocated for her job, but she still considered her a friend and knew life sometimes placed people in different places. Jasmine checked in and then surprisingly made her way towards her and took an empty seat.

"Hey girl, you are glowing, like radiantly," Vanessa said as she patted her hand and smiled.

"*Am I?*: she asked because she was feeling anything but radiant. She had missed her period and was certain she was pregnant but didn't know whether she should tell Vanessa.

"Your skin is so smooth and shiny," she told her, genuinely excited to see her friend. "You're pregnant, aren't you?"

"*WHAT THE*...." she almost blurted out loud.

"Girl, I know you too well," Vanessa said, turning her whole body in her direction.

"I think I am," she confessed to her while grabbing her hand. "I'm excited this time though."

"Are you happy with whoever the father is?" she asked out of concern.

"Yeah, I really am. It feels different." she told her. "It's like I feel like I can finally live my life without unnecessary strings attached."

"You did take on a lot with Alonzo at a young age," Vanessa told her. "I don't think I could've been that strong, not even for Avant."

"I don't know how I did it honestly," Jasmine said. "But this time I think it will be different. My boyfriend is older but more settled. He does have a young daughter."

"Well one day maybe we can do a double date, with me and Avant." she said to her just as a nurse opened the door and called her name. "My number is still the same girl, don't be a stranger."

"I won't be. It was really good seeing you," Jasmine wiped away tears that were starting to form in her eyes. Vanessa had been her best friend and she hated that they had fallen out over something so petty. But she loved how she had such a forgiving heart and spirit and had picked up right where they left off. She rubbed her belly gently as she waited for her name to be called.

Vanessa was happy to have seen Jasmine. She was even more excited to know that she was happy and surprisingly, was expecting a baby! She sat down and waited as the nurse prepared to take her vital signs and ask if there was anything she wanted to note about for the doctor to speak with her about regarding her health. She then waited for her doctor to come in and do her physical and examination. She looked around at all of the anatomical pictures and models on the floating shelves. She saw a baby in utero model in front of a poster showing different stages of pregnancy. It kind of made her depressed when she thought about her pregnancy. She did have questions about what could've caused it and if she had anything to worry about for future pregnancies. She came back to reality when she heard a slight knock on the door.

"Good morning, I'm Dr. Maxine Jaemison. How are you feeling this morning?" the doctor asked as she took a seat across from Vanessa.

"I'm fine, just wanting to make sure I'm in good health," Vanessa said softly while not making eye contact with her.

"Are you sure, you appear upset," the doctor noted calmly. "Are you sure there isn't anything bothering you?"

"I just had a flashback about my ectopic pregnancy as I looked at the poster on your wall," she confessed. "I just don't understand."

"Well ectopic pregnancies can happen even with the most healthy moms," Dr. Maxine began. "They're unexpected and can happen at any time. Miscarriages on the other hand can be spontaneous, just happening out of the blue, and others can result from different predisposing factors, such as genetic disposition, family history, anatomical or physiological issues, etc."

"Is there something wrong with me?" she said as she felt herself becoming emotional. "Is something wrong with my body?"

"I did look into the family medical history and noticed your mom had what's called cervical insufficiency, where it looks like she had a genetic issue that affected her collagen production. We can test you for it to see if that's what caused or contributed to yours. Based on your past examinations and labs, everything else came back fine."

"I think we should do that because I'd like to know before we decide to try again for a baby, which until then won't be anytime soon. It just feels like everyone else I know is having babies or getting pregnant and I am unable to carry one for myself. I also know that my first pregnancy was an ectopic one. Is that genetic, or just a coincidence, and a potential problem for the future?"

"Well don't jump the gun or put the cart before the horse, as the old folks used to say," Dr. Maxine said, trying to reassure her. "Let's take it one step at a time. We can take some blood to do the genetic testing and go from there. But know that you're not alone. I'm here and I've been where you are. I don't share my story with everyone but I can feel that you need to know that you've got someone in your corner."

"Thank you," Vanessa as she wiped her face with the kleenex she had in her purse. She kinda wished she had taken Avant up on his offer to come with her. She'd make sure to bring him to the next one.

They finished the rest of the physical exam check up without her becoming too emotional. If anything she gained a new female role model and motherly figure in her corner. She'd recommend her to and bring up Jasmine before she leaves. The samples from her blood would be sent off to the lab and her "pocket book" labs sent in to make sure she's good down there too. No lumps or bumps during her breast exam, but a mammography down the hall would also be completed just to be safe, as part of the examination. When she left she felt very relieved and happy to have gained such a supportive provider. She made sure to give her Jasmine's info so she could see if she could become her provider as well. When she left she saw her coming down the hall and gave her a hug and said they'd catch up later.

I was analyzing the latest set of financial reports that had been delivered this morning by a courier for a client that wanted me to preview before sending them off for the legal team to approve or send back for modification. I loved my job and was glad I stuck with it though I really wanted to do more with real estate. At least here I had stability and could always build on my passion with the benefits and knowledge gained along the way. I momentarily looked over at the picture collage on my bookshelf that sat in the corner. My family and closest friends were all there. I had one picture I had with just me, Alonzo and Myles, with our dad's all together on a fishing trip. I kept that one in my desk drawer and pulled it out only on special occasions. Noticing that my blinds were closed, I instinctively pulled it out and sat it on my laptop. I looked at each face and dug deep in my memory for that day when they all were together. Myles would love to see this picture, and to see his old man.

We'd called him Uncle Peanut (Booker Moses "Peanut" Banks), because he always had a peanut shaped head that had a *high and tight* cut for as long as they knew him, and loved anything having to do with peanuts and peanut butter. Myles was only five years old when he passed. I remember it vividly and how me and Pops had come over to where his body had been brought. He had died in an accident involving a military helicopter that claimed the lives of everyone aboard. He was only 28 years old at the time. Auntie Angie was distraught because she had witnessed it by coincidence as she had come that way to surprise him with lunch with Myles. She was also pregnant and wanted to break the news to him that day. They ended up losing the baby because she was so overwhelmed by the stress caused by it. Myles would turn to us for comfort and they would stay with us until Angie could get back on her feet. I brushed back the tears as I thought about how much Myles and Auntie Angie had been through and how far they'd come. I prayed for their continued healing as my mind shifted to the incident with Ollie and how it had also taken a toll on everyone. I was brought back to reality when I saw my phone light up with a message from my phone reminding me of bae's appointment.

I checked my wrist watch and noticed it was near lunch time. Bae should've been out of her appointment so I called her from the office phone. As the phone rang I hoped all was well and that we could potentially try again for a baby once she got the *all clear* from her doctor. I could only imagine how hurt she'd been from the pregnancy termination and tried my best to pay close attention to her to minimize the chance of her experiencing any postpartum depression. We were always open and honest in our communication so I truly felt like I'd know if something was bothering her…*but how much did you really know someone*?

"Hey bae," she finally answered after adjusting her seatbelt and getting the phone set in its holder in her air vent.

"What's up ma," I said smiling as I was glad to hear her voice. "How did your doctor's appointment?"

"It was okay," she answered calmly. "She's going to run tests to make sure we don't have anything to worry about whether we should try for a baby again."

"What is she testing for?" I asked curiously, and partly concerned. "Is there something I need to be aware of?"

"She looked up my mom's medical records and wanted to make sure there wasn't anything potentially genetic that might affect future pregnancies," she explained. "I think we should be careful until we hear back from her before potentially looking into reversing my tubal ligation."

"I understand and have no problem with that," I told her reassuringly. "Your well being is my main concern. I'm sure we don't have anything to worry about."

"I hope so," she said as she drove through the greenlight heading towards his job. "I'm close by, got time for me to stop in?"

"That would be awesome," I said as I looked at my calendar right quick to see what the rest of the day held. "Matter of fact, how about I leave early and we meet back at the house or a restaurant nearby. I don't have anything pertinent that requires me to be here all day today."

"Sounds good, how about *Seoul for the Soul* for lunch?" she said knowing how they both liked Korean food.

"Great! I'll see you soon," I said as I grabbed the jacket to my suit and briefcase before ensuring my computer was secured and then locked my office up on my way out. "Love you bae."

"Love you too," she said as she disconnected the call. She then slowed down and turned into the restaurant parking lot to find a parking spot so she could go reserve a table. The place was packed and she hoped the wait wouldn't be too long for them to be seated while she waited. The owner, Mrs. Kim Chou greeted her with a warm smile and motherly hug. She already knew what to order and said not to worry about the wait. Vanessa smiled as she took a seat near the bar and waited for a booth to open. Mrs. Chou brought her out a small plate of fresh cut fruit while she waited. She insisted that she eat because fruit was good for her. She had learned early on when she first started coming here that *you never turned down food from Aujimha!* She looked up at the *wall of memories* near the kitchen that was full of pictures of customers that had become family over the many years the restaurant had been in existence in the community. She spotted some of the gang when they were younger and had come for a birthday party for Avant and Myles. She then saw the family pictures of Mrs. Chou and her children. It brought a sudden air of sadness as she thought about how hard it had been to grow up without her mother's love and how she felt an instant attachment to Mrs. Chou and then Avant's mom when they met.

Damn cancer had stolen her mother! Her father had done his best to protect her and keep her around strong women that he felt would serve as positive role models for her. He never gave a thought to remarrying or even dating though he had many opportunities over the years. His heart was broken over the loss of his wife at such a young age that he wanted to devote his best years to giving her the best that life had to offer. He wasn't too happy when she wanted to start dating and kept a close eye on her potential suitors. In Avant, he saw some potential that wasn't like the usual group of boys who tried to spit game to his daughter. He prayed she wouldn't end up with someone like Alonzo, after witnessing him in action and how his parents seemed to let him get away with murder when he was younger. She reminisced about how they first met and she introduced the two and how much of a natural gentleman Avant had been then and still was. Her thoughts switched to their unborn baby that they never got to meet and pondered many "*what if's*". As tears formed, she heard the hostess call her name.

Myles arrived at the gym to check in and get his assignments for the day. It was still early but there were a couple of players warming up as he went to Alonzo's office to set his stuff down. He saw a note on his desk outlining the game plan for their upcoming tournament. He also saw the notice sent about a meeting to discuss academic status of student athletes and potential roster changes should players roles and playing status need to be shifted relating to eligibility. That was always a hard thing to do, but even he understood the importance of balancing school and sports for student athletes. He grabbed his clipboard and equipment from the backroom before heading back out and walking towards the small gathering that had assembled for his training session. They would be going over some new drills and plays that everyone was involved with creating to showcase both individual and group skills and talents for the tournament.

He set up different stations with a veteran player to take lead on helping the less experienced ones, and watched and timed them. He enjoyed helping with player development and was instrumental in convincing both Alonzo and the admin to force the players to come during this particular time of the day so as to avoid any time conflicts involving academics or personal obligations. Depending on how things go with this internship, Myles considered looking into potentially becoming an athletic trainer and coach professionally as tools to help him along his way to opening up his own training facility.

One thing he really enjoyed was after the training sessions finished, they'd run the plays in short full court games, with him testing their knowledge and retention skills. The head coach, Coach Smith, gave him and Alonzo the green light to incorporate anything they felt was helpful to player development and winning games. He even personally came and observed how well the team had progressed since they began the experiment, but always wondered what stopped Myles from wanting to pursue basketball more seriously as a student-athlete.

He kept his thoughts to himself while genuinely appreciating his commitment to helping push the players. He remembered when Alonzo and Avant played, and how similar each played, while also noting the unique differences each brought to the team during their run. The upcoming tournament was rumoured to be one of the highlights because this would be the first time former players would be able to form teams to heighten the competition and test the current players' acumen and skills. Scouts would definitely be in attendance for various professional, semi-professional, and other leagues, looking for new raw talent, from both the university and the new teams that would enter to play. So much to look forward to with the players, assistant coaches, and trainers, that helped him keep the program running afloat.

The recent promotion for Alonzo was way overdue, and depending which direction Myles decided to go, a potential assistant coaching position for player development could be in his near future. But only time would tell. The head coach would just continue to monitor how things went in between everything else he had on his plate. He had a nagging headache that he just couldn't ever seem to shake. He knew it was time for another scan and made sure to call his doctor.

VII.

Angie arrived at the City of Hope Cancer Center ready for her follow up appointment. She had been feeling a lot of unusual pain and just wanted to be sure to inform her care team to see what the best course of action would be to address them. Both Vivian and Eva accompanied her this time because of her becoming more frail and weak recently. Everyone did their part to keep the little ones preoccupied so as to not attract premature worry or concern. Once they were checked in they patiently waited and prayed and read their Bibles for strength and comfort. It didn't take long for the care team to call them back into the suite.

"Good morning Ms. Angie," one of the younger resident physicians said upon meeting her. "How are you feeling today?"

"Not too well honestly," she said while trying to smile back at the doctor. "I feel pain all over now-in places I didn't before. And I feel drained and am having trouble just trying to eat, despite being hungry. If it wasn't for these two wonderful women with me, I wouldn't have made it in by myself."

"Well I'm glad that you have a great support system here with you," she said as she took notes and pulled out a folder with reports from the last scans and findings. Another doctor stood up and walked towards the screen as images started to populate on the screen. "We think that some of these images will help to explain what's going on now, along with the reports of findings."

“This first scan shows the brain and primary tumor which confirmed the diagnosis of the glioblastoma multiforme.” he said as he pointed to each image and explained them. “During the last visit, you mentioned bone pain and difficulty breathing, as well as pain in your lower abdominal and uterine areas.”

“This second set of scans show areas of particular concern, paying attention to the bright areas.” he pointed and explained how based on the scans, blood work taken, and pain areas, it showed that her breast cancer had returned and spread very quickly and aggressively, in addition to the glioblastoma also metastasizing, all of which explains her being in constant pain.”

“What can we do, other than chemotherapy, at this point?” she said weakly, as her sister and friend held her hands.

“Palliative care to manage pain and hospice,” he responded grimly. “It’s terminal at this point and based on the latest research findings in medical literature, the median survival time frame is around 15 months unfortunately.”

Angie knew that her time was running out but didn’t expect the prognosis to be so grim. She looked back and forth between Eva and Vivian, both of whom had tears flowing down their faces. She had been dealt a very hard hand of cards when it came to her health, having survived cervical cancer, only to be diagnosed with breast cancer shortly after Myles turned 10, and aggressive brain cancer within the last year, now to be told her only options were pain management and hospice, as her body has become ravaged because of all of the affected organs, with only maybe 15 months to live. Her baby boy Myles had already survived so much trauma and pain, and just when he seemed to be getting a new sense of normalcy, now comes yet something else to try to knock him down. It became too much for her-everything went black. Vivian and Eva tried their hardest to arouse her to no avail. The doctors each went into triage mode to get everything needed to try to revive her. Her sister and friend stepped back to allow the doctors room to work on her. They prayed while an AED was being hooked up to Angie, and CPR was being performed.

"CODE BLUE, CODE BLUE, SUITE 116, CODE BLUE, CODE BLUE, SUITE 116," was announced over the intercom.

A gurney was brought in where Angie was moved onto, and CPR continued while AED analyzed her heart rhythm. A shock was delivered and her chest flew up like a fish. No change in rhythm. A second charge was delivered. No change. CPR continued as the team prepared to move her to the ICU. They followed behind but not too closely as to interfere with care. Finally a weak pulse was detected, and her heart started back beating, though very weakly.

Me and bae took advantage of their rare opportunity to enjoy lunch together, away from everyone. The owner opened up a private area for us to eat and had the chef prepare some of our favorites to enjoy. I could tell something from the doctor's appointment was bothering her and was trying to figure out the best way to break the ice without causing her to become too sensitive, or worse, shut down completely. She was enjoying some fresh fruit. I put my arm around her and pulled her close, gently kissing her cheek.

"What's on your mind?" I asked cautiously.

"Just thinking about what the doctor said and hoping for the best," she responded as she ate some pineapple.

"Give it to God bae," I told her as I turned her face towards mine. "Just give it to God. He knows what's best for us. It's painful for me to think about too."

"I saw Jasmine earlier while I was there," she said softly. "She's expecting too."

"*Oh really?*" I responded, but not too surprised. "I hope she's happy. She deserves it."

"Me too." she said in kind. "That's what I want for everyone."

"So, I have a serious question for you," I said, trying to change the subject to something lighter. "When would you want to have a wedding ceremony?"

"I honestly haven't given it too much thought," she admitted to me. "So much has gone on that I haven't really taken time to think about what I want."

"Same here, but we have to. We owe it to ourselves." I told her as I kissed her lips. "We are important too."

We finished up lunch and she was gonna head back to work to check on everyone. I knew she was doing it to keep busy and I respected it. I was gonna go check on Alonzo and Myles at the school since I had the rest of the day off. It would be nice to see the old grounds where we caused so much hell to visiting teams and finished our collegiate basketball careers. Coach Smith was a legendary figure and role model in our lives, and treated us just like his own. I pulled in and noticed both Myles and Alonzo's cars parked nearby. Walking up to the gym I reminisce on all of the good times shared at this place. *A light breeze went across the back of my neck and a scent I vaguely remembered stopped me as I reached to enter the gym.* I stopped short and looked around out of curiosity, but saw nothing. I then opened the door and went inside to check on everyone.

Myles and Alonzo both were running drills with some of the players, and rightfully giving them hell while at it. Coach Smith was in the far corner watching the action, while directing the film student when and where to move the camera to capture certain aspects. Other players were watching as well and helping to call out plays or things to watch out for. Myles set up a screen that allowed for Alonzo to be free to come in hard for a hard dunk. They didn't like that at all, especially being a buzzer beater. But in good sportsmanship everyone came together to prepare for some post workout stretching and small talk. I took this as my opportunity to make my presence known to the crew, and to get a dig in on Alonzo.

"*You lucky I wasn't guarding you,*" I called out towards Alonzo with my hands like a loudspeaker. "*I'd have smacked that ball all the way to the back court!*"

Everyone looked up as I passed by, patting Coach Smith on the shoulders to elicit a fatherly hug from him. He still looked the same, though with a little less hair on his head. Alonzo threw his hands up as I came his way to help him up. Myles was stretching with the players but nodded his head in acknowledgement. He took charge and the players followed his direction. Some gathered equipment while others cleared went to gather dust mops to go across the floor, or gather the water bottles for the trainers. Everyone had something to do. Once he had that taken care of, he went and showered up in the coach's locker area before joining us in the office.

"What's good cuzzo?" he said as he came in feeling much better after that intense workout.

"See you two out there giving them players much needed competition." I said giving him some love. "Good to see you making the most of your time and talent."

"Can't afford to waste anymore time man," he said as he sat down at his desk. "Not getting any younger."

"Have you considered ever playing with the team, *officially*?" Coach Smith asked him flat out. "You have too much talent to just be doing what you do."

“Being real Coach, if it as a different time and place in my life, I’d take you up on that offer,” Myles said to him. “I’m honored just to be here helping out. But I got a whole lot going on personally that won’t allow for such a time commitment.”

“We’re willing to help in anyway we can to help make the opportunity a reality foryou,” he reiterated while looking back towards me and Alonzo, “You bring out the best in the players. You’re fresh and raw. A natural leader. Just like these two were back in their days. But most of all you’re humble.”

“Give it some thought man,” Alonzo said to him. “*You deserve a chance to do something for you. You already handle your business with everything else. We all see it.*”

“And you know the family supports you,” I chimed in, pulling him in close as he was sitting next to me.

Just then his phone rang. He saw my dad’s name pop up and jumped up as he answered the call. We watched and waited. Next thing we knew, he was sprinting across the gym towards the parking lot. I wasted no time going after him, leaving coach and Alonzo behind. Whatever it was that was going on, I knew it had to involve Auntie Angie. I caught up with him just as he closed the door to his car. I stood looking through the window until he acknowledged me. He was trembling with his hands on the steering wheel. I went to get my car and pulled up blocking him in. He didn’t need to drive. I got out and opened my passenger door and went to open his door. He got out and knew what to do. I locked his car up and jumped back in, heading towards the hospital. The ride was quiet but full of emotion. He was calmer thankfully but I knew things would change upon arrival. We managed to navigate through traffic without much incident and find parking easily. Pops was standing outside when we arrived and Myles stopped.

"She's waiting for you," he said as he pulled him close and we all walked in towards the elevators.

When we arrived at the ICU, we saw mama and Mrs. Eva in the room. They both came out so Pops and Myles could go in. I waited outside in the waiting room as they made their way out. Dried tear streaks were on both of their faces and I just stood and embraced both of them, before we all sat down. The silence was overwhelming, but I felt comfort knowing that they were with her at her appointment. It was only right for Pops to be in there with Myles. Aunt Angie was his sister-in-law, wife of his late brother Uncle Peanut, and he was the closest father figure that Myles had in his corner. Not long afterwards, Alonzo and Coach Smith arrived, with Yvonne who had the dynamic duo with her. Alexis had to take her big exams to finish out her specialization, so she let Malachi spend the night with his buddy. and Vanessa had called, but gave Myles his space. We all sat quietly in the waiting room, mostly watching the boys play with the few toys that were in a small corner, and waiting for the door to open to the ICU.

Not long afterwards, a nurse came out and asked for Malachi. He looked up and smiled. He came my way and reached for my hand, obviously wanting me to accompany him. I obliged and let him lead me, behind the nurse, to see his grandmama. Upon reaching the door, I stood outside but let him go in to be with them. I grabbed a nearby chair and sat down. My dad soon walked out and stood by me.

"It's okay son, she's just resting." he said as he put both hands on my shoulders and made eye contact. "Myles is being strong and understands what's going on. The doctors spoke with him. He wanted Malachi in there with him."

"I just hate that he's had to go through so much man," I said trying not to cry. "He's got to be a strong warrior because Lord knows he's definitely been dealt a hard deck of cards in life."

"I couldn't agree with you more," his dad replied. "But God is still God. And He knows exactly what He's doing. Even when we don't. We just have to trust and believe."

"That's so true," I said just as the door opened and Myles appeared in the doorway. I looked past him and saw Malachi had climbed up into the bed and was laying next to his grandma. I stood up and gave him a hug. He appeared numb-his eyes in a place far, far away. He looked at Pops and shook his head slightly, which was a signal to notify the others. He then ushered me in to say my goodbye. I went up close and held her hand and gave her a kiss. I told her I loved her and that I'm glad she's no longer in pain. That I would continue to look after Myles and the family. I stood up and then made my exit, so that others could come in to say their goodbye. Myles patted my shoulder as I tried to save face for him. One by one, everyone rotated through, with Myles sitting in the chair outside of her room, keeping a careful eye on Malachi in case he needed him. Alonzo stopped short of going in and just leaned in the door frame. This was especially hard for him, mostly because of Myles. Kyjuan walked over to Myles and tapped his hand. He looked up and saw his little buddy and smiled. He then saw Alonzo and stood up, grabbing lil man hand, so they could all go in. Malachi sat up when he saw his sidekick come in, and climbed down. The two gave each other hugs, and Alonzo helped him up to give Auntie Angie a hug, before getting back down. He leaned down to give her a hug and kiss and squeezed her hand. She had always treated him as a bonus son, and brother to Myles. He wiped his face of the tears that started to fall, for Myles and the boys. Myles gave him a hug and whispered that it was okay, as he then made his exit with Kyjuan.

The machines next to her started making noises, as her vitals started to change. Malachi started to whimper, eliciting Kyjuan to start as well. *That broke Myles's heart.* He went to pick him up-he fought him off all while holding tight to his grandmama. He let him lay next to her and rubbed his neck and back, trying to sooth him as he cried softly. Alonzo tried to comfort his son, but he wanted to be near his buddy. They took a seat near the bed, next to the window, so the two could see each other. Myles sat in the chair next to his mom, grasping her hand gently. A nurse came in and they made eye contact. There was a DNR in place, so he knew what she had to do. Her doctor and nurse admin came in shortly afterwards, and told the attending nurse to let whomever needed to come in, come in, and they'd handle whatever happened later. Pastor Johnson knocked on the door and came in. Myles looked up and smiled. He made his way over to him and gave him a fatherly hug. Alonzo also came and gave him a hug, Kyjuan holding a tight grip around his neck. He asked if it was okay to pray with them. All of the immediate family gathered in the room and held hands, as the Pastor prayed for Auntie Angie as the Lord prepared to take her home.

Then everyone filed out and back into the waiting room, leaving me and Malachi in the room. All of the machines had been disconnected and she was breathing on her own, and appeared to just be resting. I had fallen asleep with her hands on my head as I leaned next to her bed. Malachi was asleep too. I felt a slight movement of what felt like her fingers move gently across my cheek. I didn't move though. I just looked towards the window. It was dark in the room. Just then I saw what appeared to be a silhouette of a young man sitting in the far corner dressed in a uniform. I blinked my eyes to make sure I wasn't imagining or dreaming. *Then it spoke.*

"Hello son. It's me, your ole man. Yeah I'm still young but it's me. I know life has been tough for you and I am sorry for leaving you and your mom so long ago. God had other plans and when He called, I had to answer. But I've always been around, looking after you and your mom. I'm proud of the young man you've become and how you've stepped up with my grandson. Your mom is also proud of you. You've turned your life around for the better and don't let anything stop you from achieving your goals. Follow your heart and live life for you for once. Don't worry, Malachi will be fine. Your life will be fine. I came to visit Avant earlier today. Trust Coach Smith. He wants what's best for you and will watch over you if you choose to pursue basketball under his guidance and leadership. Just know that we're proud of you either way. But time is winding down, and I've got to complete my task. I've come to reunite with the love of my life. I

got it from here, son. Take care of your brother Jordan. Your watch is over for your mom. I got it from here soldier. "

I watched as he stood up and pressed his hands down his uniform as if to knock out the wrinkles. He had made his way to admire his grandson and rubbed his head before also giving him a kiss. Then everything around me lit up and I watched as what looked like my mom's spirit lifted up from her body and sat up on the far side of the bed. It concentrated on Malachi, and I watched her rub his face as he slept. She leaned down and gave him a kiss. She then turned my way and reached for my hand. I looked on as tears ran down my face. I couldn't speak. But I could feel her wiping the tears away and holding my face in her hands, trying to comfort and prepare me for her departure. She gave me a hug and kiss, and stood up and walked towards my dad, who was waiting at the center of the window on the far side of the room. They both smiled as they looked my way. She looked the same way she had the day he passed, with her belly showing the unborn baby inside. I was fully sitting up by this time, and moved to stand. Wanting to move towards them, I tried to but felt frozen from the legs down. I wanted to hug them so bad.

> *"Don't fight it son. You won't be able to come any closer. It's about that time. Will you do me this one final favor?" my dad asked as they held hands looking back my way. "Will you allow me to escort my wife, your beloved mother, home?*
>
> *"Yes sir," I cleared my throat and answered hoarsely. "I love y'all both."*

Just then I heard a soft heavenly melody play and a lit path opened up for them to follow. They then turned to go towards it. Just a ways ahead, a white chariot appeared and Mr. David stepped down to open the door and help my mom inside. My dad looked back my way and rendered me a final salute. I instinctively stood and returned the salute, watching as a single tear flowed from his left eye while he lowered his hand, removed his beret, and stepped inside. With that Mr. David lifted up the steps, and closed the door. He tipped his hat in my direction then returned to his place behind the horses, lifted his reins, and off they went along the dirt pathway towards the light. Soon they blended in with the light and I saw a metal door close behind them, returning everything back to darkness. At the sound of the doors shutting, Malachi woke up crying out for me, and I went over to pick him up. I felt for my mom's carotid pulse but didn't feel anything. Her body was cool to the touch. It was all over. I gave her a final kiss, and let Malachi do the same. He kissed his hand and placed it on her cheek.

"*Love you Gigi*," he whispered softly. With that my watch was over and I walked towards the door. I stopped at the nurse's station. They handed me a clipboard to sign off and fill in who to notify for her body to be picked up and transported. After all was done, we exited the ICU hand in hand to the waiting room, where I saw Jordan waiting patiently. He looked up as Malachi made his way towards his Godfather and opened his arms. He swung him around in the air, eliciting a much needed smile and laughter from him. I headed to the nearby restroom to relieve myself and wash my face. When I returned, I hugged Jordan and we all walked to his rental car. We drove to a nearby Waffle House to get some food. I put my coat around Malachi so he wouldn't be cold while we waited for our food.

"When did you get in?" I asked as we previewed the menu. I wasn't hungry but knew Malachi wouldn't eat unless he saw me eat.

"A few hours ago," he said as the waitress came over to take our orders. "I didn't want to disturb you."

"Good evening," the waitress said. "My name is Lisa. Can I get you all started with something to drink?"

"Good evening," Jordan answered with a smile. "Can we get two coffees and one small orange juice?"

"Sure thing," she said, returning the smile. "I'll give y'all time to look over the menu in the meantime. Your little man is too cute by the way."

Malachi looked her way and cheesed hard. "Thank you. I'm *Malachi."*

"It's nice to meet you Malachi." she said warmly. "I'll be right back with your drink orders."

She then put her pad back in her apron with her pen and headed to fix the drinks. Jordan laughed while Malachi tried to stand up to see which way she had gone.

"She'll be back lil man," I told him as I made him sit back down. "What do you want to eat?"

"He's looking for his girlfriend," Jordan snickered from behind his menu. "Can't deny that's you in rare form."

'Man, *what you say*!!!" I said in agreement. Malachi pointed to some waffles and sausage. I would get a simple two eggs and bacon meal. Jordan got his usual All Star meal. By that time the waitress had come back around with our drinks. Malachi cheesed the whole time she was there. She had no clue why he was smiling so hard but soaked in every minute of it. Jordan went over to the jukebox and put in some quarters to select some tunes. "*Sadie*" played softly from the speakers as he made his way back to the booth.

"Appreciate you coming down, for real man." I told him knowing he didn't have to make the trip since everything was so unexpected.

"It's all good man," he responded. "My aunt and uncle had planned to come check on the new facility, and we just happened to be in town when Alonzo called me. Don't worry about anything regarding the arrangements. My folks are going to take care of everything, *and I do mean everything.* So you take your time and pick out and plan with the family."

I stood up and gave him a strong hug. Malachi looked on not knowing what was going on, only that I was crying. We sat back down and he came over to hug me and to tell me that "daddy ok", as he patted my back. *God was too good!*

Part 4: Count On Me

I.

Auntie Angie's homegoing service was one fit for the Queen that she was in Myle's eye. Coach Smith and the entire basketball team helped Aunt Genevie and Uncle Julius with setting up everything for the ceremony. Her final viewing was held privately for only the immediate family to attend, before having a closed casket service. A huge blow up of a portrait of her with Uncle Peanut and Myles as a baby was placed on an easel next to her rose gold casket which was covered with an American flag and full length spread of pink roses, indicating her as a triple cancer survivor. Everyone part of the ceremony had some shade of pink, black, and gold, in her honor. In lieu of flowers, a request for donations to be made in her name towards the Agape Cancer Institute. A military detail performed the military honors for her since she was the wife of a veteran. Myles received the flag and both he and Malachi returned the salute that was given by the leader of the detail.

The ceremony was packed full of love from all around. The cancer center staff and her care team were all in attendance, and all came up to speak on their experience with being around their favorite "auntie". They all gave wonderful stories of Avant and Alonzo's mom bringing them goodies and snacks, while ensuring they did their best to give her round the clock care whenever she was there, and especially during the final visits. Members of Myles' care team also showed up and spoke on her behalf. There were even folks from Uncle Peanut's old Army Unit at Fort Mason that came to pay respect on his behalf. My ma and Mrs. Eva sang a tribute of "Count on Me" by Cece Winans and Whitney Houston, to their dear friend. Me, Alonzo, Myles, and Jordan, all came together to sing a soulful rendition of "A Song for Mama" for him as Pops accompanied us on the piano.

Finally, My dad and Myles surprised everyone by performing an instrumental duet of "I Will Always Love You", Myles on the piano, and Pops on the vintage saxophone gifted from his late brother Peanut when he first enlisted. There was not one dry eye in the sanctuary by the time Pastor Johnson began reading her eulogy and then his sermon titled "*A Mother' Love*".

When it was time to go, the basketball team lined up next to each aisle, and the pallbearers got in place to carry Auntie Angie's casket to a horse and carriage awaiting outside. There was a special carriage behind it to transport Myles, Malachi, and to the local Veterans Cemetery. Upon arrival there, a small ceremony was held for her with full military rites. The sounds of the rifles shooting off in the distance started Malachi, who instantly started crying. Kyjuan, sitting beside him, leaned over to comfort his friend, as Myles patted his back. Everyone soon filed out, leaving them to have some time to themselves with her. I wanted to cherish this final moment with her before I left, knowing that the workers would inter her after everyone had gone. This would be my final goodbye to the first love of my life. I never told anyone about what I'd witnessed at the hospital. It was still all too surreal, but I knew what I saw right now was reality. I lifted Malachi and gave him a rose. I placed the rose I held on top of the spread and lifted Malachi up so he could do the same.

I kissed my hand and placed it on the casket, whispering "I love you mama, always and forever. Take your rest. I got it from here. Tell dad me, Jordan, and Malachi said hello, and we love and miss him. Until we meet again." Malachi kissed his hand and put it next to the print left by his dad. Jordan came up to place his rose next to theirs. He looked at Myles as he held Malachi and put his arm around his shoulder. *"Let's go home brother. I want you to tell us about mom and dad."* Caught off guard, all he could do was embrace him. They were all they had now. With that, they each gave one final salute to the picture of their parents. Jordan, taking it with him, held it close as they started walking out. *He was with his two best friends.*,

II.

KyJuan has been quite the little helper for his mom while I've been working hard getting things ready for the arrival of our little girl. My boys are clowning me about how she's going to have me wrapped around her little finger and that I'm going to change now that I have a daughter of my own. I see it as a good thing though honestly. My mom even said that she knows I'll be fine when it comes to raising my children. Other than Myles no one else knows, but I'm planning on proposing to Yvonne soon and I'm hoping to be able to give her a nice intimate wedding ceremony. I miss my pops like crazy and wish he could be here physically, but I know he's always with me.

Mama Dukes finally retired and has been allowing my father's CPA to take over handling most affairs so she can relax. Myles has been a champion balancing all that he's been doing. We're preparing for this basketball tournament and I can't wait to see him doing his thing with the team. My boy got them skills for real and we've all been watching game film with the team to get them ready. This tournament is especially special because some of the alumni are reuniting in a special game against the current team players as a closeout to the tournament. This meant me and Avant would be back on the court playing with Myles against the university team. Win or lose, it would definitely be one for history books!

I recently found out that Jasmine is also expecting a baby boy soon and I sent my well wishes and a baby gift through Vanessa. I'm glad she's happy and finally able to do her own thing. It was fun while it lasted and I'm eternally thankful for all she did to help me become a better man and father towards KyJuan.

I've been learning more about the world of sports management while gaining more experience and responsibilities in the athletic department of the university. I was recently promoted to the Head Athletic Director and Assistant Coach for the Basketball team, couldn't have come at a better time. I was now able to deal with more students one on one and help make an impact on them in ways that would help them stay on track. Sometimes it meant dismissing students from the program that were not living up to the university and athletic standards because of academics, or off field behavior. In those times, I always thought back to how my dad was tough on me and tried to show the same courage and strength through tough love to my students. While some of them left cursing and angry, eventually I'd hear back from them about how they needed that type of tough love to help them grow as individuals and get their acts together. Others continued down their own paths and sad to say, even a few would end up locked up or with me attending their memorial services. Can't help them all, but that doesn't mean I won't bend over backwards trying my damndest to.

Myles took Coach Smith's offer on joining the basketball team as an official trainer while he completed some of his college classes online, until he can officially get into his major. He wants to learn more about coaching and sports management/administration, so it's a good thing for him to be around that environment. Naturally the coaching part is easy for him to handle, but it surprised me to see he had no problem getting in the trenches with me learning the ins and outs of administration and day to day operations of what it took to run the athletic program at the school, in addition to monitoring the players and everything that came with that.

We have an upcoming basketball tournament that the University would be hosting, and he definitely put in work helping out with both the individual and group training sessions. He mentioned wanting to eventually open up a training gym to help attract young boys and girls to learn different sports so they wouldn't turn to the streets and trouble. He knew first hand what could happen. In between my work tasks, I observed Myles giving some of the players hell on the court. He was very hands on. He'd explain what he saw them doing, critique it, and then have them set up so he could show them how to improve or fix any weaknesses.

While they were initially resistant at first because he was an outsider, the players quickly caught on when they'd catch us playing full court one-on-one where he'd be giving me a run for my money. They'd soon come out to play him, with him taking the time to slow down and do skills development in the middle of their games. He would come out and train with them, but never considered wanting to actually play on the team. By the time the tournament came around, the players had improved their individual and team acumen drastically, and it showed! Thank God for all of his blessings!

III.

The tournament was everything expected and some! The teams that came out definitely brought their “A” game and the University team definitely had to stay focused throughout it. The first couple of rounds were a breeze since they were ones that had been no problem throughout the regular season. But once they advanced to the semifinal rounds, the ante was upped quite a bit and we as coaches had to pull out our full secret arsenal of tactics and strategies at just the right time. Coach Smith let us take the lead since we were more familiar with the plays. The family came out to watch because they knew the last game would feature us as part of the special team of alumni.

They sat behind the team in the VIP section to see all of the action. Malachi and Kyjuan got to see their father’s in rare form out coaching the team with cousin Avant egging them on. The elders sat back and enjoyed the festivities. After battling fiercely, the University came out on top with a final score of 107-86. Congratulations were in order, handshakes were given as the final teams gave due credit and props where due. Then it was really game time. After the visiting team cleared out of the locker room, the players for the special teams made their way to get ready to show up and show out, all in love though of course.

I was too hyped to play in my first collegiate game, albeit an alumni/special teams/family exhibition game. I was more hyped because I would be playing alongside Avant, Alonzo, and Jordan, as part of the alumni team that was formed. Outside of playing with the fellas exclusively, and Jordan back home, I almost exclusively focused on boxing and coaching. I stepped into one of the single stalls, shutting the door and saying a private prayer to God to have His way and to let the game be one of fun and enjoyment. Allowing no violence or animosity to be present, we were here to just enjoy the time and opportunity together with family, community, and friends.

After I finished, I rejoined the group where Coaches Curtis and my dad, Coach James, were getting ready to give their pep talk. They were true legends and everyone listened closely to everything that was said, before we huddled up and headed out to the court. As Coach Smith and the University team was being introduced on one end, we lined up on the opposite side, awaiting our introduction. The rules of the game were then announced and the real fun began.

Myles was chosen to do the tip off for our team. Lauryn and Malachi cheered loudly as he humbly made his way to the court. The other guy from the university had a clear height advantage over him and used it rightfully to secure the ball in his team's favor. But what he didn't expect was the metamorphosis of *Coach Myles* to *demon-savage player Myles* when it mattered most, and was completely caught off guard when he was stripped and left looking confused while Myles shot passed him with the ball connecting with Alonzo for a tomahawk Jam slam dunk! That sent a clear message very early that no sympathy or mercy would be shown, and they turned up the heat accordingly.

Back and forth, with every play, the alumni team challenged the university players play for play, basket for basket. Each player on the alumni team had an equally matched player on the university team, with the exception of Jordan. Myles's versatility allowed him to switch out easily to wherever he was needed. The university players had a hard time guarding him. Alonzo and Avant showed no mercy launching far away three pointers, layups, and repeated slam dunks, either from themselves, or their former alumni teammates.

They decided to slow up a bit since it was a community event, and let the team think they had the advantage when they managed to take the alumni on a 15 point run, unchallenged. But it was clearly all in the tactics because they ran their "A" team ragged, and had to resort to subbing in most of the team's "B" team players. The alumni team did the same, except their "B" team included Jordan, who up to this point had just been observing silently from the bench. Just a little bit smaller than Myles frame wise, but equally as fierce, Jordan was the secret weapon Myles really wanted Coach Smith and the team to experience in action. Right off the rip Jordan came out swinging with all of the smoke with a screen set up so smooth that it opened up an opportunity for his 5'6 frame to do a windmill dunk on one of the best players on the university team for his first score. Not happy with that at all, the two would go head to head in battle for each bucket made afterwards. Coach Smith continued to sub players in and out of rotation to help him out, but to not much avail.

Myles would equally be subbed in when least expected, showing the opposing team that just them two alone could and would wreck any play, screen, box, or defense they tried to set up. Fade away here, lay up there, charge, slam dunk, they did it all flawlessly and effortlessly like it was a normal game for them. Alonzo and Avant were going crazy from the bench along with the rest of the alumni.

Eventually they would go in for the final few minutes of the 4th quarter to finish up with the dynamic duo. Coach Smith picked up on it and subbed his players accordingly, or so he thought. The best of the best from both sides battled it out in a display of both individual and team skills and talent. The game would end with each of the players doing their best from their respective teams, and the university losing to the alumni 89-112. All of the alumni players presented each senior and junior player with trophies for their hard work and dedication to the team.

The Coaches were all given trophies as well. Jordan and Myles would each get an MVP trophy and be given the titles "Smoking Demon and Bandit" for their nonstop assault on the university team players. Malachi and Kyjuan ran on court to join their father's as they were presented their trophies and took pictures with the press team, with Malachi holding up the trophy over his head while he sat on his dad's shoulders. Soon the family made their way onto the court to congratulate everyone. It was truly a memorable moment for the entire family. *But the fun wasn't over just yet.*

Man oh man! Just when I thought I would be ready the second time around *dear God was I wrong!* We had not long gotten into the house from finishing up a big basketball tournament at the university and Kyjuan ourselves settled into bed when Yvonne started having contracts, accidentally swinging her arm into my nose! Startled, I got up and tried not to panic with her. Taking a minute to catch my breath, I opened the nightstand drawer and looked inside the emergency folder. Thankfully the to-do list was there, and I used it to start checking off items on it while monitoring her. I went to wake up my mom and let her know what was going on while simultaneously looking over at lil man sleeping peacefully. She gave us her blessing and ushered me out the door where Yvonne was already in the hallway. The contractions were becoming closer and closer and I could only hope we made it to the hospital in time. I didn't have time to call the crew, it was only me and her. As I got her safely loaded, she told me that we didn't have much time because her water had already broken!

"Try not to push baby," was all I could tell her as I sped down the highway with my hazard lights flashing.

"IT HURRTTSSSS!" she screamed as another contraction rippled through her body. "I DON'T THINK THE BABY'S GOING TO WAIT!"

With that all I could do was pray as I ran the next red light and speed through the ER parking lot where the ambulances usually park. The police officer on duty looked at me sideways as I got out and started to say something when Yvonne yelled out "*THE BABY'S COMING NOWWWW!*" He jumped up to get a nurse and a stretcher. Just as they were getting her on it, I saw the head starting to crown and jumped between her legs to catch in case she delivered right then and there. By the time we got inside the OR, I was holding my baby girl in my arms, completely covered in blood, but thankful she was crying-signaling a healthy newborn. A nurse took the baby just as she started to deliver the after birth…*truth be told I don't remember much after that because I blacked out at the mere sight of it!*

IV.

Myles and I were up early working out on the terrace when I got a call from Alonzo saying their little bundle of joy had arrived. We went to wake the girls up and get dressed so we could all go see the family. We stopped to pick up his mom and son along the way. Alexis also met us over there with Malachi. We each took turns rotating in and out so as to not overcrowd them and the doctors and nurses trying to do their job. Myles and I almost hollered when Alonzo recounted how he passed out and fell off the stretcher after handing off lil LaNya Danielle Carlson.

He was sitting in a wheelchair playing guard over the baby bed next to him. Yvonne looked relieved that the hard part was over but knew that it was technically only the beginning. Mama Eva knocked and came in with KyJuan who was holding a pink balloon for his mom and pink elephant for his baby sister. Yvonne smiled as he climbed up to give her a hug, careful to avoid her belly. He gave her a kiss while he peeped over to see his dad and the new baby. Alonzo looked over his way and he made his way to climb up into his lap to get a look at his baby sister. He carefully rubbed her hair and placed the elephant near her. He put his hands on his mouth to kiss and put it on her cheek. Everyone “aww'd” at his gesture.

Malachi wanted to see too so he made his way over as well, dragging Myles with him. He lifted him into a nearby chair so he could look too. I managed to sneak a picture of that kodak moment. Vanessa, Alexis, and Lauryn checked with Yvonne, and tried to fix her hair, though she didn't care how she appeared at that moment knowing the birth part was over, and that *no more would follow*!

I went over to give Yvonne a hug before going over to check on Alonzo and get a closeup of the bruise on the side of his head. Myles leaned over to give his bro a congratulatory hug with Malachi in tow. Malachi, never one to disappoint, noticed the knot on his Godfather's head and poked at it curiously-eliciting laughter from everyone, as Alonzo moved his head away while he gave him the side eye. KyJuan then did the same and *it was on from there. Myles and I laughed at the dynamic duo double teaming him*. It was truly a happy moment for everyone though somewhat bittersweet for him. Alonzo motioned for us all to step outside, and we followed with the little people in tow.

"What's up man, you alright?" I asked him as they walked down towards the waiting area and stopped by the window showcasing the skyline.

"Yeah I'm cool man," he said as he looked out at the scenery down below. "Just thinking about Pops man and hoping everything will go right this time around with my daughter."

I put my hand on his shoulder. "I know it's still fresh in your memory man. I don't speak on it, but I always think about my ole man too. I miss him so much."

"You don't have anything to worry about man," Avant told him. "You've come a long way from when KyJuan was born and everyone saw it. Don't be so hard on yourself. You've made sure to cover all of the bases."

Alonzo turned our way and we all gathered in a brotherly hug before he almost broke down. Myles hugged him tight as he shook full of emotion. That was his other big brother and one who'd helped look after him after his dad passed so many years ago. He and Avant always included him and their dad's never made him feel left out. Myles was forever grateful for that and had always felt more like brothers to them, then friend and cousin. Though he favored his cousin in skin tone and other physical traits, everyone could tell that his bond with Alonzo was just like that of Malachi and KyJuan.

They ran the streets together whenever he came to visit, when Avant was busy working with his dad or chasing after Vanessa. That's how he came to meet Alexis, though he'd later learn that they (he and her) shared mutual contacts back home in Chicago that would twist and entangle their worlds in more ways than either could've ever imagined. Alonzo knew things that Avant didn't because Myles knew his cousin wouldn't be able to handle it if he did. Alonzo eventually collected himself and went to clean up his face in the restroom and go back to check on everyone. He and Myles had been planning a surprise proposal and needed us to help him keep his nerves together. We prayed and then headed back down the hall where we met with one of the nurses caring for the baby. She had changed her into a new onesie that was purposely put on wrong to force Yvonne to go into OCD mode, setting the stage for his surprise.

I pushed the baby cart back in and Yvonne ushered me to bring her baby to mama. Everyone watched as she tilted her head ever so slightly as the disheveled mess that was her baby's onesie. Her face was priceless! But before she could open her mouth to express her disapproval, Malachi and KyJJuan on cue, interrupted her.

"*LOOK*!" they both said cheesing hard at her, completely shattering any type of anger she was harboring towards Alonzo. "*We helped*!"

She looked at their "attempt to dress" her baby haphazardly, and just laughed as she worked to unbutton the onesie and get her situated. She then made a weird face as she muttered "*I Swear*", before coincidentally noticing the shirt saying *"I Swear",* and looked up to see us fellas surrounding her bed, the ladies looking back and forth trying to figure out what was going on.

"*By moon and stars in sky….."* Malachi and KyJuan both said softly.

"*I'll be there,*" we all joined in. "*And I swear, Like the shadow that's by your side. I'll be there…*
For better or worse, 'Til death do us part. I'll love you with every beat of my heart…I swear…"

Myles and Alonzo continued on with the song, alternating singing the verses, and me joining in with the chorus. Everyone was awestruck as we serenaded Yvonne. Tears streamed down her face as she held her daughter completely dumbfounded. The ladies wiped their tears as well. Then, to make things ever so much better, KyJuan walked up to *Yvonne* with a small box. KyJuan even got down on one knee, just Alonzo did without anyone noticing.

As she opened the box to reveal the engagement ring, he asked innocently, *"Mommy, will you please marry daddy?"*, prompting everyone to look past them, noticing Alonzo still down on one knee, and Malachi now holding a small bouquet of red roses. Mama and Mrs. Eva both screamed in joy, while Yvonne boo hoo'd, breaking in happy tears. Yvonne hugged them both while saying "*yes*", prompting him to come forward to place the ring on her finger and give her a hug and kiss.

Jordan prepared to make the trip down to Georgia to check on the business operations and update the crew on the housing arrangements secured for their Miami vacation trip compliments of his aunt and uncle. They would be staying at their penthouse right in the heart of downtown, with access to their private gym. He was looking forward to getting away for a bit and spending time with his best friend. He was also excited because he was going to be able to link up with his other friend Lamont down in Miami. He was the one promoting the Plies and Ne-yo concert, and the two of them had an on-again, off again situationship.

Lamont didn't identify himself as gay, but merely said he liked to have variety in his life. Jordan respected that as he also didn't identify with it himself. He just went with the flow and enjoyed the time they spent together. He knew Lamont was very much in the public eye because of his profession and career, and didn't want to do anything to bring discredit or notoriety to his image. No one ever suspected anything was going on between the two because of how they carried themselves, but he didn't want to take any chances. He also didn't want to ruin this trip for Myles because he had definitely earned this much needed vacation.

He was excited to learn that he had a new god daughter from Alonzo, and looked forward to meeting her when he arrived. He texted Myles to let him know he was about to hit the road and would be there by that afternoon. He then checked to ensure he had his permit and his *equalizer* close by in case things got ugly. He wasn't afraid to throw hands if necessary, but also kept a piece handy, along with his secret arsenal at the condo. He also hit up Lamont and after receiving his reply, smiled and started the car to commence his trip.

V.

Jasmine and Calhoun met up for lunch at the legendary *Madame Laurent's Seafood with Seoul*, which was an establishment that blended the Louisiana seafood culture with Korean infused culture-it was an ode to Madame Laurent's husband, the late General James "Jimmy" Kim Lee, who helped her bring her dream of a fusion restaurant to fruition after meeting him on a chance visit to Korea during the Korean Conflict while on tour with the USO. The two kept in close contact and a romance that lasted for over 60 years before his eventual passing. The restaurant had become a staple in the *Sugar Cane* community that had seen many other businesses leave, close down, or relocate due to the changing dynamics of the neighborhood and community. The two looked over the menu while their waiter sat down the silverware and took out her pad to take their drink orders.

"I'll have sparkling water with lemon," Jasmine told her as she turned from the menu. "What about you bae?"

"Same, for me as well." he said smiling.

"Okay, I'll get those right out and give you all time to look over the lunch selections," she said as she replaced her notepad into her apron.

"Thanks, we won't take long," Calhoun told her warmly. He was glad to be back around Jasmine. She was his peace and he appreciated her loyalty and genuineness. They looked over the menu and after selecting their meals, sat them on the edge of the table for the waiter to pick up upon her return. He grasped her hand and just smiled at her. She was a naturally beautiful young lady that carried herself with just enough confidence. He knew he wanted her to be his wife.

"What was the news you had to share?" he asked calmly while looking into her eyes.

"I went to the doctor today," she said slowly. "You're going to be a daddy."

"Oh *Word?*" he responded, his mood cheering up almost immediately. "How do you feel about that?"

"I mean I'm excited," she told him as she thought about her career plans and still wanting to relocate. "Just thinking about how it's going to impact my relocation and career."

"We can still do that. Come visit my place and see how you like it?" he asked her. "Then you can meet Azuri."

"Does she even know about me? About us?," she asked him. "Are you ready for us to be a family?"

"'*Family',* I like the sound of that," he said as he rubbed her hand with his. "A family together-me, you, lil baby bundle, and my daughter, all together."

"Yes, that sounds wonderful," Jasmine responded. "But we have to do it the right way."

"Formal wedding to make everything official," he asked. "Small and intimate, or all the way out?"

The waiter came back around with their drinks and took their orders before disappearing with their menus to go put them in. They made small talk about taking some time off to celebrate the good news, like maybe taking a trip to Miami Beach to get away and relax. Jasmine was excited and couldn't wait to go. Even though it would be part business, part vacation, she didn't mind as long as they were there together. For the first time in a long time, she finally felt like her life was finally coming together. Running into Vanessa and rekindling their friendship, getting confirmation that she was expecting, and then knowing that she was with someone who she felt would protect and grow with her together as they planned for their futures. She couldn't feel any more blessed than at that moment. Their food arrived and they enjoyed their meals.

I was changing the baby and watching the clock to make sure I was still making good time. I still had to get KyJuan up and ready before fixing breakfast and getting him off to school while Yvonne caught up on sleep. Thankfully I was able to take advantage of the paternity leave which allowed me the necessary time to not only bond with our daughter and help around the house, but also give Myles time to get into the groove of coaching and training the team during the offseason. Jordan helped us plan a "guys" trip to Miami to celebrate our win in the tournament. He was coming down early to update us on the business and join us on the trip.

VI.

I used part of the inheritance money to pay off the house for my mom, me and Malachi so I'd have a place for when I wasn't working here. It was structured as a loan to help me build my credit and financial profile. It had a small balcony in the back that overlooked a garden similar to that of my Aunts' that my mom fell in love with. She deserved the best and I wanted to ensure she had it while she was still able to appreciate it. She had stairs on both ends that led down to it, where there was also a small koi pond with a waterfall/fountain combination that was inspired by one of my dad's overseas assignments to Japan and Korea. Simplicity yet mindful. I had surprised her with it on Mother's Day secretly before she passed away along with the announcement that I'd qualified for my college degree at the end of the upcoming semester.

Pops and I drove up with Malachi, to help Jordan set up new furniture in the old house. Myle's old suite had been renovated, and Pops guarded it with his life. There were lots of boxes that held Uncle Peanut's belongings that were off limits to everyone else. It was set up like a music studio/lounge mixed with a museum-like memorial vibe. I sat on a nearby recliner and watched as he meticulously inspected everything. He was over at the vintage record player flipping through the collection. I knew which one he was looking for, and just waited til he found it and set it up for us to listen to. That familiar scratching of the pin hitting the record as it spun made me reminisce back to when me and Myles were little and his dad and Pops all would be down here jamming.

The sounds of Thelonius Monk filled the room through the tall speakers. Pops sat down near me and closed his eyes. He had his glass on a coaster nearby filled with rum and coke, ready for sipping. I cherished these moments. I wish Myles was here with us. It would be perfect by the time he came to visit. Jordan got a text from Myles and made his exit. My physical scars have healed completely thanks to Aunt Vivian's home remedies and made from scratch shea butter cream to help even back out my skin tone. I've finally come to terms with what happened with me and Ollie and took time to visit Jordan's aunt. She took me to her private garden area where my mom had gone to say her last goodbye's to him. It felt good to release all of that pain and anger and start the journey of healing and forgiveness. Despite all that's been going on, I'm thankful to be alive and able to provide for my family.

Sometimes I cry when I'm alone because though I know she's no longer hurting, I felt like we both got cheated out of what could've been a really good life. She was really around to try to keep me grounded when I turned to the streets. Don't get me wrong, Avant and Alonzo's fathers were both instrumental in keeping me on my wayward journey to the straight and narrow when I came down to visit. But living up in Chicago was a beast in and of itself. Jordan was my ace and looking back, I don't think I'd be here if it wasn't for him surviving in the trenches with me. We protected each other through thick and thin-even when he ended up getting temporarily locked up during a situation where he was apprehended in case of mistaken identity. I've never forgiven myself for getting separated from him...he was vulnerable while locked up and if only I'd been there with him, *that* would've never happened! I might still be locked up to this day,rather than what I know happened, and how its lingering effects still haunt him to this day.

My mom did her best to raise me to the best of her ability after my father passed. I haven't thought about him in so long that it's hard to imagine what life was like with him. Distant memories of him flying helicopters and showing me how all of the buttons and gauges worked. I remember the day of his accident though I've tried to forget it to no avail. Momma and I were bringing him lunch and he was supposed to take me flying in the helicopter. They were returning from a quick trip from nearby Ft. Mason to pick up a recently serviced older model huey to bring it over for a showcase to take place honoring some Vietnam vets later that week. I remember waiting inside the building with the big glass windows watching and waiting for his arrival.

Just as I saw them begin to descend something went wrong and the helicopter began to do a death spin with the rear blades malfunctioning. My dad wasn't piloting that day, just a passenger. A more experienced pilot was operating it and couldn't regain control in time. The huey came down in a crash so violent that the entire building shook upon its explosion, and caused the windows of the building to shatter. My mom screamed as she pulled me back from the glass so I wouldn't be cut. All I could think of was that my dad was superman and he'd make it out alive, if only injured. My mom picked me up, and turned her back to everything, and held me to shield me from seeing the fire rescue crews fight desperately to extinguish the flames. There were only two survivors. My dad's area took the brunt of the impact and he was found with his body protecting the younger soldiers nearby when the rescuers finally got to them.

The days and months afterwards were a blur as a joint memorial service was held on the base for them, with special tributes given by the 130th Bomber Squadron that he was part of. The Vietnam vets that were supposed to be honored all came and gave each of the families of the deceased flags and tributes, and spoke kindly of their honor and appreciation for our loved one's sacrifices. I remember Avant and Alonzo sitting on either side of me during the private family service. A big portrait of my father was displayed alongside a metal container draped with an American Flag. That was the first and only time I ever saw Uncle James cry.

He couldn't hold back as he went to and placed his hand on his baby brother's casket. I remember getting up and walking to him, pulling on his pants leg. He turned to see me and picked me up, and allowed me to wipe his face with my hands. I hugged him as he held me. Avant and Alonzo would eventually come up with each holding onto a leg and giving him extra support. The two soldiers that he protected were able to attend, and visited with the family privately following the service. They kept in touch with us through the years.

I'd eventually move in with Avant while my mom was busy trying to settle his estate with Uncle James, and grieve herself. The trauma took a toll on her and we truly believe that led to her eventually being diagnosed with cancer. Avant and Alonzo looked after me and kept me engaged so I wouldn't think much of what happened. They knew I had seen everything but never brought it up. We instead engaged in sports and other activities to pass time and help me try to enjoy my childhood. I never spoke of it nor asked any questions. I blamed myself at first but learned that there was nothing I could've done to change the outcome. I later learned that my dad had named me after his favorite musician *Myles Davis,* only because my mom absolutely refused to have a son with the name *Thelonius*! *Thank God for my mom saving the day!* I laugh to myself thinking about that. *"Coltrane" would've been cool no doubt.* Ole Peanut, as they used to call my dad, was a man of jokes and pranks. He loved music and I guess that's where I get it from.

My mind turned to also wanting to open my own gym to help train other aspiring athletes and fighters to develop their craft if they wanted to learn, and off the streets. I thought about how much I had experienced growing up and how fortunate I was to have a family to help keep me grounded despite my sometimes disregard for my own life and wellbeing. Things could've turned out much worse had Uncle James' family not kept me under their guidance and supervision while mama dealt with my father's passing in her own way. She didn't abandon me but merely just sent me to where she knew I would thrive and be able to keep my mind off the trauma. She was thankful for her village coming together during her time of need. Though they never did approve of Ollie and how he treated us, they let her deal with that in her own way, much to his own demise.

Ollie's replacement, Mr. Tymell, arrived at the Crematory and grabbed their tool bags. It was time for the routine service of the facility's main furnace located on the backside of the property. Mrs. Geneva had been expecting him, and so had a staff member posted to let him in. She was watching the installation of a new waterfall in the recently drained pond in the children's section when she turned to nod in approval of his arrival. She was excited to soon be able to add some koi fish once everything was completed. Inside the facility, the staff showed them to the inner furnace area. They left the door propped open for free access to and from the truck as they worked. Should the inner door ever close, no one would ever know anyone was inside if they didn't watch the security cameras for it was completely soundproof from the outside. One couldn't get locked though because of the large yellow push button on the door, as an additional safe proof method.

A shipment of cement and other stone fixtures, along with bulk soil bags were expected to be delivered so she waited to ensure proper placement took place upon arrival. So many moving pieces kept her occupied. Jordan would be bringing his friend Myles by to help around the grounds. They were hardworking young men, and needed very little supervision. They kept each other out of trouble for the most part, though they did tend to disappear at random times. Work always got done in a timely manner and exceeded her standards. Everything seemed to be going according to her schedule so she'd soon be able to check in with her husband to figure out where they'd jet off to for a rare private lunch. Jordan would be able to oversee things with Myles in the interim.

Julius Harris was busy looking over paperwork and listening in on a conference call when he noticed the new guy in one of the cctv screens working on the furnace. He watched his coming and going, taking notice of how efficiently he was working. That was a very good sign, as he wanted to hurry up and finish his affairs so he and his lovely wife could go enjoy some lunch at their favorite restaurant, a rare treat for the both of them. He texted Jordan to see his location and ETA back to the grounds with Myles. It didn't take long to get a response, and with that he worked to wrap up everything. Jordan and Myles pulled up ready to work.

They were accustomed to helping out on the grounds whenever they didn't have to do any "processing". Aunt Geneva had taught both of them about horticulture, gardening, and landscaping from an early age. They knew she could depend on them to oversee any tasks while they were off grounds. Jordan spotted the technician's truck on the hill a little ways back from where he'd parked. Myles went to help load her prized bonsai trees for display in her greenhouse while Jordan went to see what the delivery guys were doing close to the crematory. As he approached the crematory, he could see newly delivered stones and other landscaping items arranged orderly but strangely placed in the wrong location. He motioned to one of the forklift drivers to show him the error and where it needed to be moved to. Once that was completed, he opened the door to see the inner door closed as well and went to see if the new gut was inside since he was nowhere to be found outside.

"Hello??" he called as he opened the inner door that led to the crematory furnace.

"Yeah," Mr. Tynell managed to call out from where he was working.

"Ok, just checking on you sir," Jordan said to him. "The doorway had been blocked by the delivery people. You're good now though, I have the door propped open for you to come and go as needed."

"Thank you young man," he called back. "This job is going to take some time, so I definitely appreciate it."

"No problem," Jordan said before heading back to where Myles was to see if he was needed before going to check with Uncle Julius. Myles and Aunt Geneva were riding back on the cart towards him, and stopped so he could catch a lift to meet Uncle Julius. As soon as they pulled up, he greeted them at the back entrance, already carrying her purse and shawl so they could head straight to the waiting black suv that would chauffeur them. After receiving further instructions, the elders whisked off, leaving the two *demons* in charge.

Myles and Jordan didn't have much to monitor since the funeral home was closed for the remainder of the day minus any urgent matters. The deliveries had been completed and those workers were gone, as well as the groundskeepers. The only person remaining was Mr. Tymell, still taking his time to maintain the crematory machine. The two went to check on him, Jordan taking the lead while Myles hung out on the golf cart. He brought some food and drinks with him in a cooler that his aunt had prepared earlier that morning by their personal chef. Mr. Tymell peeped his head out from the machine and acknowledged him. Jordan wasted no time leaving him to his work. He walked back out to the golf cart and the two headed back to his office to hang out until it was time to lock up shop.

Tymell finished up in the crematory after ensuring everything was in working order. He cleaned up his work area and went about packing his tools and equipment back in his work van. One final test run would be performed to test efficiency. Tymell hit the button on the control panel. From there the furnace was automated to cycle through testing all aspects as if performing an official cremation. He notated the time of testing to ensure all proper documentation was in compliance. Because of the automation that came with the new upgrades and services, the new system was self-sufficient-with automatic shutoff would occur upon completion, and any emergency signal or alarm activated from inside the furnace would signal a separate shutdown procedure. He then closed up the building and hit the intercom to call up to the office where Myles and Jordan were.

Jordan acknowledged the message and hit a few buttons to activate the alarm, and watch the cameras as he drove down towards their location. Another button and the sliding gate opened to allow his exit. Jordan waited for him to come drop off the necessary paperwork and invoice for his service. Ollie might have been a fucked up individual but stood on business when it mattered, and had trained Tymell well before his untimely demise. Jordan always treated him as such mainly off the strength of his Aunt and Uncle. Tymell walked in and acknowledged Myles in the far corner. He quietly observed the business transaction take place, never losing sight of him. Jordan signed off where necessary and handed him a check. They shook hands and off buddy went. Jordan waited until he had left the premises before turning to his ace.

"Well we're done for today homie," he said as he shut down his computer and proceeded to grab his jacket and keys so they could lock up and head out. "Where you wanna go?"

"You wanna grab something to eat?" I suggested. "We could swing by the house and pick up lil man, Unc and cuzzo."

"You already know I'm down to eat anytime," Jordan shook his head in agreement. "Hit them up and see what they say."

"Bet," I said as I pulled out my phone to dial Avant's number.

"Hello," I said, picking up after fumbling to find my phone.

"Yooo, y'all down to go eat?" He asked, sensing I had been asleep.

"*Food*?" I asked, hearing my stomach faintly growl. "*Hell yeah!*"

"Okay," He said, chuckling. "We'll be there in about 15-20 minutes."

"That's a bet," I said looking over at Pops who had long finished his drink and nodded off with Malachi against his chest, in the other recliner. I knew him well enough to know he wasn't sleeping, though he was much more relaxed than earlier.

“So where are we going?” he said calmly, without opening his eyes or moving.

“Knowing them two, there’s no telling,” I said smiling as I watched a smile start to form on his face. “But it won’t disappoint.”

“That is true,” he said as he sat up carefully so as to not disturb him,and stretched. “Come help me with the youngin,”

I stood up and went towards him, extending my hands out to get Malachi as he stood and brushed invisible wrinkles from his shirt and pants. That was my old man and I loved him more than he ever knew. He looked around and grabbed his glass while I returned the record back to its jacket and into the collection folder. I then wiped off the record player and closed the top back down to protect it from dust. After ensuring everything was turned off and back where it belonged, we turned off the lights, locked up, and went to wait out front. We settled in the rocking chairs on the porch. It wasn’t long before they pulled up.

“Good to see you Uncle James,” Jordan said as he walked up to the porch and leaned in to give him a fatherly hug.

“Likewise young man,” he said in return. “Where are you two coming from?”

“We were helping out at the business,” he answered. “Deliveries, ground keeping, and maintaining things.”

“Keeping busy doing productive things,” Pop responded in approval. “That’s good.”

“Come over here Myles,” he said as he stood up. I walked over and looked him in his eyes. He embraced me like his own son, one hand on my back, the other on the back of my head. His body language let me know it was ok to let my guard down as I hugged him back. So much was conveyed through this action that there was no need for words. I felt him release me, opening up for Malachi, Avant and Jordan to join. This was one of those rare moments that he outwardly expressed his love and affection. All of his boys, minus Alonzo, together. Just as we were about to head to the suv, Ollie’s work van pulled up with Tymell. We all continued walking while Pops stayed behind to watch the man in the van. We watched as he headed towards the garage and stopped upon seeing Pops. We all waited in silence as a bag and keys were handed over. They shook hands and the young man headed back past us to a waiting taxi. We watched as Pops locked up the garage and calmly walked our way.

“Ready to go eat fellas?” he asked calmly as he readjusted his Vietnam War capand smoothed out his starched slacks before fastening his seatbelt and checking on Malachi, who was eagerly awaiting forhis new partner in crime.

“Yessir,” we all said as we eyed him and then each other, chuckling to break the ice.

We ended up going to this Caribbean place called *Jazzy’s* that had a deck that faced the waterfront. We chose to sit on the deck since the weather was nice and calming. Pops ordered a perfect margarita while we each ordered iced tea and some fruit punch for Malachi. I watched as Myles seemed like he had something on his mind. When he got up to go to the restroom, I followed him just to check on him.

"You good man?" I asked as I stopped at the stall next to him to relieve myself.

"Yeah I am," he answered as he flushed the toilet and fixed his clothes. "Just happy that things have changed for the better."

"What do you mean?" I asked as I finished up and joined him at the sink to wash my hands.

"*Malachi*," he said looking up at the mirror as he washed his hands. "He's truly been my saving grace."

"You said it would all work out," I said while drying my hands and handing him some paper towels.

"Yeah, but it's bittersweet," he said, looking me dead in the eyes. "Uncle James and them knew before I said anything."

"They seem to always know," I said as we walked out the door back to join the others.

When we got to the house, we were eager to show Myles the new terrace set up. Pops stood in silence for a minute before he motioned for us to follow him. We walked behind as he led us down to a door not far down the hall. He nodded towards the door and

Myles opened it for us to see. Inside was like a miniature version of his own living area, with smaller rooms within the room for sleeping or studying. There were pictures on the walls of them together, Myles and his dad and Mom, along with different themes to captivate 's imagination. They had been preparing a space for Malachi whenever he came to visit. I placed a hand on his shoulder, patting it in silent approval. Myles looked my way and saw me hold out my fist to dap him up. He and Malachi left us in the room temporarily and he continued the tour. A lot of time and detail had been put into designing, picking out furniture, and arranging everything. Jordan showed Malachi shelf full of books. He had a special book put together that he couldn't wait to read to his god son.

As we finished looking around and made our way back towards the outer area and prepared to exit, Pops met us in the doorway. We walked towards him as Myles closed and locked the door, before we went back to his entertaining area. As Myles and lil man sat down, Pops handed him a box that looked vintage. He looked up at him as he received it. He took a seat nearby and watched as Myles opened it. He pulled out an old leather book of sorts-a scrapbook of sorts. It was Uncle Peanut's from when he was in the military. He immediately returned it to the box and took it to the studio for safekeeping in his safe. He came out and hugged his Uncle tightly.

I could tell he was crying and just left them to have their private moment. More and more he was starting to show his vulnerable side knowing when and where to though. Their bond was different, and I respected it. I grabbed some water and went outside to shoot some hoops. I zoned in like I was back training, mentally running drills to see if I still had it. I was a bit rusty but easily found my rhythm and was soon going full in until I was drenched in sweat and breathing hard. I sat down in the shade and sipped on the cool water.

They all joined me not long afterward, and we were going full court-them moving effortlessly, me catching my second wind to keep up the momentum. Both Myles and Jordan were naturally gifted athletes but never wanted to play formally; yet at the same time both were too disciplined to resort to *street ball* tactics-that came from his Uncle James. He taught us to treat the game of basketball with respect and stay grounded on the fundamentals and most importantly, sportsmanship and conduct. Everything he taught us came with life lessons that extended far beyond the court. Even dad put up a few shots, with Malachi on his shoulders, adding to the intensity-*if only Alonzo was here to even everything out.*

Julius and Geneva arrived at Jimmie Dee's and were escorted by the hostess to a private section reserved for them to enjoy in privacy. A special menu lay on the table along with a bouquet of red roses and a bottle of vintage red wine chilling in a decorative bucket of ice. A young waiter came out to uncork and pour them each a glass while they surveyed the menu. Julius marked their selections on a small pad and handed it to the waiter to place. After he was gone, they cuddled up to enjoy each other's company.

"You always know how to surprise me," Geneva said, leaning to give her husband a kiss on his cheek.

"You deserved it baby," he said smiling, happy that she was happy. "We have to do this more often."

"I know," she sighed, sipping the red wine slowly. "Jordan and Myles are working well together. I think he's almost ready for our expansion project."

"I agree," Julius said, clinking his glass against hers lightly. "It will be a good distraction for Myles too. He's a natural but I can tell he likes to be in the background-kind of like myself."

"That foolish ass Ollie has put him and his mother through so much," she exclaimed, fighting the tears that threatened to fall. "I'm so glad that he spends his time doing constructive things instead of being in the streets. Lord knows we don't need them to reverse course back to that time."

"They're going to be just fine doll," Julius said, dabbing her tears. "Don't get yourself all worked up about them. This is our time. Enjoy the ambience."

Rockefeller oysters and caesar salads arrived just as they turned their attention towards the waiter setting the table. He stood back awaiting their approval before asking if they needed anything else, and disappearing so they could enjoy their meal. Julius carefully picked up one of the oysters and squeezed a hint of lemon juice on it, before turning towards his lovely wife, feeding her carefully. She loved when he babied her. She blew on it before taking hold of the shell. *Exquisite!* How all of the flavors fused together and the oyster was grilled to perfection. Julius was enjoying them just as much, in between his salad. He added a touch of pepper sauce to a few of his before indulging in them. They had just barely enough time to digest before their main course of grilled red snapper with asparagus and five cheese-lobster mac and cheese, arrived.

VII.

Downtown Miami was a sight to see. Culture everywhere and beautiful women, expensive cars and homes. Jordan's family had set us up in their private penthouse that had spectacular, panoramic views of the ocean and city skyline, with private pool access. We were located about ten minutes from all of the city's hotspots-beaches included, and had exclusive access to one of the premiere training gyms that catered to fighters and boxers of all types. This was right up Myles's alley since he wanted to get some training while on vacation. Jordan had linked up with his friend Lamont to get us tickets to an exhibition fight that would feature one of his cousins, Memphis Lanier, and a VIP tour of the venue. We all got dressed and headed over to the exhibition site. Myles was too hyped. He saw a picture of the event and caught a glimpse of Memphis Lanier. He had read up on him and had studied film of past fights and sparring sessions. Memphis was definitely the truth when it came to throwing those hands and was known to many on the streets for being a brutal, vicious but honest fighter. He was definitely certified with his hands. He had three older brothers, Ross, Kingston, and Harlem. Together their names commanded respect from the streets. Jordan knew them because of his family ties and had filled the fellas in. We actually wanted to meet them because we had worked together indirectly with the *Clean Up Crew* when handling packages through the processing facility at the funeral home that Jordan's family had expanded and opened near them in Miami.

After that we walked the beach strip checking out everything it had to offer. We found one of the basketball courts free next to a pullup bar set up and went to see what it was all about. Surprisingly it was pretty empty for such a lovely day. We took that as an opportunity to get a small workout and game in. We took off our shirts and set our gear down before heading over to the pullup bars first. Apparently a bar was located right across from us, and was full of college girls on vacation from one of Florida's HBCU's, unbeknownst to us. Alonzo went first to see what he could do. I watched and then mimicked him on my setup, with ease. Avant and Jordan then took turns doing the same. Not long into our session we switched to the basketball court where we engaged in a heated game of two on two.

Not realizing it, we started hearing cheers coming from the distance and turned to see a small fan club from the bar. And what a beautiful sight was to behold. Some of the ladies had on thongs covered by small see through skirts, while others were dressed in sundresses. There were groups that were color coordinated and some were shouting out different chants, based on what colors they had on. Alonzo and Avant recognized them as sorority members from AKA, Deltas, and Sigma Gamma Rho, sororities respectively, and gave me and Jordan the 411 on them.

"Do we have any active black fraternities and sororities back home on campus?" I asked Alonzo and Avant.

"Delta Sigma Theta, Zeta Phi Beta, and Alpha Kappa Alpha," Alonzo told me as he pointed their colors and members out. "And fraternities wise, Phi Beta Sigma, Alpha Phi Alpha, and Omega Psi Phi."

“Those guys over there are members of those fraternities respectively,” Avant pointed out, not too far from where our fan club had gathered. “They seemed to be noticing our little fan club.”

We all laughed as we noticed some of them mean-mugging and smirking as the ladies watched us. We paid it no mind as we finished our game, knowing that they wanted none of the smoke we’d unleash on them, and headed towards the bar area for some food and drinks. They smiled and waved as we walked past and we returned it back to them. This particular bar specialized in Caribbean food, and had an awesome menu selection. The bartender asked what we were drinking, and we all ordered some coconut water since we needed to rehydrate from our workout, along with ginger beers to enjoy. We asked her what the best authentic meals on the menu were for first time visitors, and she took her time describing each of her favorites. When she was done, we each ordered a different one of her favorites based on our preferences, knowing we’d all share the food amongst each other, and take some back to the penthouse. While we were waiting on our food and nourishing our beverages, a couple of the ladies made their way over for conversation.

“Lovely day gentleman,” the first one said as she stopped at our table. “What brings you to Miami?”

“That it truly is,” Alonzo replied, flashing his signature smile. “We’re actually here on a little vacation.”

“Must be nice. We’re here for a little bit of both *business and pleasure,*” she said smiling, looking for the bartender. “My name is Sharice. These are my friends, Layla, Tanisha, and Ariel.”

“I’m Alonzo,” he said as he pointed to the rest of us. “These are my boys Avant, Jordan, and Myles.”

“Are yall twins?” the one named Layla asked, looking at me and Avant.

“Naw, ma,” I quickly answered for me and my cousin. “We’re cousins.”

“*That’s bullshit,*” said Tanisha, clearly not buying it. “Ain’t no way yall aren’t twins.”

“Girl, stop tripping,” Ariel said, coming to their defense. “Anyway, my name is Ariel.”

“Nice to meet you,” Jordan said, smiling and laughing as Tanisha was clearly embarrassed.

“Shawty we don’t have any reason to lie,” Avant replied while sipping on his ginger beer.

“*Scouts honor*,” I chimed in, cheesing hard at Tanisha, who still had a cloud of doubt overhead. “Have a seat, drinks and food on us.”

"Are you all sure?" Sharice asked, looking around. "We don't want to interrupt or be caught off guard in case your wives or girlfriends come up asking questions."

"Not to worry," Avant spoke up for us. "It's only us. We're just catching some lunch before we head over to see the exhibition fight over at the Klimaxx arena later on this evening."

"Okay, well in that case, why not," Layla said while making herself comfortable next to Myles. Tanisha sat next to Alonzo, Sharice with Avant, and Ariel next to Jordan. The bartender noticed the extra people at the table and came to take their drink and food orders. We all made small talk as we waited for the food and drinks. The ladies were also visitors, coming on a girls trip from Florida A&M. Sharice was studying chemistry for pharmacy school preparation. Layla was studying dance and theatre. Tanisha was studying dual aerospace/mechanical engineering and waiting to hear back about an internship with NASA, and Ariel studying psychology and criminal justice, to prepare for a career in criminal profiling with the Navy.

We all shared our backgrounds, with the ladies shocked to know that all of us were college graduates, and with Myles being the most recent to graduate with his degree. Tanisha still couldn't believe me and Avant weren't twins, so we pulled out our ID's to settle the matter once and for all. After that was tabled, we all continued small talk and enjoyed our food and drinks. They invited us to a dinner party they were going to that would include some of the other ladies we saw earlier, as part of a big fraternity and sorority conference they were attending. We took them up on their offer since it wouldn't interfere with any of our plans…*what harm could it be*? Ariel and Jordan exchanged numbers and then headed our separate ways, glad to have met each other's acquaintance.

"Mannnnnnn, sad that only *two of us are* single," I confessed to the crew as we made our way back to the penthouse. "*Alonzo, I might need to transfer to an HBCU for grad school, buddy, so I can truly get the full college experience.*"

"*Hell yeah we could be roommates*," Jordan chimed in with a smirk of his own. "We're both *young, single, and most definitely willing to mingle."*

"*Damn you, dammmmn you both,*" Alonzo said, shaking his head. "I'm not gonna let you two lil goofy asses get me in trouble. Avant ain't got nothing to worry about."

"Hell naw," Avant replied, throwing his hands up. "All is good in my neighborhood; I ain't tryna have those problems."

"All is good on my homefront as well," Alonzo told us. "Yvonne aint about to kill me!"

"More fun for me!" Jordan exclaimed, kinda feeling both Ariel and Layla. Somewhere in the back of his mind though, Lamont lingered. We all headed to shower and rest up before we had to get to the fight venue. We picked out outfits that would fit both events for later on that night. Tomorrow was the concert and they'd slick hope to run into the ladies again before then, sans the attitudes and third degree that they had received initially from Tanisha.

Calhoun was on the phone finalizing plans for their Miami getaway while Jasmine finished packing her bags. *A girl could never overpack for a beach trip*! She was barely showing at all, so she wanted to take advantage of the sunshine and beach while able to in her new bathing suits. They'd be attending an exhibition fight being promoted near one of his new lounges that had recently opened. Horatio had wasted no time helping to get it set up after the destruction of *Lights, Camera, Action*, had mysteriously gone up in flames. It was confirmed to be an arson case, but no definitive leads on who was responsible had been successful. Calhoun managed to do damage control and give Charlotte the send off she deserved, and compensate her family generously to keep them from becoming too nosy.

Azuri took it hard and that pulled on his heart strings. Charlotte helped him raise her after her mom, Aaliyah, passed away unexpectedly due to complications after her birth. She'd saved him from getting more active in the streets. He could never repay Charlotte for all she did for him, but he made sure to do the best he could with the motherly guidance and shrewd business tactics she taught him. He went to check on Azuri and bring her bags to join theirs.

"You ready baby girl?" he asked as he walked in her room where her nanny was finishing her hair.

"Yes daddy," she said softly smiling wide at him. She'd recently lost two teeth and had gotten a visit from the tooth fairy in the form of both money and a new baby doll.

"Well as soon as your hair is finished we will be ready to go." he said as he grabbed her bags.

"Senor, I'll take those for you," an older man stopped him as he headed out of her room. "I've already loaded everything else. Take your time."

"Thank you Henry," he said, handing over the bags. "Always looking out for us."

Azuri then joined him as he walked back to check on Jasmine. They were two of a kind. They walked back to his ensuite where he found her putting on her shoes. Azuri went up to her and gave her a hug. They had on complimenting sundresses and hats, and Calhoun just smiled as he watched them interact. He secretly prayed that he'd finally get the son he always wanted with Jasmine. He'd then have a pair and be done with kids. They all loaded up in the Sprinter van where Henry was waiting to transport them to his house to drop her off, and then to the airport for their trip. They'd taken a small family trip to Malibu and enjoyed the scenery. Everyone enjoyed themselves and he was glad since he was almost always away from home on business trips.

Once they arrived at his mansion, he helped Azuri inside and gave her nanny the itinerary and updates. He hugged and kissed his baby girl and told her he loved her, before heading back out so they could catch their flight. It was a thirty minute drive to LAX, and Henry managed to get them there without incident. They went pre-check and bypassed the long security checkpoint to make their way to their private terminal via a small passenger cart. He helped Jasmine board as she fought to keep the wind from blowing her sunhat away. After their luggage was brought onboard, they settled in for their flight. She'd make sure to bring her anti-nausea medicine just in case things got woozy on the flight. She took in the scenery from her window while Calhoun reclined back to get a much needed nap in. She put his coat over him as he slept and gave him a kiss, which he returned with a smile. *Life was good*.

Vanessa kept herself busy working with the catering company preparing for yet another big event. This time it would be for soldiers returning home from a recent deployment in the middle east. Their families were being honored and treated to a welcome home event sponsored by the USO at the W hotel in Atlanta. came through to help with plating and food, while Alexis and Yvonne offered to help set up the children's area. Their parents helped coordinate everything with the units, USO, and other military veterans. It was the first time in two years that some of the families would see their loved ones, so it was very bittersweet. Mr. Curtis helped Mr. James set up a special table dedicated to the fallen soldiers, ensuring that each had a name plate setup, candle, and wine glass. Mrs. Vivian and Eva were helping with the programs and floral arrangements. Everyone pitched in wherever they could. They all missed the fellas but knew they'd earned their trip to Miami, and just prayed they'd be safe while there.

At around three o'clock, the plane arrived at the tarmac with the soldiers. They would disembark and line up in formation for roll call before securing their belongings for storage so they could reunite with their families. From there they'd be transported via Coach buses to the hotel where they'd be welcomed to feast! kept track of the time for Vanessa as she checked on food in the kitchen and the setup stations surrounding the entertainment space. Everything was going according to plan. They then went to check in on Yvonne and Alexis at the children's area. They were jealous! The kids had a much better set up and they slick wanted to hideout and chill there instead. They all couldn't wait for the families to arrive. And they didn't have to wait long as the first to arrive were some of the older veterans and their families, along with dignitaries, and other VIP people. The Color Guard entered with the unit colors, American Flag, followed by a special detail holding a picture of a fallen soldier, and made their way to their designated areas. Everyone stood silently as the detail filed through and each set their picture down at its appointed place at the memorial table. They had special tables reserved just for them towards the front. All stopped and saluted the memorial table setup and flag as they made their way to their designated tables.

After getting the VIPs settled in and situated, the first buses arrived and soldiers and families started flowing in. "America Soldier" by Toby Keith played loud and proud as they made their way through the Patriotically decorated corridor and into the venue. The staff and volunteers lined up on both sides to welcome the soldiers. The VIPs and Dignitaries stood from their seating and saluted them. The videographer and photographers captured the memories which displayed on large projector screens throughout the venue. The Chaplain then made his way to the podium to introduce himself and say a very moving prayer. Whitney Houston's rendition of "Star Spangled Banner" followed with the soldiers all saluting the flag held by the Color Guard. The serving staff then made their way to their stations in the back, where they sat down and waited to execute their duties. Those working in the children's area made their way there to prepare as well.

VIII.

Jordan was awakened by his phone buzzing and rolled over to see Lamont's name appear across the screen. He smiled while wiping the crust from his eyes, and answered the phone.

"What's good man?" he answered the phone, stretching the sleep away.

"Nothing much, just handling last minute fires around this concert," he told him. "Have y'all touched down yet?"

"Yeah we got in late yesterday," he responded as he headed to the bathroom. "We rested up and went to check out the fight venue for tonight's event and grabbed lunch."

"That's wassup," he said. "What are your plans afterwards?"

"We're supposed to meet some ladies for a dinner party," he replied, trying to see where this was leading. "They're here for a fraternity/sorority meeting."

"So when will *we* get to see each other?" he asked him. "I've missed you."

"I have too," he confessed. "But I know you've been busy. Maybe after the concert, we can link up?"

"That will be cool. Y'all try to get here early so we can do a meet and greet." He told him.

"Awesome! I'll make sure to let them know."

"Bet. See you then *J-man*."

J-man. That was the nickname he'd given him when they'd first met. He still had that charm that made him fall for Lamont. He turned on the shower and undressed to get freshened up. The water was so refreshing. As he lathered himself up, his thoughts turned to how fine Ariel and Layla were and he felt his manhood respond. He stroked himself as he thought about how he'd like to smash either one, or both in a threesome if they were down. Or maybe he could introduce Lamont to one of them, and they all hang out. That turned him on even more, and before he knew it, he'd released a nice load of baby batter into his hand. It had definitely been a minute since he'd done that, but shit just wait til the real deal happened…whomever it was would be in for a good hurting! He washed himself up and went to get dressed before checking on the others.

I heard a knock on my door and turned to see Jordan peep his head in to see if I was awake. I motioned for him to come in and close the door.

"What's up?" I asked as I turned from the tv to give him my undivided attention.

“Lamont called to see if we could all get to the concert venue early tomorrow,” he said casually. “He wanted us to do a meet and greet with some of the performers.”

“That’s wassup man,” I said, giving him some dap. “Alonzo and Avant are gonna be too hyped.”

“Yeah, it’s very nice of him.” he responded.

“So are yall gonna try to see each other while we’re down?” I asked cautiously, knowing it was a sensitive topic.

‘It would be nice, to be honest.” he confessed though he sounded doubtful. “But you know it's complicated.”

“Yeah, y'all do have a complicated history,” I agreed thinking back. “Just be careful man. You know I got your back. I’d hate to have to fuck him up over you but I will.”

“Yeah we not tryna do all that,” he told me. “We’re here to have fun and enjoy ourselves.”

“Hell yeah, so are you feeling that Ariel chick or Layla more?” I asked him, eliciting the smirk he tried so hard not to display.

“Layla honestly, though Ariel does have her advantage too,” he said thinking back to their conversations during lunch. “What about you?”

"Man, all I'ma say is that they better watch their backs," I said laughing at the thought. "I'm still single........"

"*AND WE DAMN SURE READY TO MINGLEEEE....*" Jordan exclaimed as we both doubled over. "*SAVVVAGGGEEEEE LIFEEEEEEEE!!!!!!*

"True, true," he agreed with me. "Someone needs to throw it down on Tanisha's big boned ass."

"That would probably knock that stank ass attitude she had earlier, right outta her," I told him. "Shit, I'd take one for the team just to get her to ease up on us."

Jordan grinned wide as he tried to keep from falling off the bed. "I bet she got that fye mouthpiece too and supersoaker *wet wet.*"

"Push up on her," I told him, tryna boost his confidence. "Whoever takes the bait, run with it homie. I got the protection on deck for ya as always." Reaching for a drawer that opened up full of sealed magnum boxes and other condoms.

With that I got up and stretched before heading towards the window to check out the views. My left ankle had been aching a little bit so I tried to rest it as much as possible. *Another reminder of my past.* I shook it off and went to relieve myself in the bathroom. Jordan noticed my limp but didn't say too much. He waited till I got out of the shower and dressed, and taped and wrapped my ankle for me. Luckily I'd be wearing jeans and my timberlands so no one would notice. We then went to check on the other dynamic duo to see if they were ready.

"*Cuzzo!*" I called out as we walked into the living room area. He was sitting in the recliner and Alonzo was at the counter stuffing his face.

"What's the word fellas?" he said, turning down the TV volume and looking our way. Alonzo looked up from his plate.

"You *still eating???*" I said, shaking my head while watching him inhale his food.

"*This food is bussing,"* he said as he licked his fingers. "*As much as we paid for it, damn right Ima eat!"*

"He is building up his strength for Tanisha, big ole juicy booty," Jordan chimed in.

"*Naw that's all Avant right there,"* he deflected it back to cuzzo. "She ain't ready for me!"

"Avant wants no part of that either," he exclaimed, waving his hands and shaking his head. "I'm a *one woman* man."

"Ahhh man, lighten up," Alonzo told him as he threw the now empty container in the trash and headed to wash his hands. "You scared she might put it on something good."

"Could be, but we'll never know now will we?" he shot back. "But knowing you, if drinks are involved and the opportunity presents itself, you gone bend the hell outta that big boned heifa's back in that room over there!"

"*Ima changed man!*" he said, shaking his head all while cheesing hard at me and Jordan.

"My boy just said the same thing back in the room!!!" Jordan said pointing my way before doubling over.

"*Really now?"* Alonzo said, giving me the third degree with his eyes. "Myles would end up taking one for the team if anyone did anything. And Tanisha would definitely be the one he targeted because of her disposition."

"I'd fold her voluptuous ass up like an *Auntie Annie's pretzel*!" I said proudly. "And *if the head right, Myles'll be there all night!"* with that Alonzo came to dap me up. None of them knew about that one time me and him hooked up with two of the cheerleaders from the school one summer when I spent the night over his house after we went to his basketball practice. Boyyyy them were some wild times back then. Tanisha could definitely be the next conquest for us both, and no shame would be given. *What can I say,* I'm a ladies man; and shit I'm a young man that's in *Miami Beach* of all places, with my crew at that. Hell yeah ima try to get my dick wet while i'm here. Gonna play it safe and strap up though. We may not be in Vegas but the rules still apply, and we can't afford to bring back any unexpected gifts!"

With that we waited while Alonzo went to brush his teeth so we could head out to the fight venue. Jordan called King and Harlem to check in so we'd all link up and sit together. They were Memphis' older brothers. We headed out towards the venue, taking in the scenery along the way. More people were out and about wearing from just about everything, to barely anything. It didn't take long for us to reach the location and it seemed like we were early, which meant no long lines. We stopped by the ticket window and Jordan gave our names to the lady for our tickets. She placed a wristband on each of us with a special stamp allowing us access to the VIP seating area. As we entered the venue, we looked around and saw many posters of past fights and events that took place. We stopped at a poster that showed the main event, *Memphis Lanier Vs. Tytus Jones*. Jordan pointed out some of the other names of people he recognized that would be fighting smaller battles before the main event. He dialed his cousins again to see where they were so they could all link up, and before long we were face to face with *two of the infamous Lanier Brothers, Kingston and Harlem.*

"What's good fellas?" Jordan and I said reaching out for brotherly hugs. "Long time no see."

"It has been a good minute," Harlem said as he showed love and pointed towards Alonzo. "Yo, ain't you Alonzo?"

"Yessir," Alonzo said, stepping up to give some love. "I remember you from some jobs we did a while back."

"This is Avant. Myles's big cousin," Jordan, introduced Avant to the crew. "He kinda stays out of the way for the most part."

“Good to meet yall,” Avant said as he showed love to everyone. Kingston gave him a strong brotherly hug. “I know about you. You a whiz with the numbers.”

“Im all right with them,” he said, trying to be modest. “It’s definitely hard work and time consuming.”

“Hell yeah, we could use someone with your acumen on our team,” Kingston told him as we all began to walk inside the main arena area. It was like being around family all over again. Kingston took us over to where Memphis was sitting with his coach and trainers, taking in all that they were saying while getting his wrists taped and wrapped.

“What’s good Memphis?” Jordan called out to him, catching him off guard, and eliciting a big grin.

“*YOOOOOOOO,”* Harlem exclaimed as he hopped up and made his way over to the crew. “When did you get in?”

“Just the other day with the crew. We’re here on a small vacation,” Jordan said as he began introducing us. “These are my boys Myles, Avant and Alonzo. Myles and Alonzo you probably recognize from past jobs back home. And Avant is the brains behind the operations.”

“Yo Jordan man, chill out fam,” Avant told him, clearly not liking to be the center of attention. “I just handle business and help with damage control as the need arises.”

"It's all good fam," Memphis responded, giving him a fist bump. "We all have our strengths and weaknesses. But you'd definitely be an asset to whomever is smart enough to bring you on."

"Kingston was just telling him that as we were walking in," Harlem cosigned. "Are you ready to deliver this beatdown to ole buddy?"

"Oh most definitely," Memphis said confidently. "And I say that as humbly as I can. *Scout's honor.*"

"*Definitely heard that one before?*" Jordan asked, giving me his bombastic side eye. I cheesed and threw my fist up in agreement with Memphis. He had to go back to his trainers so we all made our way to the concession stands to get some drinks before returning to the VIP area to take our seats. The smaller events started soon afterwards and were definitely worth catching. Both men and women competed against each other in different events from kickboxing, mma, and boxing, from different age groups. Two young kats in particular, one who the announcer said was active duty Army, Ace Hill, put on a show integrating something called *combatives* training with his mma and it showed as he was ruthless towards his opponent. The other guy was named *Moon* and he was the truth! When we say the fight literally lasted *seconds*, by the time the bell rang, he had ole buddy wrapped up like a pretzel tapping out!

Then it was time for the main event and the place went pitch black. Next thing we knew, *DMX "Ruff Ryder's Anthem"* came on and the tunnel across from us lit up as Memphis and his crew made their way to the ring. The lights slowly illuminated the place as he checked in-pointing in our direction before stepping up into the ring. Then *Makaveli "Hail Mary"* came on as Tytus Jones came from the opposite direction and made his way to the ring. They both had similar stats frame wise, though Memphis was more new than he, but was more known in the streets for his fighting style. Myles had shown us some film of him fighting and he was definitely nothing to play with. The announcer went over the rules and had the two bump fists before stepping away and allowing the first round to commence.

Memphis wasted no time ducking and dodging sloppy thrown punches and jabs while making sure to connect both rib and other lethal body shots, sending his opponent backtracking into his corner. He came back ready to give him hell as he focused and managed to connect a couple of hits to the face and ribs. Memphis let him think he had the advantage for a bit. Kingston and Harlem were hollering his way to *ante up*, which egged him on even more. Jones made a grave mistake of letting down his guard and turning his back after launching what he thought was a powerful combo, not knowing that Memphis would use that as his opportunity to seal his fate. Turning back around, he was met with a fury of fists, jabs, upper cuts, so fast and furious that the judges had a hard time keeping up with how many connects had delivered in the few seconds his all out assault lasted before delivering one final blow that knocked ole buddy straight off the ground, *And the fight was over*! Harlem stood back, taking a knee, as the referees and his opponents coach and manager came over to check on him. It was a clear KO. The referee then called the fight. His opponent ended up being taken out on a stretcher.

Harlem checked on his opponent before coming back to collect his trophy and take pictures with his team, family, and fans alike. He then made his way back to the locker area to shower up and change and meet back up with the crew. We told the crew our plans to meet up with our new found lady friends for their fraternity/sorority dinner, and the Lanier brothers agreed that we'd meet up tomorrow. After that we headed back to freshen up and change since the venue had folks smoking and we didn't want to show up with that scent all over us. About an hour later, we headed to the Omni Hotel, where Jordan hit up the ladies to see where they were so we could link up.

We waited in the piano bar and ordered some drinks. Henny was the drink of choice, straight with no chaser. When the ladies arrived, we bought them whatever drinks they selected, and then ordered some more Henny, this time on the rocks, before following them to the conference area where the dinner was being hosted. The room was decorated very elegantly though the dress code was business casual, so no one felt out of place. We found a big table and pulled out the chairs for our ladies. All eyes were on us as we were clearly strangers in the mix of this semi-formal affair.

"Yall look very elegant in your sorority attire," Alonzo said genuinely as we all took note.

"Why thank you," Layla responded while nursing some Stella Peach in her wine fluke. "Ya'll look *quite dapper yourselves.*"

"We tried our best, given the short notice," Avant chimed in. Coincidentally each of us managed to color coordinate with our lady friends.

"Yall did well," Tanisha admitted with a genuine smile. She was finally talking with some sense.

"*Fine as hell might I add*," Ariel and Sharice both exclaimed while sipping their Moscato.

Jordan looked my way and grinned while I dropped my head trying to hide the smirk growing on my face. Avant and Alonzo sat back, with their arms around their "dates", and watched us cut up. The servers came around to offer hor dourves and other treats, while a speaker was up front making some kind of announcements related to the evening events. We all watched to see what the ladies selected and just finally settled for fish, salads, and the fresh fruit selection, to not risk eating anything that would go against our drinks from earlier. Throughout the event we witnessed the different fraternity and sorority members do their chants and strolls around different tables and areas. The dinner selection was awesome and we were on our best behavior, etiquette wise. We surprised the ladies with knowing what utensils and drinks paired with what meal selections. Major points thanks to Jordan and Avant. The ladies then excused themselves to the restroom, and we held down the table til they returned.

"Man this is awesome," Avant said looking around the conference room. "I didn't know they did all of this as part of their organizations."

"Man, who are you telling?!" Alonzo said, pointing out different items of interest. "Yvonne invited me to some of her Delta stuff, but me being young and dumb, shit I just wanted to be seen with her. But I definitely respect them for all they do."

"Makes me want to consider looking into some of the fraternities to see which one I might be a good fit in," I told them looking at the different fraternities displayed along the wall.

Alonzo spotted the open bar and nodded his head in that direction. Soon as the ladies returned, we excused ourselves to the restroom for some much needed bladder relief from all of our libations. We washed up and headed back, stopping by to ask the ladies if they wanted some drinks from the bar since we were headed to reup. After getting their orders, we went over to place the orders, bringing them back, and then going back to order some bacardi and coke, and henny straight. Just as we were making our way back, we noticed the wait staff moving tables out of the way to make way as the DJ started playing different jams.

The ladies stood up and had us accompany them to the dance floor as "*Set it off*" played through the speakers and they wanted to join in on the electric slide. We all managed to get in step with them as they started dancing to the beat. Me and Jordan were cutting up something serious with our dates while Alonzo and Avant stuck to the basic steps. All was well when all of a sudden the frats and sorors started strolling through from every which way. We ended up getting divided across the floor as they all did their organization chants and strolls. Our dates joined in when their respective sororities came through, and we eagerly cheered them on. So much fun with such a wonderful crowd. No fighting, just pure camaraderie. The DJ put on *"Rhythm of the Night" by Debarge* as the final cut of the night and Jordan and I went crazy as this was one of my late pop's favorite jams. Tanisha and Sharice stayed in step with us as best they could. The others cheered us on as we got down, careful not to spill our drinks.

Once everyone started filing out, we escorted the ladies back to the piano bar for a few more drinks. They had room reservations in the hotel so we just chilled out making small talk till the wee hours of the morning. Jordan pointed to the empty piano, and I looked around then towards the bartender, pointing that way. After getting the okay, I made my way towards it and lifted the cover from the keys. I sat my drink on the nearby bar after taking a sip, before proceeding to play Tupac's "I Ain't Mad At Cha", while Jordan rapped the lyrics smoothly while sipping his drink. The ladies were definitely feeling the mood, as they rocked along to the music. I then slowed it down but keeping the same melody except in a different key, and transitioned to Blackstreet. Alonzo and Avant joined us at the piano as we belted out "Before I let you go" as our final number for them, before the bar closed. The ladies gave us standing ovations for our efforts, and we all brought our glasses for the bartender to collect, and paid our tabs with generous tips for allowing us to stay late and use the piano.

We then accompanied the girls up to their floor where we made sure they got in safely in their rooms. Layla and Ariel were out for the count while Sharice and Tanisha were up and active. I aint gone lie, I was *gone off the Henny and ready to fuck something*. I knew Jordan would be down too, and shit I wanted my boy to get lucky too. I slipped a box of condoms in his back pocket as he walked with Sharice back down to the lobby. I had Tanisha's fine ass wrapped around my finger. We hailed taxis and headed back to the Penthouse. Alonzo and Avant turned in early, leaving me and Jordan to invite the ladies out to the hot tub. We gave them their privacy to change in my room, while we stripped down to our boxers in his room, joining them out on the balcony where the hot tub was bubbling. We brought some beer and wine coolers out to enjoy.

The water wasn't too hot so we were able to get comfortable without frying our crown jewels. The ladies soon joined us. They were beautiful and we stood to help them down into the water. They each grabbed a wine cooler and sipped while we nursed our Coronas. Jordan started kissing on Sharice's neck and she returned the favor to him. I turned towards Tanisha and spread her legs to get close as I explored her neck and voluptuous breasts. She moaned softly as I kissed her all over.

I let my fingers slip between her panties and massaged her pussy. She tried to get away by sliding up out of the tub, but I held her in place as she sat up on the edge and I pulled her panties off. I grabbed some ice and used it and my tongue to go to town on her pussy. She held my head there as she moaned between pleasure and pain from me using the coolness fighting against my warm tongue assaulting her clit. I could feel her cumming and become really wet, releasing all of her juices in my mouth and all over my face like a geyser, as I continued to please her. I held her legs up as I dived in deeper with my tongue, taking her to unknown levels of ecstasy, before coming up for some fresh air. She was breathing hard and fast as I lowered her legs onto my shoulders. I turned to see Sharice giving my boy that A-1 dome. He held his beer bottle up cheesing and I nodded as I turned my focus back to Tanisha. She started licking on my chest while her hands reached down to free my aching soldier. I leaned back and removed my boxers, giving her full access to him. Her eyes grew big as silver dollars-she wasn't expecting to see me packing *all that*. Little did she know....the *Myles effect was about to go down and claim another victim*!

I sipped on my corona and laid back as she went to work on me, using just her throat and tongue. Damn her mouth felt like pure heaven as she topped me and made sexy slurping noises. She stopped long enough to take a swig from her wine cooler, and then went back to work giving top notch neck work. I guided her head with my hand and held her down til she had me all the way down her throat and her tongue was touching my balls, before letting her back up. She kept her magic up til I was about to nut, when she started working her mouth and tongue like a possessed demon, causing me to bust hard all down her throat. She took it all like a champ, and kept going till I was back rock solid. I sat up and noticed Jordan and Sharice had long disappeared, so I followed suit, taking Tanisha with me back into the room, where I laid her back on the bed and spread her legs to dive back into that pussy with my tongue. She shrieked out in pleasure as I explored from the inner parts of her thighs, all the way as far as my tongue could reach inside til her inner waterfall saturated my face.

I came up long enough to grab a condom. She took it from me, not ready just yet. She pulled me up and had me lay back against the pillows. She walked to the very edge of the bed and I watched as she took her place between my legs. My soldier was in need of some more serious *CPR* from earlier, and she was ready to help him out with some *mouth to wood resuscitation.* Starting with my balls, she sucked them gently while stroking me. I was up on my elbows admiring her handy work before she gently pushed me back til my head was against the pillows still watching her work. She took her time slobbing on my tip before taking me gradually all the way in. My toes reacted instantly as she worked my soldier like a pied piper. I closed my eyes and moaned as she did her thang.

I eventually looked over to see the condom next to me and opened it up. She obliged and slipped it over my sidekick. I slid down while pulling her up to where she was hovering over top, slowly lowering herself onto my soldier-we moaned as I entered her temple, inch by inch until fully inside. *She was soooo wet, warm, and super tight,* letting out audible moans as my soldier stretched her pussy walls and traveled deeper into what felt like her belly. *OOOOOHHHHH WEEE she had that gripper for sure!* She rode me nice and slow, trying to get her rhythm. I caught her wave and pulled my legs up to go even deeper as we rocked together. She reached out for the headboard to steady herself. I was face to face with her twins, and gave them equal attention with my mouth and tongue. She threw her head back while pulling my head in closer as we held onto each other still going at it, going at it, making the headboard knock against the wall. I was ready to give all of my thug passion.

Without warning, I then threw my left arm around her as I flipped that ass on her back (she screamed out *"OH FUCK" and held on*) to give her what she thought was a break....*shiddden me;* I teased her with slow, gentle deep strokes at first as I found my positioning, then without warning went into *straight drill mode*-rocking her body something pierce with powerful deep strokes against her flat belly. I was on my tippy toes with her legs stretched to capacity as I dug deeper and deeper into her pussy, my head positioned perfectly between her velvety soft breasts, which I also sucked and nibbled on. She put a pillow over her head to keep from moaning too loudly. Her pussy seemed to get wetter and wetter as I went to work on her. She sucked on my neck as I grinded up against her knowing I was truly putting in that work. She had a tight grip around my waist with her thighs, no lie. I tried to pull back just as I felt myself start to nut and fought hard to free myself so I could pull out, moaning loudly while releasing all my seed into the rubber, hoping and praying it didn't pop while still inside-I collapsed onto my back, breathing hard while lying next to her.

It took me a good minute, but I was finally able to get up and limp to the bathroom to tie the rubber up and flush it down the toilet. I wet some face rags with warm water and soap and washed my soldier down. My ankle was hurting something serious. I brought another one out to wipe her down too, and cover her up with the blanket. I put on some basketball shorts and hobbled out to the kitchen to go get some bottled water and percocet. I could hear Jordan giving Sharice the business next door and congratulated him silently before heading back to join Tanisha, who was still breathing hard, but much slower now. *Damn, I was rehydrating to give her round two of my thug passion! (Ode to the realest OG, Tupac). Instead I stepped outside onto the patio to find a much needed blunt while propping my foot up and looking out at the late night skyline.*

Sharice was working Jordan like a stallion, with her legs wrapped tightly around his waist. He sucked on her breasts and held her close as he had her bouncing up and down his dick. She held on as he flipped her over and went deep in the missionary position. He lifted one leg to position himself better as he dug deep in her pussy. He somehow managed to flip her around into doggy style, and got on top of her, stroking slow and deep while kissing on her neck and ear. She moaned softly as if he was giving her the best dick of her life-partially thanks to the Henny, and that it had been a long minute since he'd been active. He wasn't about to come up short! He worked her like a maintenance man, *making sure she wouldn't forget him or his tune up*. He felt himself about to finally nut and stroked deep, one last time before pulling himself out and rolling over. She surprised him by helping him remove the condom and nursing him with her mouth something serious, until he was completely drained of his baby juice. "*FUCKKKKKKKK!*" He moaned.

Once he caught his breath he headed to the bathroom with the used condom. He relieved himself and flushed it down the toilet before washing himself off and bringing a warm wet rag to do the same for her. She then headed to the bathroom to handle her business. He peeped the empty box and other empty condom wrappers next to the bed and gathered them up to dispose of in the trash can by the nightstand. When she returned, he had put his basketball shorts on and was sitting with one knee up, lighting up a blunt-waiting as she got under the covers to cuddle next to him. He played with her hair with his fingers as he waited for her to drift off to sleep. He looked towards the window and saw me sitting with my back to him, the faint red light of the blunt as I took a hit from it, staring out into the night. *He always had my six.* (“*Brothers and Friends”, by Micah Stampley & Micheal O’Brian played in his head)* He and I would ensure the ladies made it back to their hotel room safely but not before getting another round in with them for good measure (he showed me his weapons arsenal hidden in his walk-in closet safe that was ready in case anything happened).

IX.

Jasmine and Calhoun had touched down at the Miami Airport where Horatio met them as they walked through the ground transportation doors. They followed him to a black on black SUV where he opened the doors before walking to the back to load up their luggage. Once everyone was in they jetted off to his condo to rest up. They were cutting close on time because of an unexpected landing delay but hoped to make it to the amateur boxing fight taking place that evening. Horatio had already gotten their itinerary. He unloaded their luggage while they waited to head to the fight venue.

Thirty minutes later, they were pulling up to the valet entrance where they entered the building while Horatio handed off the keys. He made sure to keep his strap on him just in case anything popped off as this was Miami. They briefly stopped at the concession stand before making their way to the VIP seating. Calhoun's head was on the swivel as they took to their seats. He immediately spotted Kingston Lanier with his crew not far from them and made a mental note to keep an eye on them. He put his arm around Jasmine after she took a seat. She looked around as well, and did a double take to make sure she wasn't crazy, when she saw Alonzo sitting on the other side of the VIP area with Avant, Myles, and Jordan with some other unknown people. *Talk about a fucking coincidence!* She crossed her legs, pulled out her compact to check her makeup, and applied some lip balm before securing them back into her bag. She offered some to Calhoun who smiled and let her hook him up. He kissed her to show his appreciation.

They watched as some smaller matches took place until the main event started. Jasmine had never been to any live sporting event outside of watching Alonzo play basketball in high school and college. This was definitely something new to her, and very physical! She looked at Calhoun as she watched fighters and boxers alike, pounce, punch, kick, and slam each other all over the cage. He got a kick outta watching her cover her eyes to avoid seeing some of the attacks taking place right in front of her. He rubbed her shoulders and pulled her close to him, kissing her on the side of her head.

There was a short intermission afterwards to allow for the cage to be modified to a boxing ring for the main event. He turned and watched as Kingston and some of his crew got up to head towards one of the tunnels leading to the back. The announcer then announced that the main event would begin in ten minutes and gave details of the fighters, their sponsors, and shouting out any celebrities in attendance. Jasmine was caught off guard when she heard Calhoun's name announced and he threw his hand up in appreciation and acknowledgement. She watched to see if Alonzo and his crew would notice her, secretly hoping that they wouldn't. She was in luck because they had gone to the concession stands where they couldn't hear the announcer, and returned afterwards. She had to admit he was looking fly as were the rest of the crew and looked like he was truly enjoying himself. She was truly happy seeing him outside of work mode.

The place suddenly went pitch black and DMX started playing through the loudspeaker and light came from where Kingston had gone earlier. They both looked and watched as Harlem Lanier and his entourage made their way to the ring. They went around the other side of the ring where he stopped to bump fists with some of his crew and brothers, before walking up the steps into the ring. Then light came from their side and the intro to “Hail Mary” by Makaveli blasted as Tytus Jones made his way through the adjacent tunnel, passing right by them on his way to the ring. He peeped her and winked his eye, triggering an unexpected response in her panties, that caught her off guard. *Jesus take the wheel!*

The fighters bumped fists as the announcer introduced them, and gave the rules and other relevant announcements. The bell sounded and it was on from there, with Tytus coming out swinging full force towards Harlem, making a few initial contacts. The crowd cheered him on while Harlem continued to watch his every move and adjust accordingly. He saw an opportunity and went for it, hitting buddy with a fury of shots to his face, body and ribs, all in rapid succession, startling him into a temporary daze as he shook his head to regain focus. Memphis and Kingston cheered proudly for their little brother. Myles and Jordan egged him on as they knew he was the truth with his hands! With the crowd definitely fired up now, Tytus shifted his strategy and tried to catch Harlem off guard with small but effective hits. Harlem let him get his mere seconds of fame as he kept his guard up, taking the hits with ease like they didn’t even faze him at all.

Alonzo watched his footwork, pointing out to Avant that he was preparing to unleash holy hell. Myles and Jordan stood up, yelling for him to *ANTE UP*, just as the same song started to play through the loudspeaker. Tytus made a crucial contact that led to him letting his guard down and turn around, falsely thinking he had stunned Harlem. Kingston walked over to where he was and yelled, *4th quarter finisher,* to which Harlem looked his way, shaking his head in acknowledgement of the assignment. Just as Tytus turned around from looking at his cheering fans, Harlem connected a hard right hook, left hook, jab to the ribs, and body, completely catching him off guard, not knowing where to guard as the full on assault rain down on him too fast for even the judges and referees to keep up.

Harlem then arched back and landed a hit so hard on buddy, his whole body spun around off the ground. When he finally did come back down, it was with a forceful thud! The fight was over. He stood back and watched as his opponents team, coach, manager, and referee went to check on him. Realizing that he wasn't moving, he instinctively dropped to one knee out of respect, saying a prayer that he hadn't hurt him *too bad*. You could hear a pin drop. It was so silent. Once the referee and team realized he was okay, just literally KO'd, they tapped the floor, and the bell rang, calling the fight.

A stretcher was wheeled over to help get him off the floor and safely to be evaluated for further treatment. The announcer then made the official announcement declaring Harlem Lanier winner by KO, with the crowd erupting in cheers and whistles. "*The Show Goes On,"* by Lupe Fiasco blasted as he jumped around the ring throwing up his fists exclaiming his excitement. He then went over to his opponents team and shook hands and gave them love. He ran towards the stretcher as it wheeled away and gave a fist bump and brotherly hug to his opponent before letting them go to the back. He came back to join his family and crew in the ring to celebrate.

Calhoun was still speechless at just how bad his fighter had been pummeled by one of the Lanier brothers. To say he was pissed was an understatement. He had invested a lot of money into sponsoring him, but always knew there were risks involved. He clearly had underestimated Harlem Lanier's fighting ability. Another lesson learned. He waited until the crowd faded before they headed back to check on Tytus. Jasmine accompanied him but kept a bit of distance to allow him to handle his affairs. She overheard them say that the EMS had transported him to the local hospital for concussion protocol and observation. They'd swing by to check on him before heading to have a late dinner. Though she didn't know the fighter from a can of paint, she still prayed that he wasn't too seriously injured.

Vanessa and the family held it down and helped the military reunion dinner truly be a success. Accolades from the dignitaries, VIPs, service members, and their families, showered everyone who had any part in the event. It didn't take long for the area to return to its normal look, thanks to the help of everyone in the building. It was truly a family affair because even the soldiers and their families pitched in with the cleanup. New connections, friendships, and bonds were formed, truly making it a memorable event. Once everything was done and the building was secured, everyone headed home to get some much needed rest. The elders offered to watch the kids so the ladies could have time alone to rest up and tend to their personal affairs.

Alexis had passed her specialization boards and wanted to take the girls to go celebrate with her. Despite them being dead ass tired, they all jumped in one of the Sprinter vans to head down to Klub Krucial for drinks and fun. Dressed to impress, they stepped out the van looking like pageant royalty in their gowns and stiletto heels. The night air was perfect and their makeup and hair flawlessly fell into place. All eyes were on them as they carried themselves with an air that exuded confidence and class.

The bouncer escorted them straight to the VIP section where they had a private booth and bar to enjoy, without unnecessary interruptions. Moet and champagne bottles on ice were bought for them to enjoy, courtesy of the house. They recognized some local musicians and other entertainers not far from them that had their own groupie fan club vying for their attention. They just sat back and enjoyed the privacy because they just wanted to have their drinks, enjoy the music, and then go home honestly. Yvonne kept a watchful eye because this was honestly her first time back in any type of club scene since her incident. Luckily she was positioned between Alexis and Vanessa on the far end of the booth, with direct access to the restrooms without having to leave their area. That brought her some sense of comfort. She missed Alonzo and wondered what he was up to while in Miami. She couldn't wait to be back in his arms. Lauryn hoped that Myles was on his best behavior considering who he was away with. She didn't know much about Jordan, but prayed he was a better influence than Alonzo. She knew and respected that Avant would watch over him but still let him make his own decisions since he was a grown man, and single. After all he was going to do whatever he set his mind to do-accepting whatever consequences that came with it.

She was brought back to reality when she heard the DJ announce that a new R&B singer, *J. Holiday was* about to perform, along with *Lloyd, Trey Songz, and a few other special guests!* They truly did not expect this and very much looked forward to it! Vanessa was still over the moon about the success of yet another catering event that featured some of her original recipes that she'd been experimenting with as part of a cookbook she was preparing to hopefully have ready for publishing considerations very soon. She had something on her mind that she wanted to approach Lauryn about when the time was right, but kept it to herself for the time being.

X.

Alonzo and Avant were sitting in the living room scrolling through the tv channels hoping to catch some March Madness game highlights when we walked in with food. Alonzo greedy ass eagerly hopped up to help us set the table. Jordan sat the drinks down and went to sit down near Avant. I knew we were about to get the third degree and just poured some orange juice before taking a seat in a nearby chair, sliding out of my Jordan slides, to prop my ankle up on a pillow.

"The dynamic duo finally returns," Avant said finally breaking the silence as he put the remote down. "*How was y'all evening?"*

"Shidddd, pretty good, pretty good," Jordan responded in between sipping his bottled water.

"Same here," I said as I drank my juice. "Nothing too exciting."

"*OH REALLY NOW?"* Alonzo chimed in walking towards us as he chewed on a limp piece of bacon.

"*Scouts honor*," Jordan said keeping a straight face, while side-eying me to see if I was gonna break or not.

"*BULL FUCKING SHIDDDDDDDDD*!!" Avant said, jumping up as he walked towards his ace,trying hard to get a confession out of us. Me and Jordan didn't crack a smile, nor say a word.

"*Scouts honor*," I repeated, reaching my arm out towards Jordan who met me halfway slapping it in agreement, before returning back to his seat, propping up his feet on the coffee table.

"Yall two muthafuckers are hell!" Alonzo said as he went back for more bacon. "I thought *we were hell (pointing towards him and Avant). Scratch that! Myles, I thought me and you were a force to reckon with. But goddamn, when you link up with Jordan, a whole different demon side comes out of you!"*

"ENTIRELY.DIFFERENT.DEMON!!!" Avant exclaimed as he smiled and shook his head. "Yall two are a hell of a team. We don't have shit on yall, truth be told. Complete choir angels. So spill it!"

I looked at them, then towards Jordan who looked their way and then back towards me. Then as if we read each other's mind, *I went in*, holding up my glass of juice.....

"Blame it on the Goose, gotcha feelin' loose
Blame it on the 'Trón, got you in the zone
Blame it on the a-a-a-a-a-alcohol
Blame it on the a-a-a-a-a-a-a-a-a-alcohol"

Jordan then jumped in right on cue with his water bottle high in the sky...

"Blame it on the Goose, gotcha feelin' loose

Blame it on the 'Trón, got you in the zone
Blame it on the a-a-a-a-a-alcohol
Blame it on the a-a-a-a-a-alcohol"

Then we both together, cheesing hard as hell at them while trolling....

"Blame it on the vodka, blame it on the Henny
Blame it on the blue tap got you feeling dizzy
Blame it on the a-a-a-a-a-alcohol
Blame it on the a-a-a-a-a-a-a-a-a-alcohol"

The only thing they could do was shake their heads in pure disappointment while holding their sides from laughing so hard at us. Jordan came over to help me up and we made our way over to the table, me leaning on his shoulder so I didn't fall as my ankle wasn't dependable at all. Alonzo pulled a chair out for me as I hopped to it. I went past him to the sink so I could wash my hands and refill my juice before doubling back his way. I pulled out another chair so I could keep it propped while we ate. Everyone sat down and we said grace before diving into the food. Memphis and Harlem had texted earlier seeing what our plans were for today. We let them know about the concert we were supposed to attend, and they invited us to an afterparty at King of Diamonds to celebrate Harlem's birthday and victory from the night before. We told them we'd get back with them, because we wanted to check on our lady friends to see if they were willing (or in any functional capacity *in the case of Sharice and Tanisha*) to join us. They said to just let them know so we could all ride together as part of their entourage.

After wrapping and taping my ankle up I put on a pair of comfortable basketball socks before sliding into my favorite Kobe's. I looked over at myself in the full length mirror outside of the closet before putting on my fitted cap. I walked out and sat at the counter while the others finished getting dressed. Alonzo was the first to emerge.

"How's your ankle feeling?" he asked as he took a seat at the table, facing me.

"It's good for the moment," I told him. "Jordan showed me how to tape and wrap so I could put a better sock on when I want to switch out shoes and boots."

"Yeah they definitely do make a significant difference," he said. "That's the same one that you hurt back home right?"

"Yeah, it truly hasn't been right since then," I admitted, hating to think back on that situation. "Honestly, I don't know how I didn't injure it further during the tournament."

"God's grace and mercy homie," he responded, pointing upwards with both pointer fingers. "Give Him all the credit, because you definitely weren't supposed to show out the way you did."

"Amen to that!" I said, giving him some dap. "I'm done with playing basketball with that kind of intensity. I'm glad that we were all able to play together with the other alumni. Closest I'll ever get to playing organized ball. I'd rather stick to what I've been doing though. My heart has never been into being a player myself, but more so as a coach or trainer. I only learned the game to give yall hell honestly. Jordan just helped me develop my skills when I was back home. He'd be the better one for you and Coach Smith to pursue recruiting wise. He loves the game just as much as you and cuzzo do."

"I can do nothing but respect your honesty man," Alonzo responded sincerely. "I never thought anything about it when we'd play around whether at my house or Avant's. But I truly see it looking back now. Jordan definitely needs to be playing for somebody's organized team. I'll talk to him before we leave Miami to see where his head is about it."

"That's a bet," I said, nodding in agreement. Avant and Jordan opened their doors at exactly the same time. We all gave each other a look over, a thumbs up, and grabbed some water before going over our game plan for the day. Jordan had reached out to the ladies and they'd agreed to meet us at a nearby seafood restaurant close to their hotel for lunch, and then we'd all check out the strip before meeting up with Lamont for the Concert. Later we'd link up with the Lanier brothers to head to King of Diamonds for the afterparty and celebration.

The Bayshore Club Bar & Grill was located right along the beachfront, with fantastic views of the city and the beach. We didn't have to wait long after pulling up for the ladies to arrive. They were also going to the concert, coincidentally, and were dressed ready to have fun. Avant and Alonzo just smiled as they took in all the beauty, knowing that they could only *window shop*. They all gave us friendly hugs, and me and Jordan, held Sharice and Tanisha hands up at arms length, so they could twirl around, showing off their outfits. We all then headed inside where we chose outside seating to be close to the water. It was too nice of a day to sit inside. The ladies headed to the restroom on cue, and we headed to the back patio to wait.

"*Mannnnnnn,"* Alonzo said, shaking his head in disappointment. "*Why the devil tryna tempt a playa?"*

"*Playa??"* Jordan looked at him sideways. "*I thought you were a changed man?"*

"*Yeah buddy*," I chimed in, grinning his way. "*You and cuzzo over there are supposed to be choir angels, remember?"*

"Hell, I am," Avant said confidently as he smiled, showing his pearly whites. "*Damn Smokey & the Bandit over there!"*

Me and Jordan looked out towards the water to see who it was that cuzzo was talking about, before turning back their way, with our best poker faces. Before either of them could say anything incriminating, we were saved by Ariel and Layla, who sat down next to us. Tanisha and Sharice sat across, between him and Alonzo. The waitress came our way to give us menus, a run down of the day's special, and take our drink orders. Since we knew we'd be out for a while, we all selected something light that would pair with the seafood appetizers we would select. No one had any food allergies thankfully, and was down to try just about anything. We ended up ordering a combination of raw oysters, cocktail shrimp, rockefeller oysters, and salads, to keep things simple. She collected our menus and went to put in our orders. The weather was lovely and we were engaging in small talk.

Jordan and I were on our best behavior, as we would occasionally catch Tanisha and Sharice looking our way, which would then lead Alonzo and Avant to look their way. Ariel and Layla were completely clueless as to the nonverbal communication going on. I could tell they were enjoying the sitting arrangements, though truth be told, if they thought anything further than friendship would come out of it, they'd be in for a reality check, quick! Well, I think Alonzo was still on the fence honestly, but it was definitely a white flag when it came to 'Vant.

My level of respect for him only grew as I watched how much of a stand up guy he was and also a positive influence on the rest of us, mainly Alonzo. He and I already had an understanding, and I knew he always meant well when it came to any guidance handed my way. Same with Alonzo-he was definitely my older partner in crime, but making positive changes since he had a growing family now. *Jordan was my evil twin-my ace boon coon. All bets were off when we linked up. Hell or high water couldn't stop us*. Our drinks arrived and the appetizers followed not long afterwards. The food looked and smelled delicious. Everything was set in the middle with utensils and napkins, while small saucers were situated on either side for us to pass around as we selected our food preferences.

Everything was cordial and everyone enjoyed each other's company. Ariel put her head on my shoulder and I watched to see what the response would be across from me. Like clockwork, both Alonzo and Tanisha looked my way. I picked up my beer and sipped in between eating my food. I peeped Jordan and cuzzo on the far end, side-eying me with their peripherals. *What the fuck man?* Sharice broke the ice by flicking some cold water on her, causing her to move her head, and everyone to redirect back to the food. I excused myself to the restroom, signaling to Jordan as I passed by, who got up and followed me.

"Everything good, twin?" he asked once the door closed and we were alone. "I saw what ole girl did."

"Yeah, man. I'm wondering if she and Layla know about what went down with their partners?" I asked while taking a leak.

"I don't know but I hope things stay cordial like they are," he responded. "Things are too good for drama to ensue."

"You right," I agreed as I finished up, flushed the toilet, and went to wash my hands. "No need for it to get any messier than it already is, considering how the sitting arrangements are."

"Man, I don't even think Layla and Ariel have a clue how awkward they made it," he said as he dried his hands. "But shit, they did it to themselves."

"Very true man," I chuckled, adjusting my cap before we headed towards the door to head back to rejoin the others. Jordan did the same and was rubbing his hands together as we rounded the corner. We had stopped to get some Henny on the rocks along the way. All eyes were once again on us as we took our seats, this time on opposite sides just to fuck with the crew. Cuzzo instantly cocked his head while nursing his beer. I gave my signature smile as I held my drink up in his direction. Alonzo dropped his head and chuckled, already knowing *something was in the works*. Jordan was busy fixing his plate from what was left of the appetizers, trying to avoid making eye contact with Sharice. I slick peeped Tanisha playing with the stirrer in her empty cup before picking up the pineapple slices that garnished it, eating them piece by piece-eliciting a response from my soldier. *Be on your best behavior lil homie*! The ladies then started getting up one by one to head to the restroom. I sipped on some water as I waited for them to disappear behind the door.

"What the hell yall up to?" Avant asked straight up, looking back and forth between us.

"Shit, being real." I told him as I drank my water. "Not wanting to mess up the chill vibe we got going with everyone."

"Hell naw," Jordan added, shaking his head in agreement. "Everything is going just fine. Why fuck up a good thing?"

"Lucifer and Chucky, *actually tryna be civil out in public?"* Alonzo asked, looking at cuzzo in amazement.

"Bro, don't you fall for that shit," Avant said as he sat his beer down, and went for his sweet tea. "You do remember what was in their glasses when they returned from the bar?"

"That damn *Henny,"* he confessed, sounding defeated.

“Blame it on the vodka, blame it on the Henny.
Blame it on the blue tap got you feeling dizzy
Blame it on the a-a-a-a-a-alcohol…Blame it on the
a-a-a-a-a-a-a-a-a-alcohol,” we started back, swaying our water glasses back nd forth.

“*You done got they asses back started!”* he threw up his hands in defeat, signalling for the check. “We gotta get ready to head to the concert area anyway to meet Lamont.”

“Let me hit him up to see where he is,” Jordan said as the girls were coming back.

“Hey guys, we’re gonna head back to the hotel.” Sharice spoke up. “Ariel isn’t feeling well so we're gonna all head back to make sure she’s okay.”

“It’s all good. We were about to go pay for everything,” Alonzo said as we all gotup. “Definitely hope it wasn’t the food.”

“Naw, it’s the usual girl problems.” she confided. “Alcohol probably didn’t help honestly. But we hope y'all enjoy the concert.”

“No problem. Hope she feels better,” we all said as we walked to the cashier. “We’ll check on y'all later.”

“Cool. We will wait for yall. Hopefully the fresh air will help her.” she said as they sat in the waiting area for us to finish up. We paid and left a generous tip before heading their way to hail two taxis. A van pulled up first and we opened the sliding door for them to get in. Once they were secured, we told the taxi driver where to go and closed the door. They waved as he took off.

A Sprinter van pulled up next. Lamont stuck his head out and motioned for us to jump in. We all dapped him up as he gave directions to the driver. The drive to the venue was very brief as we were maybe a couple of blocks away, but judging by the traffic that surrounded it, we'd never make it on our own. The driver hit a one way street that could easily be missed and backed into a loading area where we got out.

A gate closed behind the entrance way. We followed as Lamont led us through a back door and long tunnel which took us out to another upper entrance just behind the stage. We looked up to see a large screen that showed the crowd building at the front of the stage. We noticed some of the fraternities and sororities had tents, lawn chairs, and grills set up very close to the stage. Lamont pointed to another area where some of the performers and celebrities would be entering in and we headed that way to hang out. So many beautiful women walking around wearing bikinis, thongs, sundresses-you name it, they wore *or barely* wore it-in all shapes and sizes! A black paradise for a group of young black men such as ourselves.

Lamont led us back to a VIP area where a meet and greet was being set up, with photo ops, etc. As we walked through, some young teenagers mistook us for celebrities and yelled in our direction. Jordan and I seized the opportunity and stopped for photos, while they kept it moving, putting their hands over their faces to keep from laughing. Lamont turned to see what was going on, shaking his head too, but like a father trying to keep us out of trouble, came and snatched us up, so we'd eventually get to our destination. Alonzo laughed out loud as he saw us fight to break free from Lamont's strong hold. He had to tie up some loose ends but would be back to check on us. We were free to roam around the area, but not stray too far away. He gave us custom lanyards with a barcode as well as wrist bands so we could move about without incident in the meantime, before jetting off. We split up with Alonzo and Avant going one way, us the other. We agreed to meet back up within an hour to get with Lamont.

"*You two please try to act civil*," Avant pleaded, with Alonzo making a prayer sign.

"SCOUTS HONOR!" we answered, giving them double thumbs up, full grins on our faces.

"YEAH, YEAH, YEAH," Alonzo shot back. "WHATEVA YALL SAY, DAMN DEMON TWINS!"

"*WONDER WHERE WE GOT IT FROM?"* I yelled back at them.

Avant shot a bird in the air, never even bothering to look back. They disappeared around the corner on the far side while we headed towards where we spotted the tents and grills at. Jordan lifted up his hat and pulled out a blunt he'd prepared for us. Looking for a lighter, he stopped by one of the tents to see if he could borrow one of the grill lighters sitting at a nearby table. One of the older men obliged but asked that we not smoke near their area out of respect.

We agreed and thanked them, lighting up and moving on afterwards. Their symbols didn't ring any bells or didn't look like any of the ones we'd seen the other night at the dinner. We recognized a couple of sororities and headed over to try to do a *meet and greet* without ruffling too many feathers. The ladies waved and smiled as we walked past.They were a sight to see! We were missing out on so much. We continued our walking and eventually came to some of the fraternities and stopped to look at the info packets they had laid out on display.

The first were black and gold, we learned they were the "Alpha"s, the *first* fraternity to be founded in 1906. One of the members gave us a brief history of their organization, significant people who crossed, and their mission. We were impressed and got a good positive vibe from them. Another member started pointing out the other organizations, and pretty much schooled us on each one, and how they were all connected under the National Panhellenic Council and were collectively known as the *Divine Nine*. While listening we realized the organization tent we had first passed was that of the last of the five fraternities, founded in 1963. It was then that Myles recognized them from the trip he and Alonzo had taken to Historic Atlanta. There was an older guy on the tour that had on a jacket that had their insignia, a shield, not a crest, on it that caught his attention.

Avant and I found our way to the food court area and you know we had to sample a little bit of everything! I looked for a place to wash my hands before picking up a small saucer to dive in. Avant shook his head as he followed suit.

"Take it easy now," Avant told me. "Especially out in this heat. Don't want you getting a hold to some potential food poisoning."

"You're right about that man," I said as I looked around the different vendors. "I wonder where Batman and Robin are?"

"4 Letters," Avant said, looking far off in the distance as he waited in line. "H-B-C-U."

"True that. You think they'd seriously look into doing any type of pledging?" I asked. "Did we ever consider pledging? Everything happened in such a blur that I can't even recall too much going on after Josiah came along, and we all went our separate ways interning."

"I mean I had been recruited heavily by the Alpha's and Sigma's. But nothing came of either of it mainly due to my hectic schedule. My old man encouraged me to loosen up and have fun, but I just wanted to be in and out honestly, after basketball."

"I can see you going with either one truth be told," I told him. The Kid was a whiz when it came to the books, and was naturally gifted when it came to athletics.My boy was certified and maybe we could look into possibly alumni chapters of different fraternities when we returned. I'd talk with Yvonne about itand see what her thoughts are about it too. Her sorority definitely had far reaching connections.

We found a shaded table and sat down to enjoy our two plates of food. I watched over as Avant went to find beverages. It was great to be on vacation, but I missed my family something serious. My pops would be proud of the man I was becoming. Though I did find the ladies that we'd befriended while here attractive, I felt it being more of something platonic than anything, but wouldn't try to keep it ongoing to keep down potential complications at the homefront. Not long after he returned, Lamont joined us looking like he needed a break. He asked if we'd heard from the other two, and we nodded back. He then pulled out one of his phones and sent out a text to Jordan for them to meet us over this way since the meet and greet was going to start soon.

"Yoooo we gotta go bro, it's about that time," Jordan said looking at his phone while listening to the pledging process for joining fraternities and how to search their home websites for local chapters near their hometowns.

"Oh man, time flew fast!" I told him looking at my watch and back at the elder (Mr. Gregory), who had stopped us on our way back to Lamont's office, to pick our brains and give us information about their fraternity. He said that we didn't fit the typical mold of college students and that's what made him want to talk with us. He was part of an organization that was founded by *nontraditional* students who wanted to be the change they wanted to see. We thanked him for his time and headed towards the food court where we saw the others. They pointed to the food which we gladly partook in once we washed our hands. We joined them at the table to chop it up right quick in between bites.

"What's good Lamont, fellas?" I said as we sat down. We kept our selection light due to the heat and limited access to decent restrooms.

"We're waiting on yall," they both said, looking in our direction. "Had fun while on your exploration?"

"Most definitely," Jordan said as he bit into his wings. "Got educated about those Greek organizations and met some people we plan to keep in contact with."

"That's awesome man," Alonzo said, smiling with approval. "We were just talking about it ourselves. If time allows before we leave, we'll all go back to get more info."

"You're gonna like OG Gregory," I told him. "He's old school."

"Y'all goodfellas ready?" Lamont said finishing up his sparkling strawberry lemonade. "If so, follow me."

XI

The crowd was going crazy as the concert got underway. Local talents came on stage and hyped the audience with their performances. The fellas watched from backstage. The crowd stretched so far back, but there were large screens set up to allow everyone to see the performances. This was the largest all black college crowd the crew had ever witnessed in one place. There was even one of the HBCU bands present to accompany some of the musicians. They were lighting the crowd up with their short performances in between the other festivities. Such a wonderful experience for everyone in attendance. Lamont and Jordan sat behind the crew as they observed everything. He had his arm around Jordan discreetly.

Myles was positioned to where the other two couldn't see when they slipped back to his office. He knew Jordan would be all right, but had already let him know he was prepared just in case. To anyone else, it looked like Lamont was escorting him around as a young VIP guest so no one paid them any mind as they walked around, picking up odds and ends, to eventually end up back at his office. He sat down on the sofa kicking his shoes off along the wall as Lamont worked on his computer. Something as simple as this was all that was needed between the two of them. He eventually stood up and got comfortable beside Jordan who took no time removing his shirt so he could give him a much overdue massage.

"You still got the magic touch *J-man*," Lamont moaned as he rotated his head and neck.

"Thanks man," he said as he made sure to give equal attention to his arms and midline. "You're kinda stiff in this area. *Stressed*?"

"The usual honestly," Lamont responded. "But I know you're gonna get me right."

"Hell yeah," he confirmed as he worked his way down to his legs, removing his shoes and socks so he could continue on his mission.

"Relax man, I got you." Jordan said as he sat down and gave his calves and feet the attention that they craved. Lamont always took very good care of himself, and knew Jordan always found little ways to make him feel special. It didn't take long for him to fall asleep. When he was finished, he replaced his socks and shoes, and just sat watching him sleep. That made him at peace-some was better than none at all.

Plies and Neyo were on stage giving an all star performance. It had me reminiscing as they performed *"Bust it baby, Pt. 2"* back to *that* summer. A lot transpired but I chose to only focus on the good. I saw a vendor with a cooler of drinks and waved him down so I could see what he had available. I got the others' attention so they could pick their beverages. Once everything was totalled up, I paid the young vendor, letting him know to keep the change as his tip. The young man looked back at us, humbled by our generosity. He thanked us profusely and fist pounded us all. We felt good about paying it forward to the next generation. I excused myself to go to the restroom and also to check on Jordan. The chilled bottled water was refreshing against the heat from the sun. I found the restroom to relieve myself, and then washed up. I located the office fairly quickly. Instead of knocking on the door, I called Jordan.

"Yo," Jordan responded.

"You good, *fam*?" I asked as I stood outside the door. "I'm outside of the office. Just wanted to check on you."

"Yeah, just chillin man," he reassured me. They were cuddled up on the sofa enjoying the simplicity.

"All right. Ima head back to the others." I said before disconnecting the line. I went back to the refreshments area to get some food and found a shaded table in the corner to sit at. I opened my drink and took a swig. It was a good burn going down my throat, complementing the food as I watched my surroundings. I momentarily glanced at the picture of me and Malachi that was on my screen background. I missed my lil guy.
I called his grandmother to check on him.

"Hello?," she answered after a few rings.

"Hi Mama Jacobs," I responded. "How are you all doing?"

"Aw well just the usual," she answered while readjusting the phone. "Working in the yard. Malachi is enjoying being a big helper to his Papa on the riding lawnmower."

“That’s wassup,” I said, imagining him sitting on Papa's lap, hands on the wheel. “I was just calling to check on yall. I didn’t want to disturb him. Yall need anything?”

“Well that’s kind of you,” she replied, watching them make their way back to the carport. “They’re actually just finishing up. Hold on just a moment.”

I could hear the lawn mower cut off and Mr. Jacobs talking to Malachi as he was trying to get him down safely. Mama Jacobs was telling Malachi to come to the phone. She switched it to speaker so he could hear me.

“What’s up Malachi?” I said into the phone. “It’s your dad.”

“*Daddy?*” he said softly into the speaker. “What you doing?”

“Eating lunch,” I answered him in between sips of my drink. “What about you?”

“*Helping Papa cut grass*,” he said proudly. “On the tractor.”

“That’s great, I’m sure he’s enjoying your help,” I told him.

“*Oh he’s a great help!*” Mr. Jacobs yelled in the background. “*He’s going to be driving it himself in no time.*”

“Train em while they’re young,” Mama Jacobs added in. “He really does like to be outside helping.”

“I remember those days,” I said, shaking my head. “Nothing wrong with a littlehard work.”

“Yes sir, you were definitely a big help with keeping this yard up,” they both said. “He’s got your work ethic already instilled in him.”

“I learned from the best,” I said, giving credit where due. “Ya’ll kept me out of trouble. Gave me a chance when most others wouldn’t look around kids myage’s way.”

“And you stood on business every time!” They both said in agreement.

“*Daddy, you come see me soon?*” Malachi cut in.

“Yessir, I’ll be back in a couple days,” I told him, happy that he wanted to see me. “You be good and continue to be a big helper to your Gigi and Papa.”

“*Okay,*” he said into the phone. “*I go help Papa. La you daddy.*”

“Love you too Peanut,” I said proudly.

“He’s gone to help wash the grass off from around the lawn mower so they can eventually move it back into the storage area.” she said switching back from speaker mode.

“All right, well I won't hold you up. I thank you for letting me talk to him.” I said to her, “I truly appreciate everything.”

"No problem at all. You enjoy yourself and we will see you when you return," she said.

"Yes ma'am. Love yall." I responded.

"Love you too son," she said before disconnecting the call.

I was on cloud nine after that call. I got another bottle of water to finish off my meal with. I peeped Jordan and Lamont and whistled to get their attention. They turned and headed my way. They looked refreshed and ready to pick up where they left off. Jordan grabbed some food for them as they made their way to the table. It didn't take long for Avant and Alonzo to join us, of course with Alonzo bringing two plates back with him while trying to also carry his drinks. Good food, good camaraderie. *What more could we ask for?* Lamont looked at his clipboard to see what was next on the itinerary-VIP meet and greet with the performers within the next hour.

We had time to enjoy our meal and drinks, use the restroom, and make our way there. We made sure to put on our lanyards so we could access the restricted areas. Just as we were heading towards the VIP gated area, we heard familiar voices calling our names. The ladies were standing not far away waving at us. Jordan stopped and said something to Lamont before pointing in their direction. Lamont went over to hand them the same lanyards and opened the gate for them to accompany us before closing it back. *This was really about to get interesting* I thought as we all walked into the meet and greet area.

XII

Yvonne couldn't be more grateful to have Mrs. Eva around to help her maintain her sanity while Alonzo was gone on his trip. KyJuan also did his part to not stress her out too. He had gotten himself into a routine that proved just how much he wanted to help-only bring out the toys he would play with wherever he went and return them back to his room. He kept the living room neat, and helped watch over his sister whenever she was in the bassinet or rocker. He even helped try to feed her whenever he could. He had watched and followed behind Alonzo so much that he felt it was his duty to take his place when he was gone. His mom and grandmother couldn't have been more proud.

At one point one day, he had become too quiet prompting them to see what he was up to. When they peeped around the corner to the living room, they saw him laid out with his mouth open as he leaned against the armrest, bottle danging from his sister's mouth as she sat in her carseat equally *out*. One went to grab the camera while the other kept watch to ensure they didn't miss out on this opportunity. Alonzo would be so proud of his little helper. That scenery reminded them both so much of how he was when lil man was born. Thankfully there wouldn't have to worry about anymore little Carlson's joining the family-she had the factory shutdown for good. The girls had been also helping where they could in between helping to run the new funeral office location for Jordan's family while the fellas enjoyed a much overdue trip.

Jordan had a crew set up to handle the "processing" while they were gone. He had carefully chosen and had his people screened by

Alonzo's Mom and Avant's parents, since they were the administrators of the facility. His aunt and uncle had given him full autonomy and authorization to set up his new location. He'd already proven his acumen at the main location, with his *Clean Up Crew* company becoming a vital partner to help with their ever expanding clientele. He and Myles were the eyes and ears to the streets. They had connections and networks all around town, so no one bothered them when they or any of their workers came through to pick up bodies. Where most other funeral homes would turn down such clientele due to heightened violence and retaliation targeting churches, funeral homes, and cemeteries where services were being held, they didn't have that worry. His family's name and reputation carried significant weight and power within the city. The new facility didn't have as much processing since things had calmed down in their area, but they stayed on the ready in case they were needed.

Alexis was up early to get Malachi ready for daycare. He would be at the same one as KyJuan so he'd have a partner in crime to keep his anxiety down. She knew the change of scenery was necessary to help him grow and develop as he needed more socializing before starting school. Little did she know what she was setting that daycare up for. Her parents had taught her to be a good steward with her finances, so she made sure to do right by the account Myles had set up for him. He really wanted to make sure they were well taken care of. She needed to cut ties completely with Calhoun because he was now involved with Jasmine, and she didn't need any static.

The business dealings would have to cease as well because she wanted to respect her friend dating him, and not risk backtracking-her recovery had been a long and painful process, but thanks be to God and her family, she'd made it through. Myles also kept check on her. It came as a complete surprise when she found out she was pregnant because between her dealings with both Calhoun and Myles, she'd never gotten pregnant before. As her business dealings evolved with Calhoun, she knew she had to be careful since she didn't always know who he was messing around with. Myles always respected her and she didn't want to put him at risk so she always tried to be careful when they linked up. He had gotten a good OB-GYN referral from Vanessa for her well woman's care. Partially due to caring for his mom and him being really close friends with her, he knew way more than most young men his age when it came to women's health.

When he found out that she was pregnant, he knew that there was a strong possibility he was the unborn child's dad. He had had a gut feeling early on because they had been a lil too careless around the time Malachi was said to have been conceived. He had taken full advantage of the fact that her family home and townhouse were both located within close driving distance from Avant and Alonzo's jobs. So depending on who he was with at the time, he'd coordinate with her for them to arrange a link up.

Jasmine woke up refreshed from her sleep. After an eventful first day and evening in Miami, the two lovebirds opted for a late night dinner downtown. Thankfully the different aromas filing out into the streets as they were chauffeured to their destination didn't make her nauseous at all. The driver eased along a one way street where he navigated into a private parking deck. Upon the gates shutting down behind them, they saw a carpeted walkway dimly lit as the valet opened the door for them to step out. Calhoun had wanted to surprise Jasmine by taking her to an upscale Cuban dining establishment called *Cabassas's*. The interior gave off a fusion of the *Harlem Renaissance & Roaring Twenties* vibes with a Cuban twist intertwined within the decor and furnishings. He gave the hostess their names and reservation number for confirmation. They were then led to an elevator to the balcony area that overlooked downtown. This part of the restaurant rotated very slowly to allow for them to take in all of the waterfront scenery.

Calhoun wanted her to experience authentic Cuban dishes, so he ordered some Ropa Vieja, tostones, paired with sparkling water with lemon since she couldn't drink. For dessert they shared some Cuban Flan with Cuban Espresso. The dinner was light enough to where they were able to walk around the local boardwalk close to the penthouse. The slowed pace of the late night dinner and stroll was much needed in contrast to the earlier events of the day. When they returned home, the night breeze allowed them to keep the windows open throughout the night. Calhoun laid with his head against her growing belly and spoke softly to their baby as *West Side Story* played on the tv. They drifted off to sleep at some point in the wee hours of the morning.

Calhoun was out on the balcony working on his macbook. Work never ended for him, not even while on vacation. He had gotten a lead on some properties becoming available soon in an area he'd had his sights set on since the unfortunate loss of his club. Horatio had gotten some very telling intel as to the people behind the incident and passed it on to Jimmy. Dots were finally being connected and a clearer picture was slowly emerging, allowing for him to theorize why he had been targeted. *Renegade and Diablo* had become very reckless and sloppy with their movements and tactics, leading to a lot of far reaching unnecessary collateral damage for many people, including *Ms. Charlotte.* Not only that but also it seems like their attack on the Lanier brother's family also had widespread consequences. He thought back to his recent spotting of them at the amateur boxing exhibition on the day of their arrival. He saw some unfamiliar faces, but *three of them were vaguely familiar….*

XIII.

We all entertained the ladies while at the meet and greet. What we didn't know was that we'd be getting access to special performances and opportunities to show our own talent in front of Neyo, Plies, Flo Rida, and some of the other performers and managers present. The scene turned up now that the ladies were able to make it-the vibe was all good the entire time. Lamont had disappeared to make sure everything was still going as scheduled while putting out small fires as they arose. This allowed Jordan to mingle with Ariel and Layla. He and Sharice were cordial with each other, as was Tanisha and I.

They were being entertained by some other fans that tried to shoot their shot at getting their numbers, which brought us some relief. He really hoped his indiscretion wouldn't harm his chances. Layla was too busy keeping an eye on everyone to really give Jordan any attention, so he focused his attention on Ariel. They slipped off to a corner bar table to kick it and vibe. I watched from a distance. I secretly hoped that he'd vibe well with her because they just seemed to naturally click and had good energy with each other. I kept a look out for Lamont just out of precaution. Cuzzo and Alonzo were networking with some of the managers and producers. All seemed to be going well when we saw the Lanier brothers make a surprise appearance. Jordan and I were the first two to acknowledge them. We all dabbed each other up and gave brotherly hugs. It was good to see them again.

"What's good fellas?" Kingston said as we all gathered to the side.

"Just enjoying the scenery with some good company," Jordan said before pulling Ariel close to his side. "Ariel and her friends are here also. They came down to enjoy the concert while on their girl's trip."

"Harlem, nice to meet you Ariel," Harlem said, extending his hand. "Bout time he made time for himself. He has been career focused forever!"

"Nice to meet you too," she said, shaking his hand.

"These are his brothers, Kingston and Memphis," Jordan said, pointing their way. "Memphis participated in the boxing exhibition a couple days back. *Cuzzo certified with them hands*!"

"You know it," Memphis chimed in, doing some quick shadow boxing. "Glad you came down and brought the fellas with you. Yall still coming to *King of Diamonds for the turn up*?"

"Can we bring the ladies?" Jordan wanted to include them since they had been cool company during their trip.

Memphis confirmed and wanted to see them. Ariel waved to Layla who rounded up the others so they could be close to the fellas for the rest of the meet and greet. They all made their way over and everyone was introduced. The vibe was at an all time high when Lamont appeared on stage to welcome the VIP guests to the exclusive access area. He acknowledged the distinguished guests, musicians, fans, letting them know how much their presence was appreciated before giving a run down of the itinerary of events to come. He pointed to an area that two workers pull curtains back from, revealing booths and tables, full of gift packs, refreshment tables, so they could sit down and enjoy the performances. The group made their way to a big oversized corner booth for everyone to sit at. Two young hostesses provided slips for beverages and snack options for them to choose from, along with a separate alcoholic menu, that they could provide whenever they were ready to be brought to their tables. They were handed gift bags from a few other helpers. Then it went dark.

The melody from *"Be on you"* by Flo Rida and Neyo, blasted from the speakers getting the attention of the fans. Everyone was grooving and moving to the sounds of the music as the performance began. I sat back with my aces while the ladies went up to a small stage set up to enjoy the music. Jordan and Ariel were cuddled up-dancing to the beat. If anyone deserved a chance at happiness it was definitely him. The Lanier brothers had found a small groupie crowd to keep them company as they made their way back to the booth. We all acknowledged them and just enjoyed the ambience. One of the waitresses came over to check on us and we placed small food and drink orders. By the time they all returned, the food started arriving for everyone to partake in. Lamont came over to join us after a while, looking like he was completely over the festivities. Jordan stood up with his up to let everyone know that *Lamont* was due credit for arranging all of their VIP fan fare, and that he was truly grateful to have such a great friend. Everyone raised their cups and bottles giving him a loud cheer of sincere gratitude and applause. He went over to give him a brotherly hug. *It was always the little things*

Lamont thought as he looked around. Jordan was always thoughtful like that. The genuineness in his actions always made things better-like how he slipped away earlier just to be with him, keeping him company as he took a much needed break from the chaos. He knew Jordan deserved better and he wanted that for him, even if he couldn't provide it for him.

Once the concert and festivities were over, everyone met up to see what the game plan was for meeting up at King of Diamonds. Kingston had arranged for private transportation for everyone when the time came. They were given the number to the driver to confirm time and location. Kingston and his gang left in his G-Wagon while Lamont had the Sprinter van ready to take the crew back to their destinations. He would be there until the night shift crew came in to relieve him, but would join them at the club if he wasn't too exhausted. They all thanked him again for his hospitality. He closed the door to the sprinter van and waved them off before heading back inside to start the shutdown process. The driver took the scenic route so they could take advantage of the sunset along the water.

The traffic afforded them opportunities to check out the different festivities on the boardwalk as they passed. Once back at the ladies' destination, the guys helped them out and walked with them to the elevators. They then headed back to the van so the driver could get them back to the penthouse. Jordan and I tipped him and confirmed the details for later when we'd all link back up to go to the club. A shower and a nap was in due order for everyone. I noticed Avant slip out onto the patio and watched silently. He had been a bit too quiet lately and I knew it had something to do with sis. I could see it in his eyes. I went and grabbed a couple of beers, quietly sitting one down next to him while giving him a hug as I got comfortable and propped my ankle up. We sat in silence as we overlooked the city, nursing our bottles.

Sometimes I feel left out because of Vanessa's condition, which may or may not allow us to have children of our own. Myles told me to stay prayed up and not give up because God is still in the business of performing miracles and giving blessings. That's my other half, brother wise, so I try my best to always look out for him just as he's always done for me. He and Alonzo are the siblings I always wanted and got through my bonus families. Yvonne and Lauryn have built up a bond and help look out for Vanessa. They give her a lot of support and have been going with her to a support group to learn more about her condition and help her village.

Vanessa hasn't been feeling her best lately. I had accompanied her to her most recent doctor's appointment where I learned she does have some kind of genetic predisposition making it difficult for her to carry a baby to full term. Something to do with the anatomy of her uterus and fragility of the walls and other stuff that I didn't understand. I'd asked my mom about it and she and pops came over to help soothe bae and I. I know she wants to become a mom and that with everyone in our inner circle having kids, it makes her feel incomplete and less than a woman because she may not be able to bear children. I do my best but know there is only so much I can do. My dad has been by my side and told me to let my mom help her because of the sensitivity of the issue. She decided to freeze some of her eggs so that we could look into other options for having children in the future, and also keep the tubal ligation in place to minimize the risk of an unexpected pregnancy. She's been through enough already as it is and I wouldn't want to do anything to put her health any further at risk. I just pray she is able to overcome this setback.

The parking lot to King of Diamonds was packed to the max. We had gotten up with enough time to shower up, get dressed before waiting for the stretch SUV to pick us up to wait for the ladies at their hotel. We are all dressed to impress and the ladies didn't disappoint with their attire. Upon our arrival, we were led to a separate entrance reserved for VIP guests. Kingston and his brothers had pulled up just before us and stood with their ladies arm in arm. He had left Lamont's name on the guest list if he decided to show up later on.

We all checked each other out, giving compliments and taking pictures before heading inside. The music was booming and smokiness gave off strange vibes. "*The Show Goes On*" blasted from the speakers as the DJ announced Memphis' arrival and recent victory at the Exhibition a few nights ago. He had his signature belt across one shoulder as he had his arms around his lady with the other. We were led to a roped off section reserved by Kingston. Chilled bottles of various high end champagne sat in buckets as the ladies escorted us with flaming bottles to our booths. The cheering intensified as the dancers on stage were definitely put on a show for the crowd. We all joined in the festivities when a group made their way over to us. We all just went along with it, though respectful of our *dates*, who seemed to be more turned on by the dancer than us. We handed them rolls of bills to playfully throw out or stick wherever they could find (*which was rather difficult to find considering….*) on the entertainers. Everyone was dancing and holding their drinks up, with blunts, cigars, and hookahs.

Jasmine and Calhoun made their way through a back entrance into the club. He wanted to ensure she wasn't around any smoke or anything that could potentially harm their growing little one. He kept his eyes open, scanning the room along with his main security as they headed to their booth. It didn't take long for him to lock eyes on Kingston's entourage not far away. He motioned to Horatio who made sure to keep eyes on them. As they got settled in their booth, he discreetly pointed out Myles and Jordan. Then his eyes shifted to Lamont who'd slipped in and made his way towards the crew. Horatio immediately recognized him. They'd had past run ins and there was definitely no love lost between either of them. Jasmine sat back and enjoyed the scenery unfolding around her as she enjoyed a sparkling virgin pina colada with fresh pineapple slices as garnish. Tytus showed up and joined them at their booth. He had been medically cleared and released after an overnight observation showed nothing significant health wise. Thankfully she was flanked by Horatio and Calhoun to keep some distance between them. She was not trying to have any drama.

Jordan slipped out the booth to head to the restroom. Lamont, catching his que, followed without much notice from anyone in the group. After handling business and washing up, the two stopped by the bar and sat to have a moment to themselves as they watched the crowd.

"It's good to see you man," Jordan said as he sipped on his drink.

"Always *J-man*," Lamont said, discreetly sliding his arm around him. "Don't get many chances."

"*That's your fault*," Jordan reminded him while enjoying their secret embrace. "*But I respect your situation* and try to accommodate."

"That's what I love about you," he said, rubbing his shoulder. "Who's the lucky lady over there?"

"That's Ariel," he confided in him. "She's really sweet. Definitely a keeper."

"You deserve it man," Lamont said, holding up his bottle. "Take a chance. I know what we have can't ever be official, but I want you to be happy."

"*Why not Lamont?*" Jordan said, turning to him. "You deserve happiness too."

"*It's complicated and I don't deserve you,*" he confessed. "But as a friend, know that I'll always be here."

"Besides Myles, you're the only person I've ever confided in," he told him as a tear fell down his face.

“I know. But you deserve better and I can’t give that. You deserve the chance to have something meaningful with someone who can reciprocate back to you what you give so genuinely,” he said wiping his face. “That’s not where I am and truth be told, I don’t know that I ever will.”

“What about *earlier*?” Jordan asked as he thought about their shared time at the concert.

“That was when it truly hit me,” he responded as he finished off his beer. “I love the little things you do, how you are always genuine with your actions. But I am not able to show it back to you because I’m unsure about myself. And I don’t want you waiting around for something that might never happen.”

“I can respect that,” Jordan replied, trying to hold back the pain he was feeling in his heart. “Your honesty and transparency. You’ve held on to a lot of hurt and pain. More than I'll ever fully know or be able to understand.”

“One day I hope to let it all go,” he told him. “Because of you, I can honestly say I’m learning more about myself and what is possible.”

“I’ll always love you Lamont,” Jordan told him. “For being there for me. What we had wasn’t perfect, or not even a title, but it was ours.”

With that Lamont pulled him closer, giving him a kiss on his forehead, as he held him close. He knew this was going to be painful leading up, but necessary. They held on just a bit longer before parting ways. Jordan went to relieve himself and save face before rejoining the crew. Lamont slipped out through the back. I felt something off and pulled him aside.

"You alright homie?" I asked him as we walked back towards the bar.

"Yea, I just had to tie up some loose ends," he said, trying to avoid eye contact.

"*Lamont?*" I asked hesitantly. "*He didn't do anything to hurt you, did he?*"

"No he didn't," he responded. "If anything, I got closure, for both of us."

"Where is he now?" I asked, scanning the vicinity.

"Probably gone," he said without emotion. "Probably headed home. It took a lot for him to say what he did and I had nothing but respect in how he handled it. It hurts no doubt, but we knew it had to happen."

"He knew about Ariel?" I asked as the bartender brought us both some Crown and Coke.

"Yeah, he's happy for me and wants me to take a chance at enjoying true happiness for once," he said as he sipped on his drink.

"It's well overdue man," I said, putting my arm around him. "You've always been there for everyone else."

"I feel bad about what happened with Sharice knowing I'm trying to push up on Ariel," he said looking back that way.

"Don't stress yourself man," I told him. "Deal with it when the time is right. Until then, let nature take its course."

"That's a bet," he said, holding up his glass for us to toast before turning it back to finish it up.

We sat our glasses down, paid our tab, and started to head back when he accidentally bumped into someone. The man exchanged an icy glance his way before continuing on his way to the restroom. I didn't like the vibe that buddy was giving off and made a mental note as we headed back to join the crowd. Ariel lit up on Jordan's return and they kissed as he cuddled up next to her. All eyes were on me as the vibe in the atmosphere shifted to one of unknown tension. I tried to play it off as I kept my eyes scanning from the restroom and bar area, all the way 360. I saw ole buddy from earlier walking from where we returned from, towards another roped off area where no other than motherfucking Jimmy Calhoun and Jasmine were sitting. He looked up as Horatio walked past to take his place next to Jasmine before turning back in our direction, *we both locking eyes in a death stare*!

Alonzo nudged me, temporarily breaking the nonverbal exchange between me and Calhoun. He knew something was up and just wanted to make sure I was ok. I was honestly ready to go but didn't want to spoil the festivities for everyone else. Cuzzo looked my way and knew I wasn't feeling it anymore, so he signalled to Jordan and Kingston and his brothers. Harlem and Memphis instinctively picked up on the static and instantly started scanning. The crew shifted to protect the ladies as we all made our way towards the exits. We felt eyes on us as we passed through the club, leaving our entire section empty, to our awaiting transportation.

Not long after the stretch pulled off, I peeped Horatio step out trying to see which way we had left. I hit Kingston to let him know and he notified the driver to change routes in the event they would try to trail us. It took around an hour but we finally got the ladies back to their hotel. Kingston met us there and we let the girls know that new transportation would ensure their safe departure back to the airport once they'd packed up. Everyone had gone inside the hotel bar to sit and have drinks while we still had time, except me and Tanisha. I stepped out to speak with the driver who pulled around to the backlot for extended vehicles. He was going on break and said the keys were on the seat!

Soon the coast was clear, I stripped down to my boxers and socks and got comfortable as Tanisha pounced on my aching soldier like a tiger. *Alexis could learn a thing or two from her.* After satisfying her hunger, she pulled me down, wanting that *thug passion one more time.* I couldn't find a condom and was hesitant about going in raw. She reassured me that it was okay and she was protected and trusted me. Not gonna lie, I prayed a quick prayer before diving into her *aquafina wet wet! OOOOOOHHHH that shit felt good as fuckkkk without the rubber. She moaned as I gave her slow and intentional death strokes. I had to prop my left leg on top of my right to protect my ankle, but that seemed to give me an even better advantage! She held me close as I drilled her nonstop. Her breasts popped out of her top and I took full advantage of them.*

I held her leg up as I worked her into oblivion. I felt myself about to nut and slowed down to delay it as much as possible. She knew I was close and pushed me back gently as she took me into her mouth as I leaned against the back seat, my hands guiding her head. I moaned like hell as she continued to work me and hollered out as I busted hard-it was too much for her to swallow as she let me loose but still jerked me-both watching as some of my seed painted her chin, neck and breasts. She found a towel in one of the compartments and opened a bottle of water to wet it before downing the rest of it herself. She cleaned me up thoroughly, along with herself. Grabbing a dry one, she wiped us both off before handing me a bottle of water. I got dressed before I downed it myself.

Right on time, we got a knock on the window saying break time was over. He dropped us off along a private entrance that led to the bar area. I gave him a generous tip for looking out. There was a small crowd when we walked in so it wasn't hard to blend in. We eventually found the others and all gave friendly hugs to them and thanked them profusely for being such great company during our stay.

They thanked us for making their trip worth the while with all of their engagements. Sharice understood where she stood with Jordan, knowing he was falling hard for Ariel. She wanted them to be happy as they were a true match made in heaven, and let him know on the sly that she was *still recovering* from their rendezvous. He looked over at me behind her back cheezing like hell! Then as if suddenly *just* having a revelation, he looked towards Tanisha noticing her walk, and then back at me, smirking before looking away, threw his fist up in the air. I threw mine up in silent agreement, as we knew it was the end of a very good vacation. Avant and Alonzo watched us and shook their heads. They had watched the entire scene from a safe distance. It was almost time to get them to the airport for their early departures.

All of the ladies luggage was ready to be loaded and we helped ensure all was set when the van arrived. After everything was loaded, we all piled in for the ride to the airport. The express route bypassed all of the usual traffic and we arrived into a private loading area for them to head straight to their terminal. Through Jordan we'd all keep in touch. It was bittersweet watching them as they started to board. Just as we were walking back to the van, Jordan got a call and turned to see Lamont waving from the distance. He jogged in his direction.

"Couldn't leave things like they were," Lamont told him once they were face to face. "I enjoyed our time together and wanted you to know that."

"I know. And I'm glad we are able to say our goodbyes," Jordan said to him. "Now it feels complete."

"I agree *J-man*," he said, giving him a hug. "You take care of yourself and don't be a stranger when you come to town."

"I won't man," he told him. "You keep in touch as well, *Montee.*"

The ride back to the penthouse was quiet as we took in the scenery one last time. We decided to go back to the restaurant we'd had lunch at with the girls for our final farewell. The driver turned in and dropped us off under the valet. He was overdue for a break and we wanted to show him our appreciation. As we walked in and pointed towards the preferred patio section Kingston and his brothers were walking out of the restrooms. We all chopped it up and told them where we'd be after washing up ourselves. The patio section overlooking the water was still the same. We had some light drinks and appetizers before heading back to the penthouse to pack up for the long drive back. They offered to drive us back so the driver could have the rest of the day off. We piled into Harlem's Escalade and headed back.

Coincidentally, a black X6 was following us not far behind. Memphis was riding shot-gun hollering at the college girls along the boardwalk. Jordan sat directly behind him, equally partaking in the shenanigans. They and Myles were around the same age, all being the youngest of the crew, so their energy was unmatched by the others. He just so happened to peep the suv following them and told Harlem to make a quick left NOW! He whipped it flawlessly while allowing Memphis to get a good look at the other driver-*Horatio*! What he didn't expect was for a barrage of bullets to come flying their way in rapid succession, POP POP POP POP POP POP POP, and just as the suv rounded the corner, *Jordan suddenly went limp.* The shooter disappeared into the traffic.

Acknowledgements:

First and foremost I want to thank God for everything-especially daily undeserved grace and mercy. Perseverance as this has been a prolonged labor of love written during my early adolescence on through to the present time. To my family, both immediate and extended, you all were my inspiration and motivation to keep writing when writer's block stymied my progress. To A.T.L., C.B., D.R., D.D., and my test readers, thank you for taking time to check out my manuscript and provide constructive feedback. To K.B., you stepping out and getting your work published, really pushed me to see this project through to fruition. Thank you for many late night emails and conversations regarding character development and narratives to build sustenance.

To F.W.K., L.D., and S.D.T.H., for introducing me to the wonderful world of reading and imagination. To S.D.T.H., during some of my darkest days you gave me a light that I'll forever be grateful for. To my favorite person in the world, A.B.F., thank you for your ongoing wisdom and love. My godparents, R.G. and late C.G., thank you for always checking on me even when I'd forget to check on you all. To my lil man and his mom, J.G.D. and T.D., thank you for giving me purpose.

To my BHS family-students and adopted god children, faculty, and staff, the classroom was the setting for many pages written and brainstorming opportunities. To ARJ and BHS % 2004, my eternal love and dedication.

To my military family-Pastor Milton Johnson, my spiritual father, thank you for helping me to trust in myself and allow God to use me while under your guidance and leadership. K.C.M., L.W., C.S. (God mom), D.B. (RIP 2007), 501st STB, 3rd ID 2nd HBCT, and CA Army National Guard (Richmond, CA), thank you for being my family when I couldn't be with those back home. We made the best of every situation, thanks be to God, and each other.

Thank you to my parents, extended family, and even strangers playing music wherever I passed through, for giving me opportunities to create playlists to help with the creative writing process. Music is my first love, with reading being a close second.

To the creators, audio engineers, artists and musicians, thank you for musical creativity and genius. There are so many others I know I'm forgetting but I want you to know that my love is unconditional and specific names weren't left off intentionally-blame my head, not my heart. Again in closing, thank you to God and Jesus Christ, my Lord and Savior-nothing came about without you. Thank you-In Jesus' name, Amen. LL King Mazi and Auntie Nettie, LL Dane Balcon (love you bro-continue to rest in peace), LL M.W.-Jr., LL Godfather Charlie.

Author's Bio

Christopher Bonner is a first time author that produced this book as an extended labor of love commencing twenty-plus years. He is a military veteran-served in Army Reserve, Active Duty, and California Army National Guard, as a combat medic. His favorite duty station overseas was South Korea, where he was able to connect with his Korean roots and learn more about his heritage and culture, while meeting some of his family. He has an undergraduate degree in Public Health (magna cum laude). He is currently working on the sequel. Writing is a hobby, and if nothing else, he can say he did accomplish becoming a published author.

www.ingramcontent.com/pod-product-compliance
Lightning Source LLC
La Vergne TN
LVHW010600100826
845148LV00014B/2782

* 9 7 9 8 2 1 8 7 4 0 0 4 7 *